A Fortune Teller's Luck

Charlotte de Souza

ISBN:0994785801
ISBN-13:9780994785800

DEDICATION

Thank you to my husband for his endless support, to my editor mum who began correcting my grammar as soon as I was old enough to talk, and to members of the various online critique groups who helped get this in shape. I'd also like to thank all the authors whose works have inspired me to write, especially the late, great Terry Pratchett.

Cover design created by author using GIMP, an open-source design tool.
Corners of cover border designed by Freepik
See https://www.gimp.org, www.freepik.com

CONTENTS

Charlotte de Souza

Thomas Jansson squinted in the brilliant July sun as he made his way along the gravel trail between the creaking tilt-a-whirl and a row of shacks housing Vaudeville-era midway games. The fortune teller's tent was at the edge of the grounds near the parking lot, if he remembered correctly, before the wire fence. No more putting this off. Canal Fest would be closing up in a few hours. Already his nerves were failing him and he was glad he'd arranged a back-up plan. He took out his phone to send a text.

With so many rides and vendors, garish signs and flashing lights, carnie shouts and calliope horns, he grew increasingly disoriented. Being tall hardly helped him see past the giant stuffed toys and helium balloons bobbing into his view. His attention was so fixed on trying to see up ahead that he kept tripping over the various cables and hoses strewn across the ground, making him even more aggravated.

The path in front of him split around yet another booth selling overpriced funnel cakes and sugary lemonade. He craned his head. There it was, on his left, the white tent partly in the shade of a giant oak tree. He ambled closer. A hand-painted wooden sign above the entrance swung gently in the breeze:

Have Your Fortune Told by
The Great Madame Zharakova

Five weary-looking people were waiting in line. He sighed. According to his watch, he had fifteen minutes. Not long, if he had any hope of making it back in time.

*　　　　　*　　　　　*

Inside the tent, Lucy Zharakova was sitting on a black folding chair behind a rickety card table. A red velvet shawl covered the surface. This afternoon, she wore her full regalia: paisley tasseled scarf wrapped around her head, billowy white blouse, strands of beads in assorted colors, silver hoop earrings, and a black cotton skirt with tiny mirrors sewn along the bottom.

Cute was the word strangers most often used to describe her, which she took as a hint that she *could* be pretty if she lost a few pounds, were a few inches taller, or had sculpted cheeks instead of dimples. Across from her sat a woman who was that ideal size and height and look. Blonde, swan-necked, wearing a mint green twinset with pearls. In her, Lucy saw the nascent Wife of a clean-cut career politician. A woman who would always appear to glide through life no matter how many times something came along to trip her up. And yet ...

The reading having just ended, Lucy cleared her Tarot cards away. The woman daubed mascara from the corner of her eye. No matter how perfect someone's life appeared, it rarely was, as she was reminded yet again. Far from it.

"I always knew my mother did care about me." She sniffled, her lonely childhood palpable. "The social pressure of being in the public eye is what made her so aloof."

"Now that you understand her better, hopefully you'll be able to mend your relationship." Lucy smiled and watched the woman's shoulders relax. She often forgot how her smile always made strangers feel at ease. She should do so more often, even when she didn't feel like it.

"I need to cut her more slack. I was so hard on her, too." She slipped gem-encrusted fingers into her Kate Spade wallet and pulled out a stack of twenty-dollar bills. "I can't thank you enough." Still sniffling, she crammed some notes into Lucy's hand and raced out of the tent as if she'd just set it ablaze.

Lucy sat, stunned. It had been so easy to tell the woman was a clone of her mother. Her controlled movements and obsessive grooming were part of an outer mask she wore, as sturdy as a stone cathedral. Yet Lucy had torn through that facade as easily as the false front of a gold rush town.

She unclenched her fist. Oh, my. At least two hundred dollars were crumpled between her fingers. Part of her wanted to dash out and give at least half of it back but the woman was long gone and other customers were waiting. She was no psychic, just skilled at reading people.

"I guess I should be happy people value it so much," she mumbled, though it did nothing to assuage her guilt.

A buzzer sounded. Through the canvas of her rented tent, she saw the line of silhouettes getting longer. People were funny. Before that blonde woman came along, there hadn't been a single person for over half an hour.

She slipped the notes into her treasure chest, which she rolled into her cardigan and bundled beneath her chair. She sat upright again, feeling suddenly ill at ease.

"Come in," she called out. Time to put on a cheery face for her new customer.

A man in his early sixties stepped inside the tent as if he were approaching the edge of a diving platform on a dare and was terrified of heights. "I'd like a palm reading, please."

"Sure, have a seat." Lucy slipped her business card to him and glanced out the entrance. Her senses had been off; it was the person after him who might be trouble for her.

The man pocketed the card, pulled his seat in with a jerk, and drummed his fingers on the table. Lucy smiled. He stopped rapping and held up his right hand for her.

"Are you right or left-handed?" she asked.

"Left."

"Then I'll need your other hand, please."

He extended his left hand out to her, hesitantly, like a turtle quick to retreat into its shell. His fingers were tanned, with a band of pale skin on his ring finger. She studied his palm, which was broad, square, and deeply creased. Earth was his element. He had a sad and mournful aspect, a gloom that hung around him like a dark cloud. He was a widower, possibly.

She stared at his palm, slowly tracing the major lines on it with her index finger. It was part of her act. People expected the performance to unfold at a particular pace and were comforted by the little things that they, too, could predict. Often they came for the ritual, the spectacle, fate still unwoven. She moved her finger along his life line. Smooth and straight, then midway through, she saw broken lines like cross-hatching in an ink drawing.

She traced her finger along another line on his palm, and tensed. "I see you've undergone some big changes in your life. You were affected by a great loss several years ago." She wanted to say he was a widower, but kept it vague on the off chance she was wrong. In his eyes, in the hunch of his shoulders, she could see his loneliness. "It looks as if you may be ready to move forward at long last and after much soul-searching."

"I have a date tonight." He gave her an anemic smile, and then a rueful frown. "The first one since my wife passed away."

Yet again, she was spot on to a degree that unnerved her.

*   *   *

The sun beat down relentlessly. Thomas grew antsy, still keeping his sentry on the far side of the wide, dirt path. Three more people had joined the queue, shuffling from side-to-side on a patch of balding grass. Next in line was an Italian widow in her late sixties, leaning on a cane. She smiled and nodded conspiratorially in his direction. He nodded back, keeping his face blank, and checked the time on his phone.

He'd been keeping vigil for nearly twenty minutes and Dave had texted him three times now, nagging him to get back. In addition to their day jobs, he and Dave were part-time stage magicians. Their fairground routine was far hokier than anything Madame Lucy might be putting on. He pulled coins and candies out of children's ears, twisted long balloons into animals and juggled fine china. Ridiculous as it was, the highlight for him was always the cheers and jeers from children whenever he "accidentally" sent a large plate crashing onto the platform.

Feeling hot, he unbuttoned his tailcoat and ignored the strange looks he was getting from passersby. With his top hat, he could have easily looked the part of a groom, he realized. Maybe he should have gone inside the tent himself, instead of relying on a proxy, along with a story about being ditched at the altar. Then he'd get to see her up close. No, this was better.

"You're not done yet?" Dave said, stomping towards him. At six foot four, he was even taller than Thomas, and a lot larger. If his weight were muscle instead of fat, Thomas thought, he could have been a pro wrestler.

"She's just going in now, it's not my fault." Thomas gestured towards the tent opening while a man coming out held the flap of canvas up for the woman in black to enter.

"I already got a good look. Photogenic, long dark hair, dresses the part, she's perfect! Let's get back." Dave tugged his arm, but Thomas wouldn't budge.

"I still need someone to suss her out in person and Marcia's mum is as sharp as they get." Thomas kept his eyes fixed on the silhouettes inside. "You're the one always complaining I do things half-arsed."

"Five minutes," said Dave.

Thomas watched him stride past the miniature roller coaster. Above, a tiny red car slowed at the bend up top, about to take its thirty-foot plunge. Screams erupted over top of the raucous Wurlitzer music. He couldn't wait until he was back in his cool, quiet library.

He took a few light steps closer to the tent and peered through a gap. Photogenic didn't come close to describing how enchanting she was. She had thick hair the color of fine chocolate. Wide-set eyes, broad cheekbones and a pointy chin like you'd see in watercolors of faeries or elves. Before she could spy him, he ducked away again, his heart fluttering in his chest.

*   *   *

An older woman dressed all in black settled into the chair across from Lucy. Her salt-and-pepper hair was pulled back into a bun under a black lace shawl. While she sort of looked Italian, and could be a widow given her age, her clothes were a little too black, as if she'd just bought them. A large steel brooch dangled from a fold of fabric on her chest, about to fall off. Her English was scanty and she'd been vague about what she wanted, apart from wishing to contact *spee-rits*.

Lucy always discouraged channeling of any kind, but the woman was adamant. She'd seen them on TV, of course it was safe, and so Lucy felt obliged to indulge her. While some people were desperate to peer into the future or plumb the inner workings of their subconscious, others wanted a performance.

Fine, then.

"Okay, close your eyes," Lucy said. They spread their palms on the table, the tips of their fingers touching. Keeping one of her eyes slightly open, she watched the woman, scrutinizing every facial tic as she spoke.

"I see an 'M'... Mie." Lucy observed an oh-so slight shake of her head. "Mah ..." She caught the hint of a smile at the corners of the woman's mouth. "Matthew."

"Matteo," the old woman said wistfully.

"Someone from your childhood. In Italy."

Her face lit up and she nodded.

"And Matteo was your ..."

"My cousin."

"Your cousin. Ah." Not what she'd been expecting. All day her readings had gone as smoothly as a freshly oiled motor and now everything seized up. At this point, she figured she'd go for something absurd yet still plausible, just to see what would happen. Her worst fear was that no matter what she said, the old woman would start cursing her and storm out of the tent, right in front of a line of people who would then stalk off in disgust. She felt enough of a fraud as it was, thank you.

She shook those thoughts out of her head, leaned forward, and winked. "You know, he secretly thought you were the prettiest girl in the village. And he always regretted a certain choice he once made."

She clapped her hands together. "My whole life I knew! Ah, bless you." She reached into a pocket somewhere in the folds of her black dress, and shoved a wad of crumpled five-dollar bills into Lucy's hands. "Bless you, thank-a you so much, a-bless you."

Dumbfounded, Lucy watched the woman back out of the tent, crossing her chest and bowing repeatedly. How strange.

*   *   *

Thomas smirked as his Italian widow came up to him. They sidled away from the tent until they were well out of view of anyone waiting in line. She pursed her lips and handed him the card Lucy had given her. "How'd it go?" he asked.

"It was, eh, typical. Like you said." She hadn't been faking that to Lucy; her English was minimal.

Thomas took the black veil and the brooch from her. "Thank you and tell Marcia to call me when you see her."

"Bah, she always forget me."

"No one ever calls their mother enough, Mrs. Torres." Thomas winked, but he looked sadly at her as well. She nodded knowingly, her eyes glistening.

"Are you okay?"

He inhaled sharply and nodded. Three years later, it was still hard. Two deaths, a break-up, life goes on, right? Once he'd composed himself he said, "I'm fine. Thank you."

"See you, Thomas." She gripped his shoulders in her gnarled fingers, kissed both his cheeks, and shuffled off towards the parking lot where her husband would be waiting to pick her up.

His phone beeped. Without looking at the screen, he knew it would be Dave, yet again. He wanted to catch one last glimpse of the fortune teller before heading back. With her dark hair billowing out from under her tasseled scarf, she looked the part to perfection, right down to the lovely, vaguely Asiatic features. She looked so *sweet*. That smile of hers.

He flicked one corner of the card and began ambling back to the stage. She had her own shop, which was handy. Instead of having to arrange an appointment, he could drop by on his lunch break later in the week. Anything to get out of the office for a couple of hours.

CHAPTER TWO

Later that evening, Lucy sat cross-legged on the easy chair in her living room. Much like her store two floors below, the décor in her apartment was a hippy-Bohemian hodgepodge of velvet sofas and antiques upholstered in red brocade. Indian shawls and sari fabric shimmered on the walls behind her crammed bookcases.

Her best friend Athena meditated on the couch across from her and shuffled a deck of Tarot cards. The quintessential Earth Mother, she had wild, sandy-colored curls that coiled to her waist. Her face and arms were covered in freckles, and her eyes were blue and catlike. She began laying the cards out in a Celtic cross spread between their glass tumblers and a half-bottle of Merlot.

"Finished thinking of your question yet?"

"Yeah." Lucy groaned as Athena set down the next card. At the sight of yellow lightning bolts and flames, she clutched her armrests. "The Tower card!"

"You're sounding like a customer. It's reversed, anyway. All it signifies is a disruption of some kind, you know that." Athena laid down the remaining cards. "It can just mean leaving your comfort zone."

"It means I'm going to screw things up royally, because I always do, and I won't see it coming until it's too late."

Lucy threw up her hands. Disruption was an understatement. In her experience, the Tower card represented nothing short of total chaos. The last time it had come up in a reading, her laptop began smoking in the midst of a presentation on geomancy the following day. The first *and* last time she was paid to speak at Hartford Hall had been a disaster.

Athena's eyes darted to a nearby shelf. Prominently displayed was a photo of Lucy smiling and snuggling against a taller man with long, dark hair. Another Tower card curse. She and Pete had been together almost six years and were talking marriage and kids when he broke it off. He hooked up with one of her alleged friends less than a week after that fateful reading. "He moved on, so can you."

"I'm over him, believe me." Lucy picked up her tumbler and swirled the wine around. Many, many times, Athena had told her to burn that picture. She kept it around because she liked how *she* looked in it, and it didn't feel right to cut someone else out of it. She wasn't that overweight, or ugly, except in her own mind. In that one photograph, she was actually pretty. "It's just that all our other friends have settled down, had kids or are moving up in their careers, while I'm still living the same life I did at twenty-two. Only traveling less. And even more broke."

"So? Everyone's path unfolds at a different pace."

Yeah, right. *Pace* implied forward movement. In recent months, her life had been picking up speed as it moved backwards. "You know how much I made at the store on Friday? Forty dollars. I'd be better off working as a Wal-Mart greeter. Only that carnival saved me this month thanks to some of the corniest routines I've ever in my life—"

"You're an entertainer! That corny routine is part of the fun for people. Get over it already." Athena narrowed her eyes at her and reached to a nearby shelf. Underneath, Lucy kept a box of candles in assorted colors.

She took out three pink and three red candles. "Speaking of corny routines, I think what you need right now is a good old-fashioned *love* spell."

"No." Lucy took another swig of her wine. "Love spells are so cheesy, just finish the reading."

"You don't need a reading for the obvious—get out of your comfort zone. Nothing like a new love interest for that!"

"I don't need a new love interest. I need customers, I need for this endless road construction to finish, I need for the expo to go well. I'd do a money spell, but those are always cursed."

"Look. Your loneliness is what's draining your energy to where you're unable to focus on any other part of your life."

"There's nothing wrong with being single," Lucy said. "Most of the time, I don't mind it at all!"

"But it doesn't suit everyone, including you. And there is nothing wrong with that, either. I know you."

Lucy gulped. She knew what was coming next: The Lecture.

"Look. I love you, but lately it feels as if I'm the only friend you have. I'm not saying it's your fault, but you're in a trap of your own making. You hate being single, yet you will not put yourself out there. It would be one thing if you made new friends easily, but you don't."

It was true, and she knew it, but it still stung. That same blasted introversion stood in the path of both. Athena came around again and rocked her in her arms until she felt better, then sat back down.

"Thanks," Lucy said. "I'm glad you're still here for me."

"Always." Athena pushed the cards aside and set the candles on the table. Sliding a box of matches to her, she said, "You do the honors."

"I've done hundreds of these," Lucy said. "They never work."

"It worked for me last time! Come on, light them!"

"You're never single as long."

"Because I already keep myself open to meeting new people." Athena struck a match on the rough wooden surface of the table. The air filled with the stench of sulfur. "So. When was your last date?"

Lucy watched her light all the candles, and sighed. "Three months ago. That yuppie guy who went on about stock prices and football trades all night."

"Yeah, he was a dud. But what about Marc?"

"He was way too clingy." Lucy reached behind her couch and tugged the cord dangling beneath the tasseled lampshade. "He'd call me non-stop even after we'd just left each other and he'd want to talk for hours. I've always got too much to do to be on the phone that long."

"Okay, but before that, you were complaining about Dan because you never knew where you stood with him." Athena blew out the match and laid the smoldering end on a bronze incense burner.

"That's how it is with me. Guys I like are never interested and the guys I'd *want* to be clingy never are."

Athena bugged her eyes out at her. "Then that is why you need to do this spell!"

To shut her up, Lucy arranged the candles in a circle, took a deep breath, and closed her eyes. She hated these spells; they *always* backfired. Last time they did one, she developed a crush on a total player. Before that, she dated a guy who turned out to be in a long-distance relationship but insisted he and his girlfriend *had an understanding*. Ugh.

"Repeat after me," Athena said, taking the Lotus position. "I am open to attracting new love into my life."

Lucy winced. This was so corny. In monotone, she said, "I am open to attracting new love in my life."

"You have to mean it when you say it!" Athena swatted her arm. "Lose the bad attitude."

"I'm sorry. I haven't been in a good frame of mind lately." The past month or so, everything was stressing her out. Business was slow, her mother was trying to suck her into some new family drama she wanted no part of, and each week it seemed yet another friend was engaged, or getting a promotion or doing something more exciting than she was.

"It'll get better, I promise. I know these things." Athena came around to hug her tightly once more. The way her dad used to hug her when she was little. Her throat tightened and she pushed all thoughts of him out of her mind for now. Neither of them had to say aloud the true fears behind her perpetual single status.

Athena settled back down on the center couch cushion. "Now say it again: I am open to attracting new love into my life."

Lucy shut her eyes tight and said earnestly this time, "I'm open to attracting new love in my life."

"I am creating room in my life for my soul mate, someone who will understand me and love me for myself."

"I'm creating room in my life for my soul mate. Someone who'll understand me and love me for myself."

In a singsong voice she said, "Love flows freely through my life and I am overflowing with love."

Lucy's nose crinkled. Athena was getting too hippyish now.

"Lucy."

"Fine." She took a deep breath, concentrating on the sweet scents of her wisteria incense, held it in, released it. With a sincerity taken from the depths of her soul, she said, "Love flows freely through my life and I am overflowing with love."

She opened her eyes again and gazed into the candle flames, hypnotized by the flickering light. If only it would work for once. She did want to be with someone again; she was so tired of the long, lonely evenings and nights. Company would at least make her failing business more bearable.

She picked up a stick of sandalwood incense, held one end into the fire, and blew on it gently. The earthy scent filled the air as smoke eddied and whirled upward. Whether this time it would work or not was anybody's guess. She promised herself that for once, she'd do her best to keep her mind open and ready for anything.

CHAPTER THREE

Lucy stood behind the counter at the back of her store, waiting on her first potential customer of the day. The well-coiffed woman rested her knee on an antique stool upholstered with blue-green brocade, and browsed through the books perched on a tall ladder shelf. She then ambled across the creaking floorboards to where Lucy kept boxes of crystals, herbal soaps, and bric-a-brac she'd picked up from long-ago trips to Eastern Europe and Asia.

Lucy watched her thumb through a stack of embroidered silk cushion covers, and tensed. Ever since her mother had told her about the old Jewish superstition that making the first sale of the week determined how the rest would go, it had lodged into her brain like an indigent tenant. "Is there anything in particular you're looking for?"

The woman came up to her and let out a deep sigh. "My sister suggested I find something to get rid of negative energy. And bad Chi as well. I'm not sure if it's the same thing or not."

By her tailored grey suit, Lucy surmised she was a career climber who prided herself on being rational and rooted in the material world. Someone who studied, followed instructions.

"I have some reading material here that might interest you." Lucy handed her pamphlets on crystal energy and watched to which stones the woman gravitated.

"Black tourmaline is the most powerful one if dispelling negative energy is what you're looking for." Lucy picked out a strand of rough black stones from a display cabinet and held it out by each end to her. "Not only does it protect against negative energy, but it also transmutes that energy into positive."

"They're beautiful!" The woman took the string of beads. She held both ends together behind her neck, checking herself out in a nearby mirror. Lucy had long ago given up pointing out they weren't meant simply for jewelry.

"How much?"

"Fifteen dollars. Or if you want, you can buy single ones. Some people like to mix them in with their birthstones."

"What do the birthstones do?" She flipped through the brochure.

"They're used more for generating positive energy, than transmutation." Lucy was tempted to pull out a couple of garnets, January's birthstone, but the woman seemed more interested in the topaz and rose quartz.

Leaving her to rummage through loose beads, Lucy went to the back of her store and crouched in front of a cabinet. The woman followed her, clutching the string of tourmaline in her fist along with a chain of garnet beads. Just as Lucy had guessed, she was a Capricorn. "I'm a New Years baby, so I'll take these for sure."

Lucy pulled out a coffee table book the woman had been eyeing earlier. "This Feng Shui book will explain how to arrange all your furniture in both home and office so that the energy can—"

The bell on the front door jingled.

Both women stared at the entrance as a man wearing a tweed cap came in. He stopped just inside, as if he were trying to slip in unnoticed. Which wasn't possible, since he was over six feet tall and gorgeous beyond words.

Lucy flashed him a smile and went back to her customer, who was blushing now. Both of them giggled, trying not to look at him again. She felt intensely self-conscious, as if a thousand-watt spotlight shone down on her and thousands of people were watching her every move.

"Anyway," she said in a voice that was a little too loud, "you'd asked about chi and that's what Feng Shui is about, the ancient Chinese practice of arranging your surroundings so that energy can flow through your home in the most auspicious manner and bring good luck into your life."

"I'll go with that as well, and I'll take some of that sage spray you have in the window. Do you take MasterCard?"

"Of course!"

The woman pulled a thick wallet out of her purse. Lucy reached for a set of vials and spray bottles on the shelf behind her counter.

Eying the mirror behind the shelves, she watched the man standing just inside the door. He was checking out the Indian cotton fabrics she'd hung on the walls between her various shelves and display cases. Damn, he was cute.

"Is that your boyfriend?" the customer whispered to her.

I wish! Lucy thought. She bit her lip and shook her head while she rang up the sale, wrapped everything in tissue, and bundled it into a paper shopping bag. "Thanks and have a good day!"

The woman smiled up at the man as she hurried out. Once she was gone, he took off his cap. He clutched it to his chest, gawking around like a lost child. His wide-set eyes were dark blue-grey and they took in everything around him. His nose was perfectly straight and he had fine, somewhat feminine features. His lower lip was somewhat pouty, so even with a blank expression he appeared to be smiling slightly.

Neither of them said anything, as if waiting for the other to speak first. This gave her plenty of time to size him up. She guessed him for a year or two older than her, early thirties at most. His light brown hair was tousled on top, shorter around the sides and back. He wore a fitted, vintage suit with leather boots. A strange melancholy hovered over him, which grew more powerful as she came out from behind the counter and ambled closer.

"Can I help you?" Lucy asked.

Backing away, he stammered, "I'm afraid what I need might seem a bit odd." He had a vaguely English accent. "You see, this sounds so ridiculous, but ... I'm sorry. This must sound so stupid."

His anxiety was starting to rub off on her. "What's your name?" she asked, doing her best not to back away from him.

"It's Thomas. My friends call me Thomas as well. Not Tom, or Tommy. I'd kill them if they did." He flashed a grin and began nibbling on one of his fingernails. He wore three silver rings, all ornately crafted. The largest one had an uncut sapphire the same color as his eyes. "I have a problem. Something in my house."

She locked up the entrance and led him to the back of her store. "Come, we'll go to the room where I do my readings. Everyone finds it more relaxing in there. Less commercial."

He followed her through a doorway behind her cash register, past a curtain of wooden beads. The tiny back room was cozily cluttered with exotic fabrics and cushions, and smoky from incense. She gestured for him to take a velvet chair at a round wooden table squeezed into the far corner of the room.

He let out a deep sigh as she sat across from him. "I got your card from a friend who was at this fair over the weekend. See, I'm looking for someone who does séances."

She giggled. Not what she'd been expecting. "Séances?"

"You know, where a group of people sit around a table and–"

She giggled again and he sulked. "What was so funny?"

"I'm sorry!" She sucked in her breath, trying to compose herself. *Why am I being such an idiot?* "Honestly, I'm really sorry. It's just that 'séance' conjures up images of all these grainy black and white movies of floating tables and parlor tricks and little old ladies talking in these raspy voices."

"What about ghosts and contacting the dead? Is it not trendy these days?" He had to be English; he was getting snarky enough.

"You mean *channeling*," she said, feeling like a total moron. Whenever she was near a cute guy, she found some way to say or do the wrong thing. Her finely tuned abilities to read people always went haywire if she felt she had something at stake beyond the job in front of her. Thankfully, her stressing about the mounting bills for her store hadn't clouded her senses yet. It was only a matter of time.

"I suppose," he said. "Is that the word they use now?"

"It depends! Not all entities are the ghosts of dead people."

"This is a ghost of a dead person. I'm sure of it." He nodded, eyes wide, but she noted something oddly exaggerated about his expression. Too much white showing around his irises. "See, I bought this old house recently. Not long after I moved in, the previous owner admitted to me someone had been murdered in one of the bedrooms several years earlier."

"Ooh." She felt bad for giggling; he was definitely nervous.

"Every night I get woken up by these creaking footsteps. As if someone is pacing up and down in the attic. Goes on for hours."

She eyed his left hand. No wedding band. "Do you live alone?"

He nodded. "It really creeps me out! The other night when I went to investigate, something flashed right in front of me. I swear I saw a face!"

"Does this ghost ever do anything apart from making these noises?"

"None that I've seen."

"Hm." She shifted in her chair, sensing that he was sizing her up as well. He kept staring straight into her eyes, which made her feel even more awkward. The more attractive she found a guy, the harder it was for her to make eye contact with him. And Thomas was adorable.

"I wish it would quit bothering me. I'm finding it hard getting back to sleep lately."

"I don't think doing a channeling is necessary." She also had only the vaguest idea of how to conduct one, especially in line with what he seemed to be expecting. "Maybe it's just something you need to make peace with."

"How do you mean?"

"Next time you hear those footsteps, say aloud: 'This is my house and there is a higher realm for you to go vibrate in'. That should be it!"

He stood, looking bewildered and disappointed. "Oh." He pushed aside some strands of beads, holding them against the frame of the door for her to pass under.

"It can't hurt to try," she said, leading him back through her store. "Old houses contain a lot of energy accumulated from the previous residents. It's not necessarily dead people's souls. It could be their residual emotions, or an energy vortex of some kind." She stopped at the entrance and unlocked the door for him. "The apparitions you see might not necessarily be anything beyond that, even if a violent death once occurred."

Thomas still looked downcast, as if he'd really wanted a séance. He reached into the breast pocket of his jacket. "What do I owe you?"

"Nothing! I'm always here to help."

"Are you sure? You did close up your shop for me."

"It was only a couple of minutes. If you ever need anything else, come back here any time." She grinned, thinking, *please, please, please*. He tipped his hat to her, and headed out.

What a strange man. But really sweet. In his own strange way. Not for everyone but exactly her type. Once he was gone from her sight, she gazed around at the torn-up street outside. The dust had settled, machinery idled, and the workers were on their lunch break. Ever since construction had started, business had slowed to a lethargic crawl.

"Why am I always such a moron," she mumbled to herself. It would have been a guaranteed sale and she'd given it up for the stupidest possible reason: because she found him incredibly hot and didn't want to risk making an ass of herself in front of him.

Just as well. She'd never conducted a channeling on her own before, and the last time she had participated in a session, she'd spent the next several hours dry heaving. Even Athena shied away from doing them.

*   *   *

Thomas hurried down the street, dodging other pedestrians while he talked on his phone. "I told you it was a stupid idea. I felt like such an idiot in there, God." At Dave's response, he said, "No, it's not that I'd rather try a different psychic. The entire concept is ... complete idiocy!"

He stopped and looked around, trying to get his bearings. He knew the neighborhood well but felt suddenly disoriented. The endless construction didn't help. The ancient neon "Rosie's Diner" sign, which had been around since forever, floated into his view. Now he knew where he was.

While Dave babbled into his ear, he leaned against a white stucco building, keeping out of the way of people teetering along narrow wooden planks placed over the raked gravel. They'd been working on this patch of sidewalk for weeks, it seemed. "No, I said there's not going to *be* a séance. She told me to go stand in the hallway and try talking to it myself!"

He waved at an approaching taxicab. To his relief, it pulled to a stop at what remained of the curb. "Of course! Fantastic!" he said, having no clue what Dave's new idea was, since he hadn't been listening to him. He pocketed his phone and brushed construction dust off his suit. He climbed into the back seat of the taxi, reached into his breast pocket and pulled out a booklet of cab chits. "Turn left at the lights, please."

"Where you going?" the driver asked.

"Left at the lights, thanks," Thomas said. He knew the quickest route back and he'd long grown tired of arguing with cabbies about it. While the car lurched around potholes and orange traffic cones, he scribbled in the address for Lucy's store. He scrawled *Day & Night Productions* on the line below.

CHAPTER FOUR

On Tuesday, business was even quieter in the store while the noises outside were deafening. Lucy gazed out at the construction workers backing away from a roaring bulldozer. She set a binder on her counter and began sorting through some paperwork. After making sure all her receipts were in order for the zillionth time, she remembered she had to include those for the upcoming expo.

She stooped to open the lowest drawer of her filing cabinet and the bells on the door jangled. Finally, a customer.

Thomas burst in, arms flailing. "It didn't work—I think I made it worse!" He wore a velvet suit now, a deep plum that was nearly black. No hat this time. "Those footsteps in my attic. I said exactly what you told me, repeated it word for word and it tried to push me down the stairs!"

Though he looked stressed out, Lucy didn't quite believe him. Ghosts only pushed people in horror movies. "Did you say it with compassion?"

"What do you mean?" He scrunched his face. He'd seemed sweet, but today he was so tightly wound. "I wasn't rude."

"Sounds more like a poltergeist than a ghost."

"There's a difference?"

"A huge difference." Her stomach churned from nerves. How could she put this? Poltergeists were only ever caused by one thing: the person experiencing them. Saying as much wouldn't exactly endear him to her. She hesitated, dreading how he was going to react. "Are you under any stress in your life or have any deep, unresolved emotional issues?"

"No!" He looked too defiant, possibly in denial.

He also needed to learn a few things about ghosts and other entities, provided they were the source of his troubles. As gently as she could, she said, "Well, sometimes these things are products of our own unconscious. Deep-seated, repressed anger or trauma can manifest–"

"Anger?" He jerked and stumbled backwards. "I thought you were a medium, not some, some psychiatrist. This is a real entity I'm trying to deal with and it's freaking the hell out of me. Believe me; if you saw it for yourself, you'd–"

"Okay, okay! I'm sorry," she said. His eyes were so expressive and the way he got upset was almost comical. She wondered if he'd ever worked as an entertainer, or just needed a *lot* of attention from people.

"I was hoping for a professional to try contacting it," he said, his brows knitted. "You know, an expert in this area. Honestly, I have no idea what's been going on in my house lately. I only want it to stop."

"If you think it would help, I can arrange a channeling session for you."

"Perfect!" His triumphant smirk made her hesitate. Something was definitely off. Either that or she was being her usual chicken self. Her mind blanked. It always did whenever she needed it most.

"What I recommend first off, is ... A consultation visit! To the place where you want me to conduct the séance. I should feel out the room, see what vibe I get from it. Then I'll have a better idea of what you're dealing with."

"Sure, yeah. How's Thursday evening for you?"

Two days from now. Shit. Way too soon. "I'll need to meet all the attendees as well," she said, hoping to delay him enough so she could discuss it with one of her more experienced friends first. "In advance."

"Who should I invite, anyway?"

"Positive people." He seemed to have no clue what such sessions involved, outside of old horror movies, which could work in her favor. "Invite friends or family who are happily married, successful in their careers, ones who accomplish goals, are free of addictions and–"

"What makes you think I know people like that?" He winked at her, making her wonder if he was flirting. She giggled and covered her mouth with both hands.

"I'm joking. Positive people. I must know at least one. Anything else? What happens after?"

She drummed her fingers on the counter and looked around her shop for ideas. Her eyes landed on the array of wafer-thin silver pendants behind the thick glass of her display cabinet.

He peered at them too, especially ones with more ornate geometric patterns etched onto them. Only a handful of customers had the faintest clue what they were for, most just thought they looked cool. A fortuitous reminder, though. "For the session itself, everyone will have to join in a protection ritual."

"Protection? This is a ghost, not a one night stand."

She shrunk from him, still trying to figure out how serious he was. It was as if a switch had been flipped in him.

"Sorry," he said. "Saying stupid things is a compulsion for me. Perhaps you have a spell for ... never mind, I'll shut up. Is this protection ritual something that's always done?"

"Absolutely! You need to do one whenever you try any contact with the other side. All kinds of negative entities could manifest otherwise."

"I get it. Never know what you might be stirring up if you're not careful." He brought a coiled notebook out of his pocket and flipped through some pages. "How's Thursday for you?"

"Thursday's good." Enough time to prepare, but also plenty of time to get unglued about it in the meantime. Already her mind spun about what his friends would be like and if he had a girlfriend.

He jotted down a phone number and email address, tore off the sheet and set it on her counter. His handwriting slanted sharply left. "I suppose that's it, then. Apart from arranging payment, of course."

She tensed even more; billing issues always had that effect. Products were one thing, but when it was just her, she had no idea what price she was truly worth, or how to calculate it. Too bad karma didn't pay the bills.

"An invoice will suffice, if that's how you handle it," he said.

"Well, I won't charge for the consultation visit. So it would just be for the protection ritual and a few small items like candles and stuff, along with my hourly rate for the channeling itself!"

"So long as it's itemized." He smirked again. "I wouldn't mind a rough estimate for now. I prefer to pay cash. And I'll need a receipt."

She opened up her laptop and found the template she used for invoices. Ignoring her churning insides, she rattled away at the keyboard, trying to think of everything she might possibly need. It was hard with him standing on the other side of the counter. His presence alone made her nervous. Once she was done, she turned the screen around for him to read.

"That's fine," he said, barely glancing at it. "Thursday, then? Say, around sevenish?"

"Sounds good!" She grinned.

He didn't return her smile. He looked a little withdrawn now. "I'll see you then," he said, rapping his knuckles on the counter. "Have a good one." He turned and let himself out of the store.

Watching him amble past her window, her heart sank. She was definitely attracted to him. Whether he was interested too, was another matter. Knowing how her life always worked out, probably not. At least with this, she'd be able to pay her phone and internet bill this coming month.

Raindrops splattered against the glass and she settled back on her stool. It was going to be a long couple of days.

*   *   *

Thomas ducked his head and ran towards the windowless van parked down the road from Lucy's store. It was pouring now. He climbed into the front passenger seat, shivering as he pulled out the strap for his seat belt.

"I can't believe it's July. I'm freezing! Though it's getting rid of all the dust around here."

Dave started the engine. He was older than Thomas and at forty, he exuded a blue-collar gruffness women rarely found attractive. They could tell at one glance that he'd be one of those tedious know-it-alls. A bore. His countenance reminded Thomas of the need to be charming around women regardless of his actual mood.

"So, how did it go?"

"I felt like a complete arse in there." Thomas pulled down the sun visor and checked his hair in the mirror. It hadn't completely flattened against his head yet, though some of the curls were tightening. He pulled out a couple of the more corkscrewed locks with his fingers and twisted them straight.

"Get over yourself. So. What happened?"

"She's clever, I'll give her that. And the cameras will like her. She's rather, voluptuous, I'd say, but she has very good bone structure. She doesn't dye her hair either. It's naturally that dark. Like dark chocolate, with a red cast to it. Her eyes were a weird color though. Both times I met her, I had trouble figuring out if they were green or brown or–"

"Do we have our séance?"

"We have a *channeling consultation visit* set for Thursday night." Thomas wasn't convinced she was the con artist Dave insisted she was, but things like consultation visits hinted at such. He'd have to ask Marcia's mum about the protection ritual. If it was all an act on Lucy's part, it was quite convincing. "By the way, she wants a run-through first."

Dave pulled out into the street. "I'll bet. Ready to go cut last week's session?"

"Can we grab lunch first? I'm starving!"

"Way ahead of you." At the next red light, Dave reached behind his seat for a pair of bulging paper bags. He handed one to Thomas, pointed at his head and said, "See, I really am a psychic."

Thomas pulled a foil-wrapped burger out of the bag and peeked at what else was inside. Wilted fries. Packets of ketchup and relish. He'd been hoping to eat out for once, but Dave was always in a rush to get back to the office.

That's what he always said, at any rate. Thomas suspected it was because he was too cheap to tip. "You know, she's a really sweet girl. Even when I was being stupid, she was very tolerant. At first, I wondered if she believes all that crap. She seemed to."

"They know it's crap. Come on."

He opened his burger and picked out the onions, tucking them into one of the paper napkins. "Some psychic," he muttered. Dave ordered burgers so often Thomas wondered if the man was even aware restaurants served other dishes. At least there was no mustard on the bun this time.

"At first, you'd said."

"Until she listed everything she absolutely needs in order to perform this thing. Her bill was itemized down to the last stick of incense."

"Told you." Dave waited for the stream of pedestrians to finish crossing and turned right, heading towards the highway. "It's all about the Benjamins."

"To be fair, I asked her to. I'm not paying for it. They're no longer séances, by the way. Mediums now *channel* things from the other side."

"I heard you. She called it a channeling consultation visit."

"Still, it's an interesting term when you think about it." Thomas gripped the armrest while the van bounced over a deep pothole. "I suppose back in the Victorian era before radio came along, there was no such thing as channels. It's an apt metaphor if you believe in that sort of thing. Tuning in to another plane of existence or–"

"They *were* aware of the electromagnetic spectrum back then. Speaking of which," Dave switched on the radio. He always did whenever he didn't feel like talking, and it was always the same seventies and eighties anthem crap. He drummed on the steering wheel to the beat of an old AC/DC song.

"Do we always have to listen to this *cock rock*?" Thomas sneered. For once, it would be nice if Dave put it on an Indie station. Or something more recent than when stringy hair and plaid shirts were the height of fashion.

"Driver picks the music, you know the rule."

He glowered out at the passing landscape. For the time being, he tried to push Thursday night out of his mind. Originally, he'd been planning to get the séance over with as soon as possible. Her wanting to suss out the place first threw a wrench into everything. He should have learned by now; things never turned out the way he expected them to. Never.

*   *   *

Lucy leaned on the counter, gazing out the window at the bulldozers rumbling back and forth. Rain made business even slower. It was almost two o'clock and Thomas had been the only person to come in so far. She thought of him now, especially those eyes of his. They'd looked even bluer against his plum-colored jacket, matching his sapphire ring. And then here was his face. His mouth was so sensuous, the way his bottom lip always pouted slightly and whenever he smiled he …

She jumped as her phone rang. "Madame Lucinda, how can I help you?"

"Hi, Lucy, it's Stacy from Wadsworth Exhibition Place." Stacy Buchanan was the events coordinator for the annual Psychic Expo. It was happening in less than two weeks, and her voice had the strained cheeriness of someone with a gun prodding their spine. It was going to be bad news; she knew it.

She hesitated just long enough to convey that tone never fooled her and said breathily, "Hi Stacy."

"I don't know how to explain this exactly, but the organizers made a mistake when they were initially calculating the allotted spaces in the main hall."

"I have to move my booth, don't I." This would have been her second year attending. As soon as it was announced, she booked a prime spot near the entrance next to the Kirlian photographer. Expensive, but it would garner a lot of traffic.

"We did our best to secure you an equivalent location. Unfortunately as one of our smaller exhibitors, our options were pretty limited. We'll happily refund the difference for you."

Lucy let out a disappointed sigh. This wasn't Stacy's fault. The bearer of bad news always delivered it on someone else's behalf. Yet once delivered, back to her regular job and no skin off her back. Lucy had once tried to get simply a name for someone higher up, the last time she'd had a dispute with the organizers. She was met with a barricade that wouldn't have been out of place in 1980s Berlin. "So where am I now?"

"It's near the back of the floor. Zone E, section 31a."

Lucy reached for a stack of brochures on her counter next to the wall. She dragged them closer and opened out the top one. Zone E was the dead area where only a handful of people ever ventured, having already spent their money elsewhere. Great.

"To compensate, your space is quite a bit larger and we'll throw in some additional signage for you as well."

In black marker, she crossed out her location and circled the new position on the exhibitors' map. "I'd already had brochures printed up, though."

"Again, I'm really sorry. Bill us for that too, and we'll compensate you," Stacy offered.

"Thanks. Have a good afternoon," Lucy said, trying not to sound bitter. It wasn't Stacy's fault but that didn't make her any less pissed. With luck, they would put her next to some other popular exhibitor that people were willing to wait in a long line to see. Wait in line, get bored, and browse through her books or her display of Himalayan salt lamps and honey skincare products. They might even buy something or take a card for her store.

She dug through the drawer under her counter for the printers' business card. At least she had something to keep her occupied on this rainy afternoon. Anything to distract her from fretting about Thursday night.

CHAPTER FIVE

Dave and Thomas sat next to each other in the video editing suite, a cramped room in the basement of a suburban office building. The place had the atmosphere of a hospital morgue. In here, it was impossible to tell whether it was day or night. While Dave switched on the largest screen, Thomas logged onto the computer to open the various files they'd been working on.

"You have last week's ready?" Dave asked.

Thomas nodded. He opened an image file showing an assortment of people sitting on wicker sofas arranged around a table. The room they sat in was airy, rustic.

"Let's rewind the tape," Dave said.

"It's online. There is no tape," Thomas said, fiddling with the mouse. The cursor had stopped moving. Underneath, a layer of nasty build-up had formed, which he proceeded to chip off with the end of an unfolded paperclip.

"Fine, smart ass, rewind whatever the fuck you call it these days and roll from the beginning."

He blew on the mouse, set it down again and clicked to play the video. The screen in front of them flickered and showed a white stage with a white backdrop. Dave walked onscreen from the left and spoke into the camera. Instead of his usual blue jeans and t-shirt, he wore a loose-fitting grey suit with faint pinstripes. "Hi, I'm Skeptical Dave. This is my partner, the Doubting Thomas."

Thomas walked onto the screen from the right and said, "Together we are–"

"–the Debunkers!" they said in unison, striking a pose next to each other and staring mock-seriously at the camera. For their show, Thomas wore black jeans and a white linen shirt with the sleeves rolled up to his elbows. In large red font that resembled thick paint, "THE DEBUNKERS" splattered across the screen.

"In last week's episode," onscreen Dave said, "We showed you how that UFO in Florida was really a streetlight. Too easy.

Someone *really* needs to brush up on their Photoshop skills."

Onscreen Thomas winked at the camera. "This week, we tackle rock energy."

"We catch a river stone energy therapist–" Dave chuckled, "yeah, you heard me, taking these river stones out of her own driveway, and scamming people into believing that a bunch of granite pebbles hold special magicky healing powers."

Thomas opened the file containing the clip they'd filmed the other day, and edited it into the one they'd just reviewed. Dave handed him a copy of the script, which he opened reluctantly. Another perfectly nice woman Dave wanted to rip apart. The producers targeted fewer men, he noticed, but compensated by being as vicious as middle school girls towards them.

"Enough dilly-dallying. Is the sound ready?"

"Yes!" Thomas stared blankly at him.

"You're on first." Dave tapped Thomas's pathetic line in the script.

Leaning closer to the microphone, he waited until the woman with short, silver hair was crouching on a gravel driveway next to a black, S-class Mercedes. In the background, a pale yellow Hacienda-style mansion loomed. "I suppose that Mercedes energizes those rocks and holding them makes you feel as if you're riding in a brand new luxury car." Thomas cringed as his mocking voice came through the computer speakers.

The woman held a stone up to the sunlight. "The crystalline structure in granite like in this rock here."

"And cut!" Dave pressed a button to pause the clip. He should have let the woman finish but Thomas wasn't in the mood to argue. Instead, he dutifully added the stock footage of assorted geodes, crystals, and agate.

Dave spoke into the microphone now. "We will also speak to our resident geologist who will de-bunk–"

"–the entire concept of crystal energy," Thomas added at Dave's signal, finishing that part of the clip.

"Looks good!" Dave said.

Thomas stopped the video. Needing to stick it to him, he said,

"I always do!"

Dave gave him a shove. "Someday we need to debunk your big fat ego."

"That's what pitch meetings are for."

"Come up with better ideas, then."

"I do, just not ones they like."

"What the hell is your problem?"

He was in the mood for conflict after all. "Why does this show have to be so serious? It's getting so mean-spirited. I feel terrible about that magnetic bracelet salesmen a few weeks back." He had no problem demolishing stupid *ideas* onscreen, or tearing apart complete and utter charlatans who'd grown filthy rich. The bracelet salesman had been just one man selling at flea markets and street festivals.

"It's what audiences want, so we give it to them."

"How about we get better audiences? With seven billion people on the planet, there's a niche for everything. All you have to do is put more effort into finding it."

"Just roll the rest of it."

"You don't think we're getting too repetitive?"

"What would make the show better? You tell me."

Thomas knew he was wasting his breath, but at least Dave was indulging him for once. "Take light bulbs. If I'm in my bedroom or living room or what have you, I'll usually have a single lamp on. 60 watts for the bulb. When I leave the room, I turn it off. Yet we're getting these bloody CFLs shoved down our throats—practically being forced to buy them."

"They save energy!"

"60 watts! An electric stove consumes thousands. But fine. I use one bulb at a time, expending an extra what, 45 watts. What about track lighting or these pot light systems where each room has two dozen or more? That wastes loads more energy!"

Dave shrugged. "Then make a presentation and pitch it. Although it sounds about as exciting as watching concrete set."

"Of course! There are things like numbers and we all know people are terrified of maths or anything requiring half a brain in their skulls."

"Quit bitching, speaking of repetitive." Dave clicked for the sound to start recording. He spoke pompously into the computer microphone: "Rocks. Stones. Crystals. We can't get enough of them. And why not? They're useful as weapons, they make for great jewelry and–" Dave signaled for Thomas to continue.

"–some people claim they have magical properties. The right stone can cure disease, cast out bad energy, whatever that is, and perhaps even help you win the lottery." Thomas clicked to stop the recording software and opened their next video clip, of an old interview with the geology professor. He was a spry man in his sixties, sitting on a desk in a cluttered office.

"Somebody actually noticed he was wearing the same outfit in that clip on magnetism," Dave said. "As if male college Profs change their clothes regularly."

"I warned you about always using the exact same bit. Anyway." Thomas tapped on the bottom of the screen and stood. "I have sales reports taking priority. They want nice shiny pie charts for their board meeting tomorrow. At least they don't have to mean anything, so long as they look impressive and show steady growth. That's what we should debunk one of these days: dodgy accounting schemes."

"Keep in mind this has to be uploaded and online before you leave today." Dave put his feet up on Thomas's chair, stretched, and locked his hands behind the back of his head. "Have fun!"

Thomas sighed and headed out towards the elevator. The show had been his idea and it had turned into a soul-destroying monster. Instead of targeting jet-set faith healers and phony preachers who used their church's coffers for money laundering and tax evasion, they were going after small business people who were barely fit to run a lemonade stand. He could barely tolerate watching himself anymore.

CHAPTER SIX

Thursday was yet another quiet day in Lucy's store, apart from relentless jack-hammering down the road. Debbie, the owner of the hair salon next door, had closed up shop to hang out until her first and only appointment.

"Thursdays used to be my best day." Lucy opened her spreadsheet and showed Debbie a chart she'd created comparing this summer's sales to the previous three and a half years she'd been in business. It hurt to look at it. In the spring, she'd had so much momentum. At last, she was earning as much as she would if she worked a regular office job. Until orange pylons blocked off one lane on each side of Main Street, then the sidewalk, and then the giant road sign came up. The notice she'd received in the mail beforehand claimed it would only take a few weeks.

Nearly three months had passed since.

"I'm no longer bleeding rent, I'm hemorrhaging it," Debbie said. "These days, I'm making more doing house calls."

"I've had this place for eight years, but–"

"This is yours?"

"My dad died and I inherited it when I turned twenty-one."

"Oh, I'm sorry," Debbie said, and Lucy sensed a jealous vibe. "Did your dad own a lot of buildings?"

"Just two. He was old school. He'd immigrated with almost nothing, worked doing whatever he could find, and saved nearly every penny." That seemed to put Debbie more at ease. "This building was his nest egg, along with one other that's under my mother's name." Her eyes watered as they always did when she remembered the dreams cut short.

"What happened?"

"He was in a car accident. He used to moonlight as a taxi driver on top of his regular job."

"Ooh," Debbie said, looking genuinely sorry now. "Sudden deaths are the hardest to take."

She sucked a deep breath into her lungs. "It was a long time ago. You'd think I'd have dealt with it by now."

"You don't ever get over something like that. My parents are still alive, but my grandmother's death hit my dad really hard."

"Thanks." She wanted to be alone now, but Debbie's appointment wasn't for another forty-five minutes.

"I was thinking," Debbie said, "since the BIA isn't wanting to step up to the plate, we should form our own committee to get compensation from the city. It's getting ridiculous. We need to audit the contractor too! Know why those pylons and sawhorses were out a month before they started work? They rent them from their buddy's company and bill us taxpayers for it!"

"Let me know what you need me to do," said Lucy, thankful for the abrupt change of subject. "Write a letter, show up somewhere, whatever you need. It's not like I've got anything else keeping me busy these days."

"Good! I'm going to hold you to it." She checked her watch and said, "I should get back. I'm going to write up a petition to send to the mayor for now, and we'll see from there."

"I'll sign for sure!"

Debbie headed out, the rumbling engines and pile driver blaring as she opened the door. Her voice was barely audible as she called, "See ya!"

"Bye!" Lucy waved.

As soon as Debbie was gone, Lucy missed her company as intensely as she'd craved solitude a minute earlier. The appointment with Thomas loomed ahead like a swelling tidal wave, filling her with dread. She had no idea what to expect.

Yesterday he'd been bored at work and she'd been bored in the store, so they'd chatted online back and forth for hours. Small talk at first, then the topic had turned to movies. He'd seen all the ones she'd said were her favorites. He spent the next hour or so sending her links to trailers for her to check out. He then added her on Goodreads, where he was up to over three thousand books, with hundreds more on his to-read list. To her shock, an amazing number of them were on the occult, including rarer ones worth hundreds of dollars.

Today he'd sent a terse email confirming "sevenish", along with his street address, and that was it.

*   *   *

In the office lunchroom, which was decorated only slightly less blandly than a dentist's office, Dave kicked Thomas under the table and said, "What's eating you this afternoon?"

He shrugged and picked at the pasta dish he'd ordered from the cafeteria. He hadn't noticed there were mushrooms in the dish before ordering and he'd forgotten to check. He hated mushrooms.

"Remember you've got that pre-consultation thingy tonight."

"I know!" Thomas scowled. "You've reminded me a hundred times already. It's at my house. How would I forget?"

"Who's coming for it?"

"Marcia and Jeremy are coming for sure. Isaac has no choice. Ron said he might, but you know Ron. Everything is fifty-fifty with him. I invited as many as I could, but you know how people are. Ask ten and two show up."

"I see you're putting your usual effort into all this."

"If *you* had done more research, you'd know séances went out of fashion along with skirt bustles and silk umbrellas." He finished digging out the remaining mushrooms and took a bite of his penne. It was cold, mushy, and, as usual, too salty. "They don't do these sorts of things anymore."

"Then it'll be easier to spot how she's faking it."

"She's not stupid; she's bound to see through what we're doing."

"Only if you fuck up."

Thomas sulked, and glanced at the microwave on the counter next to the sink. It still had an *out of order—do not use* sign taped to the front. Bloody thing had been broken for months.

"So that's why you're in such a pissy mood today. Not used to something riding on your shoulders alone? If we don't get the footage we need, you'll be the one explaining everything to Mark and Alastair."

"This thing is not going to get views. While we still have time, we should come up with something far less, less *dated*." Something that didn't involve Lucy, he added to himself. She even admitted she had no psychic abilities and told all her customers as much. Nobody seriously expected her to contact their late grandfather or come up with this week's lottery numbers.

"There's more to it than an idea. You have to write out a treatment, estimate the costs involved, create a profile of audience demographics and potential advertisers."

"I'll do it, then." He enjoyed shocking Dave like that. "I'll start by debunking all those libertarians with their stupid obsession over the gold standard."

"How about something more marketable like watching paint dry?"

"Trolling a handful of Ron Paul forums alone, I can guarantee fifty-thousand views." Thomas stood and pushed his seat against the table.

"Just show her around the library. You make the most trivial tasks seem like a year-long expedition across the Antarctic."

"Speaking of monumental tasks, I'm going back down to the caf to see if there's still something half-edible."

"Good luck," Dave said, chuckling.

Thomas didn't head to the cafeteria once he'd left Dave. Instead, he went back to his desk. As much as he liked Dave in many ways, the man was toxic. Around other people, Thomas ridiculed the concept of energy vampires, but privately, he wasn't so sure. He always felt drained and in a foul mood after hanging around the man. They'd originally paired up on stage and had great chemistry so long as they were in front of an audience. Alone, it was like brackish water and rancid oil.

He checked his email. Lucy hadn't replied to the last one he'd sent, so presumably she didn't need directions. Lucy. Tonight, he'd decide whether she was worth sabotaging his career. He'd have to, to get out of using her as a stooge. A girl he'd known for less than a week. If he had any sense, he'd call and cancel, telling

Dave she wasn't able to make it. He picked up the phone, held it, and hung up again. Who was he fooling; he had no sense. If he had, he'd already be doing much better things with his life.

*   *   *

The bells over the front door jingled and Athena came in, carrying takeout from a Thai restaurant downtown. The scent of garlic and jasmine rice filled the store.

"Yay! You made it!" Lucy got off her stool and crouched behind the counter to fetch her wallet. "I've been so bored today. What do I owe you?"

"Get me next time." Athena set the stack of Styrofoam containers onto the counter next to the cash register. Something in one of the dishes smelled amazing, but Lucy had yet to figure out what it was. Something sweet, but definitely not coconut or any of the other ingredients she typically came across in any recipes she'd looked up.

"Back in a sec." Lucy ducked into the back room to grab two plates and some cutlery. As she caught sight of the little round table, Thomas's face popped into her mind, a ghostly memory of her first time meeting him. Three more hours until she was to see him again and she was nowhere near ready for it.

Her hands shook as she took the containers of rice and dumped several spoonfuls onto each of their plates. Thankfully, Athena hadn't yet noticed how on edge she was. Heading into the back room again, she fetched an extra wooden stool and set it in front of the cash register. The odds of them being interrupted by a customer were next to none, anyway.

"Basil beef for you, veggie Pad Thai for me." Athena opened her container and dumped the contents over her rice.

"Thanks for getting this. They aren't delivering right now and I hate closing the store on the off chance someone wants to come in." Lucy used her fork to pull out as many pieces of meat and as few vegetables as she could, then poured sauce over her rice. As much as she liked the flavor of green peppers and onions, she couldn't stand biting right into them.

Athena gulped down a mouthful. "Up to anything tonight?"

"I've got a reading at someone's house and I have a feeling the outcome of the cards might be something the person isn't going to want to hear." Lucy felt bad lying to Athena, yet she wasn't ready to tell her about Thomas. That would only lead to questions she didn't even want to think about.

"Are you afraid to be the bringer of bad news?"

Lucy stabbed her fork into a piece of beef and dipped it into the sauce. Even though it was one of her favorite dishes, she was having trouble getting it down. "Maybe. It's more a sense of unease I've had since the reading you did for me. That tower card."

"Just go with the flow. Have a bath beforehand, do some yoga. Besides, if anyone should be nervous, it should be me," Athena said, a grin spreading across her freckled face. "I have a date with the most amazing guy later!"

"How did you meet him?" Lucy asked. Not that what worked for Athena ever worked for her.

She giggled like a little girl who'd just snuck a fingerful of frosting from a birthday cake. "At this café. I was just sitting in a corner with a book when this tall, super-hot man came up to me and complimented my hair. Oh, and he was wearing this super-sharp suit. This'll be my second time hanging out with him."

A chill came over Lucy at the mention of a suit. Just as quickly, she put it out of her mind. It couldn't be Thomas, he'd be waiting for her at his house tonight. Not that it should take long. "What does he look like?"

"Tall, dark hair, really built. He works for this big advertising firm and loves his designer labels. Way more conservative than me, but it makes for interesting conversation."

Lucy continued stirring the piece of beef around in the sauce, unable to put it in her mouth. Although she was tempted to tell Athena about Thomas, she didn't want to jinx anything. "I hope it goes well. I've decided for myself, being single is not so bad. No one else's mess to deal with, no in-laws, no—"

"You always did like the easy way out."

"Better to want what you have than to chase after what you cannot have. As the Buddhists say, the source of unhappiness is desire."

Athena put her leftover containers back into one of the paper bags. "Another source of unhappiness is a defeatist attitude, m'kay?"

Lucy huffed. There was no convincing Athena that the Universe had it in for her; she didn't understand what it was like for *nothing* to go right.

"I have to get going," Athena said, making her way to the front of the store. "I'll call you later."

"Good luck tonight." Lucy waved to her and returned to picking at her cold food. Her stomach churned. She tried not to think about tonight, but her mind kept veering back to it like a shopping cart with a misaligned wheel. She checked the chat app they'd been using and he was still offline.

Fine, she'd let herself think about him. He was a little weird, but she liked quirky guys. Most of the ones she'd met since breaking up with Pete were so boring. Closing her eyes, she took a deep breath in. "I am no longer going to sabotage myself; I deserve happiness."

She switched on her cell phone and checked to see if any new emails had come in. "Who am I kidding. I always shoot myself in the foot."

Now that she thought about it, he hadn't asked how she was getting to his place or he assumed she had a car. According to the transit map, the bus ride would take between half an hour and forty-five minutes. She checked the city website and couldn't find any detour notices. Plenty of her friends had cars, and they'd be happy to drop her, but she hated asking them for favors. Lately, she felt she had so little to offer in return.

CHAPTER SEVEN

Lucy stared out the window of the city bus as it wound through the leafy neighborhood. The houses and lots appeared much larger than they had in street view on the internet. She barely recognized the same stone fence surrounding a wooded property when the bus neared the top of the hill. At the sight of a bench next to the stop, she pulled the cord and rushed to the back door.

The bus lurched to a halt. She stepped off, crossed the road and hesitated at the wrought iron gate. It stood ajar, daring her to pass through. When Thomas had described the house he lived in, she'd pictured some modest, two-story abode in need of a little fixing up. Her stomach was all butterflies as she double-checked the address, walked around the gate and ambled up the gravel driveway leading to a sprawling Queen Anne. She took her phone out and checked the email from him once more, just to be sure.

The house was certainly old enough to have ghosts and looked like it had been used as a set for some horror movie. Not the dilapidated ones in teen slasher movies, but the kind some yuppie family had just purchased, wanting to escape from the big city.

Gables with gingerbread trim and stained glass windows jutted out from the peaked roof in all directions. Below, the front balcony wrapped around one side of the house. While the only furniture he kept on it was an old wooden stool, it would be a great spot to watch thunderstorms, she thought. As she got closer, she couldn't help noticing all the little details like the bronze mailbox, the lion's head knocker, and the antique doorknobs.

She lumbered up the steps. She started as Thomas opened the door, poked his head out, and smiled at her. He was easily as cute as she remembered, though dressed more casually now, in black jeans and an argyle sweater.

"Made it here all right?" he asked, staring around at the driveway behind her.

"Bus was right on time." She hated how winded she must sound. "It didn't take nearly as long as I thought it would."

"Hm. It's never punctual when I go to take it."

"You don't drive?" she asked. A black Karmann Ghia sat on a patch of gravel between the house and a giant fir tree, just in front of a garage that had definitely seen better days.

"My car needs fixing up," he said, standing aside for her to come in. "You don't think I'd have made you come out here by bus if I was able to pick you up, would you? Now that I think about it, I should have asked. Sorry, got a lot on my mind lately."

Already she'd managed to upset him. One of her gifts. She shrugged awkwardly as she followed him into the airy front hall She stared around, agape.

The entire house was an heirloom. She felt a tinge of jealousy as she took in the beveled glass in the window above the door, sunlight sparkling through. To her left, an elegant walnut staircase swept up to the second floor. Beneath the banister sat an antique chaise lounge upholstered in red brocade. Straight down the hall, she could see into a huge, brightly lit kitchen. This was exactly the sort of place she'd live if she had the money. "It's gorgeous. This is *yours*?"

He nodded, a glimmer of sadness in his eyes.

Running her fingers around the spherical newel, she wondered how he could afford such a place by himself, especially if he had only recently moved in. "Amazing workmanship."

"Nowadays, everyone goes for whatever's cheapest," he said. "A shame, really. My uncle did a lot of the fixing up in here himself and always went for the best."

She could have sworn he'd told her he lived alone and had just moved in. "Didn't you just buy this place?"

"Come, see the library!" He took her arm and dragged her to the first door on the right, opening it wide. "This is where we'll be holding the um, channeling session."

Lucy gasped. The library was enormous. An oriental carpet covered most of the polished floorboards. A fireplace with a finely carved wooden mantle took up most of the far wall. Sofas, leather recliners, reading lamps and side tables had been arranged artfully to fill the room, except for a large, round table set incongruously on her left.

"My uncle crafted everything in here. He was incredibly handy. If I had more time I'd try making some things myself; I still have all his tools."

"It's nice," Lucy said, kicking herself at the bland response. For now, she'd ignore his little lie. Having inherited property herself, it wasn't something she liked to tell people. They'd always lecture her to sell it, or borrow against it. For all she knew, he was the same way. "Some of the pieces look like pine, but not quite."

"He stained them darker. His favorite is chestnut, but it's hard to find in this part of the world."

"I guess it's a lot more common in England?"

"England?" he asked, furrowing his brow.

Again, she'd stuck her foot in her mouth and felt a rush of embarrassment. "I thought your accent sounded …"

He chuckled. "I'm from Denmark originally. Grew up in a town outside of Copenhagen nobody's ever heard of. I did have a couple of teachers who were from England."

Now that she tuned in more, he did sound almost stuck at certain consonants. Not knowing a thing about Denmark except that it was somewhere in northern Europe, she said nothing and walked further in. If not for the books and sitting areas and desks, it could have easily been a ballroom. It was certainly large enough.

"This place is amazing," she whispered.

He checked the time on his phone and mumbled, "Everyone else is late, of course."

She wandered up to a shelf crammed with leather-bound books. As usual whenever she was around an attractive guy, her mind blanked. She hated how easily intimidated she got. She tried to distract herself browsing through titles that seemed to cover every imaginable subject. Collections of plays by Ibsen and Molière, history books on the Roman Empire, ancient India, the Ming Dynasty, nearly every literary classic she could think of. She could spend days in here, weeks even.

She stooped to check out the lower shelves and felt his eyes on her. Not only did she like everything about his appearance, but he seemed to be extremely bright. He had that same mien as certain kids she'd gone to school with, the ones who got top grades without studying, who knew a little about everything and showed up their teachers whenever they got the chance. One of the reasons she was always single was because most of the men she met were so dull, with barely any interests beyond sports or their careers.

"You must come across quite the variety people in your line of work," he said.

"I spend most of my time running the store and it's been really quiet with all the construction." Mentally she kicked herself, remembering Athena's nagging to be more positive. "So the chance to do a channeling is welcome relief for me."

He frowned, took his phone out again, and swiped the screen. "You must see some strange things, though."

"I wish. People come in with the same problems over and over again, wanting someone to fix their lives for them. I suppose I'm cheaper than a therapist." So much for being positive.

The tone of his voice changed as he said, "So the people you deal with are predictable, you'd say?"

"People face pretty much the same things in life, such as marriage, kids, career frustration, coping with the death of a loved one and so on." She gazed out one of the windows onto a well-tended yard, wondering why she was here. He hadn't asked her any details about the séance or once mentioned the ghost supposedly plaguing him. Not that she'd asked.

"Your card mentioned Shamanism. Yet your surname is–"

"It's Russian. Zharakova is my real surname. My dad's Russian originally, though his family moved around a lot. Shamans are Siberian." Again, she mentally kicked herself; she must sound like a third grader speaking in front of class for the first time.

"That's what I thought. Yet I always hear people talking about some Mexican shaman they met, or a Vancouver Island–"

"It's just another word for 'sorcerer'. As for Siberia, they think there's nothing but barren tundra. The landscape is so beautiful. Especially around Lake Baikal."

"You've been?" His eyes gleamed, the sadness, gone.

She felt hot, especially around the back of her neck under her hair. Just when she thought he was trying to trip her up, he began sounding genuinely intrigued.

"I visited family there some years back."

"I can't get my friends to go anywhere that doesn't involve the words 'all inclusive', but I'd love to go someplace more exotic. As for Siberia, have you ever read up on the Tunguska ex—"

A knock at the front door distracted him. "Excuse me." He brushed his hand on her shoulder as he went past and trotted out to the front hall. He poked his head back in and jerked it, summoning Lucy to follow him.

Two people let themselves in through his front door, which he'd left unlocked. A tall, chic woman with a pixie haircut stepped inside. She was dressed all in black apart from an olive green shawl. She had a vaguely Mediterranean look about her, with black hair, dark eyes and heavy, almost masculine features. Yet she was strangely beautiful.

She kissed Thomas's cheek and then held her hand out to Lucy. "Hi, I'm Marcia. I've never been in a séance before, but always wanted to see what it would be like. Sounds really cool. And this is my husband, Jeremy."

Jeremy, a shaven-headed bear of a man, shook Lucy's hand.

"Couples are okay for this?" Thomas asked.

"Absolutely!" Lucy was relieved they seemed so nice. No mention of any girlfriend either. So far.

Jeremy slapped Thomas's back and said, "Still up for drinks later?"

"Yeah, um—" Again, someone pounded on the front door. He opened it to three more people. First to come in, a lanky man with wild, curly hair, heavy eyebrows, and full lips. He wore overly large prescription glasses with thick black frames, and a faded blue t-shirt that read: *Beer! Helping ugly people get laid since 1862.*

"This is Isaac," Thomas said, "along with Jenn and ... Steve!"

Steve had square, chiseled features and a blond brush cut. With his weight lifter build, his arms hung away from his body gorilla-like and he walked with attitude. *Short man syndrome,* Lucy thought as she realized they were the same height.

Meanwhile Jenn was stunningly beautiful, with green doe eyes and long blonde hair pulled back into a high ponytail. Her Lululemon ensemble revealed a perfect body and ample cleavage. She was taller than Steve but had similar Scandinavian features. Definitely a queen bee. She gave Lucy the once-over and flashed a broad, fake smile of perfect teeth. Lucy simpered at her as well, feeling short and dumpy. Next to Jenn, anyone would look like a troll.

"I guess that's everyone, now?" Thomas locked the door and placed his hands on Lucy's shoulders, sending a frisson up her spine. "This is Lucy, our lovely medium who will be guiding the, uh, channeling session."

"Nice meeting everyone," she said, suppressing the urge to bolt out.

While everyone took turns shaking hands with her, Thomas kept his hands on her shoulders. She felt an electrical current coursing between them. "Seven of us should be okay?" he asked. "There's something mystical about numbers, right?"

"The number doesn't matter, so long as everyone adds positive energy." Lucy stood aside and watched everyone else go in. She folded her arms in front of her chest, hunched her shoulders, and walked into the center of the library, startled by how gloomy the place now felt. Definitely a lot of tension in the air. Negative energy. "It feels kind of depressing in here."

She eyed Jenn, Steve, and Isaac whispering to each other.

"It was upstairs in the guest bedroom where the, uh, murder took place," Thomas said. "But I read that you should never try to make contact in the exact same place, because the energy vortex would be too intense. Or something like that."

Lucy really did feel an ominous presence now that she wasn't absorbed in scanning all the book titles. "This must have been where the killer brooded first, or where he and the victim likely quarreled."

"I was told it had been a robbery gone badly. There's no evidence he actually came into here."

"Are you sure?" Lucy stiffened and darkness clouded her peripheral vision on one side, blocking the fireplace.

"Absolutely. According to the police report, the ..."

Steve, Isaac, and Jenn began snickering. She should have paid more attention to her earlier hunch; he was definitely lying about something. She pulled him aside and hissed, "What's so funny?"

"No idea," he whispered, his eyes wide. His expression seemed genuine; either that or he was a top-notch actor.

"Just so you know, people who don't take this seriously can create really bad energy."

"I'll deal with them. One moment." Thomas motioned for them to follow him out into the hallway, saying, "Eh—guys?"

As they left the room, Marcia rolled her eyes and smiled at Lucy. "I've seen you before." She had a throaty, musical voice. "You have a store, don't you? Somewhere in the student ghetto?"

Lucy nodded and edged closer to the door, trying to eavesdrop.

"I got a really cool book from there about the Coral Castle in Florida. But some guy named Pete was working at the time."

"My boyfriend. Former boyfriend." Lucy stared down at her feet. Marcia seemed nice, she loved the house and she really liked Thomas, but the only place she wanted to be right now was back at home. In her comfort zone.

*   *   *

Furious, Thomas cornered Steve and Jenn in the hallway just outside the kitchen while Isaac watched on. "Look, you can have your shits and giggles when this is over, but for now I need you to play along. For fucksakes grow up!"

Steve and Jenn glowered at him like a pair of sullen children.

"I'm sorry," Jenn said and Steve nodded.

"You promised me you'd help. She's going to see right through this unless the lot of you takes it seriously. Now I'm glad you showed up, but if you're not going to go through with it, why bother. Go home!" He turned to Isaac and said, "Especially you. This could make or break our ad contract and believe me; you'll see a pink slip long before I ever do."

"Chill, it's just an internet show," Steve said.

"This is my job."

"All right, fine!" Steve said. "But dude, you should have rehearsed your act a little more before you brought her here. Just sayin'."

Jenn winked at Steve and Thomas sighed. "All I ask is that you keep a straight face. For ten minutes. Is it really so difficult?"

*   *   *

Lucy eyed Steve, Jenn, and Isaac as they followed Thomas back into the library, looking contrite or at least pretending to be. Something was off about all of them. Her sense grew only more acute as Steve came up to her and said, "I'm sorry. I didn't know about the whole negative energy thing."

"It's okay," she said, hoping he wouldn't continue. It was rare for her to take such a strong, instant dislike to someone. She noticed Marcia and Jeremy avoided interacting with him too, beyond acknowledging his presence.

Thomas clapped his hands together and stood by the round table near the bookshelves as if he were taking the stage. He cleared his throat. "This is the table we'll use for the ceremony. You said to get a round one, right? Nice and large?"

Lucy grinned. "It's perfect!"

"What else will we need?" He turned and gazed up at the recessed shelves above the mantle. "You use candles or anything?"

"I'll bring it all with me. Maybe put out some hearty food like stew or fresh bread to attract the spirit. Otherwise." Lucy nodded toward Jenn, who stood in a corner fiddling with her phone. "As few distractions as possible!"

"Great!" Thomas clapped his hands together again and stepped forward to herd everyone back out. "I guess that's it, then. Are we still on for Saturday? Ten-thirty isn't too late, I hope."

"It's fine," she said. His abruptness threw her but she couldn't think of anything more to ask. He walked her to the front door. Everyone else lurked by the library entrance, waving.

"Nice meeting you," a few of them mumbled.

"See you all Saturday!" She bundled her purse in her arms and hurried out. As soon as she reached the gravel driveway, she dug out her phone to check the time. The bus was due in four minutes. "What on Earth am I doing here?" she muttered, relieved her wait wouldn't be that long.

She was definitely going to need Athena's help. She didn't believe for a second Thomas's claim that a murder victim haunted the house. Even if it was true, she had no idea what they expected from her.

On top of that, she had definitely sensed *something* in the library. Even with the lofty ceilings, glittering chandelier and light from a fiery sunset pouring in through three windows, the room had been dark and gloomy. With entities of any kind, the best thing to do was simply acknowledge them and politely ask them to go somewhere else. Provided that was his problem to begin with. Unfortunately, if she wanted to see him again, she'd have to go through with this.

CHAPTER EIGHT

"That Lucy was a bit weird wasn't she," Thomas said, opening the door to the Cloak and Dagger Pub. He felt guilty about being so abrupt with her, but Jenn was in one of her moods and she would've made mincemeat out of the girl. He never should have invited her. Too late now.

Marcia made a beeline to an empty table by the wall. "Weird? Quiet, maybe."

"She was quite chatty when I first met her." Thomas stripped off his trench coat and sat. "But talking to her today was like pulling teeth. Actually, it was more like my car. Whenever I thought I'd finally got conversation started, it would splutter and stall out."

Jeremy shrugged, already looking bored.

"Maybe she's figured out what you guys are up to." Marcia picked up the plastic beer menu and tapped it on the table. "She didn't strike me as dumb."

"You have to be a bit stupid to believe all that New Age crap. And it was your mum who said her fortune was a complete fraud and that she was making everything up as she went."

"Drop it." Marcia waved to the bartender. "Same as always!"

"Didn't you find her awkward? She was chatty enough in her shop, but barely said two words the entire time you were there and that was two more than she'd said right before that."

"Because you never shut up for long enough," Jeremy said.

"How's the rest of your job going?" Marcia asked.

"It's getting to be like that movie Groundhog Day. Every day seems identical, only I don't get the chance to change any of it, or ever escape." He leaned back in his chair and scanned the crowd of scruffy, tattooed thirty-somethings. Same as always in this bar, too. Whatever happened to being presentable in public?

"I thought you got a promotion," she said.

"To manager of nobody and my last raise was less than a nickel an hour. Now I don't even get overtime when they call me in."

"Maybe if you didn't slack off so much," Jeremy grumbled.

"That is *why* I slack off. So long as they're expecting twelve hours a day from me for shit pay, I—"

"You could sell that house and never work another day of your life," Jeremy said. "Invest the proceeds and live like a king."

"What, in zero-interest savings bonds or a rigged stock market that crashes every few years?"

"You could start your own business."

"Then I'd still be working; only I'd now be living in some crap apartment instead of a perfectly nice house."

"Or get a roommate like I've told you a zillion times," Jeremy said.

"I'm not tolerating anyone else's mess unless I'm at least getting a good shag from them regularly." He watched the server set down a pitcher and two glasses along with his drink. Beer for Marcia and Jeremy, gin and tonic for him.

He reached into his wallet and paid for the round. "Sorry I'm boring you. This show was my idea and it's morphed into this horrible, I don't know, it's not what I pictured it being."

"We know. It's been rough lately." Marcia looked at him motheringly and squeezed his hand.

"You need to get out more," Jeremy said. "Think about what you want in life, not what you *don't* want."

He knew what he wanted. He wanted a family, children, and stability in his life outside of work for once. Twice he'd had the chance to settle down and both times, he'd blown it. Well, the second one wasn't his fault. Nor was the first, in hindsight. His mother being sick was why he'd abandoned his life in Denmark, yet he hated the idea of holding her to blame for it. It had been entirely his choice. One he'd never regretted for an instant.

Marcia shrugged off her paisley shawl. Underneath, she wore a chunky necklace of clear, glass beads from which several much larger crystals dangled.

Thomas picked up the middle stone and turned it, watching it glint in the lights. "Very clever idea, Marcia. You took a strand from a chandelier to put around your neck."

"You are such a brat!" She swatted his arm. "What do you know about fashion? Everything you wear is even older than you are."

"It's called style. Very different from fashion. To begin with, style looks good."

Jeremy shook his head at him. "Dude, this is why you're single. You need to shut your mouth more often."

Marcia pursed her lips and stared straight at him. "Fine, I'm not going to let you see my drawings, then." She leaned her elbows on a large black leather folio that she'd placed on the table in front of her. Marcia was obsessed by the *Wizard of Oz*. She spent an inordinate amount of her free time drawing or painting various characters from the stories.

Thomas pretended to whimper and Marcia sighed, opened up the folio to show him a print of an acrylic painting she'd just finished. She turned it around so he could see her rendition of Tik-Tok, the rotund bronze robot balanced on spindly legs.

"I like it," he said. "It's very steam-punky."

"Steam punk? You are such a geek." Jeremy poured beer from the pitcher into two glasses, one for him, and one for Marcia.

"It's a cool aesthetic," Thomas said, proud of his inner nerd. "Sort of what technology would look like today if they'd never invented plastic. I always find anything with plastic tacky. Cheap-looking."

"Not everyone can afford the tastes of your majesty." Jeremy turned his attention to a game starting on one of the giant screens. Two teams stood facing each other on the ice. The arena darkened while a singer walked towards the microphone stand.

"Back in a sec, forgot to get some cash earlier." Marcia squeezed Jeremy's shoulders as she got up.

The second she was out of earshot Jeremy asked him, "Have told her yet? About Jenn?"

Anger flared in him. "Why should I? It's got nothing to do with me!"

"Uh huh."

"Just because I have an arts degree doesn't mean I'm bad in maths." Thomas glowered around at the other tables. Thankfully, Jeremy knew when to drop a matter. Jenn was the last thing he wanted to talk about. He'd only invited her because three other people had canceled on him at the last minute.

"There has to be at least one in here you think is cute," Jeremy said, nodding towards the long wooden bar.

Thomas shook his head. Pity drag-queen makeup was back in style, making even the most attractive ones look as if their faces were molded plastic. And what was it with those spidery false eyelashes? Then there were cell phone addicts who seemed incapable of live conversation, neglecting real friends in favor of fake ones. Others had that vacant stare indicating little in the way of brains inside their heads.

"You're too fussy. You don't drink beer, you don't follow sports, and you own more hair care products than Marcia. What kind of man are you?"

"I still have a dick, last time I checked." He turned stone-faced at the sight of a hen party cackling at a neighboring table. All of them wore bright pink feather boas, black tube dresses that fit their bodies like sausage casing, pink stockings, and silvery dollar-store tiaras. The bride-to-be and her friends groped the busboy while he cleared away some empty glasses.

"That is why I'm single. That is what's left to choose from, right there. It's been years since I met anyone who is single, not trashy, who is reasonably attractive and remotely sane."

"All women are crazy. Just need to find the right kind of crazy to settle down with. Trust me, Marcia is *nuts*." Jeremy's attention drifted back to the screen above Thomas's head.

"No one's flakier than that Lucy. God. In chat yesterday she was going on about chi energy and how she's in constant turmoil because of Venus being squared with her birth sign and—"

"Yeah!" Jeremy jumped up and punched the air as he watched the replay of a goal being scored. An ad came on the TV and he sat back down. "You know, for a guy who met a girl he can't stand, he sure does have her on his brain."

"Fuck you."

"Just saying it like it is, buddy. You've been yammering on about her since she left!"

"Woo!" The neighboring hen party clinked their glasses together. One woman stood to gulp her shot and green liquid dribbled down her chin. She slammed her glass on the table and staggered backwards, bumping Thomas's chair.

"She is so not my type." Even without Dave's stupid scheme, he had zero chance with Lucy anyway. She was attractive enough, but the walls she'd built around herself were as impenetrable as a bank vault. "My type is rational for start."

"Whatever. Who are you to say it's all bullshit? You only read up enough to know what to make fun of."

"I've investigated this crap for years. I even hoped to find *maybe* just one thing that's real behind any of it. But no matter how deep I dig, I find nothing but frauds and charlatans and deluded fools."

"Buddy, you are way too close-minded. Wanna know what your problem is? You shut out everything that's not guaranteed to work out like you think it should."

Thomas glared off while Jeremy turned his gaze back to the giant screen to watch the face-off. Both of them knew he always did this, talked himself out of being interested in any new woman he met, preferring to complain than put himself out there. To his relief, Marcia came hurrying back to their table.

"I want you to be the one to tell her," Jeremy said, almost growling.

"Forget it!" Thomas hissed. "It's up to Jenn."

"Your funeral," Jeremy said, faking a smile as his wife squeezed in next to him.

For whatever reason, Jeremy refused to get it through his thick skull that Thomas and Jenn had broken up and were definitely not getting back together again. Ever. Whatever Jenn had done with her life since was none of his business, or Jeremy's business, or Marcia's. She was Steve's problem now.

CHAPTER NINE

The bells jingled and Lucy looked up from her Sudoku puzzle. Athena elbowed her way into the store, carrying a white cardboard box. Although it was small, she was hefting it in both hands as if it were loaded with bricks.

"So. How'd that reading go?"

"It was okay," Lucy said in a tone to discourage any further questions.

She plunked the box down on a clear space next to the cash register. As a commercial distributor for essential oils, soaps, candles, herbs and teas, Athena liked to call herself Lucy's middle-woman. "I know you don't need anything for now, but I figured I'd still show you what came in this week."

"How did your date go last night?" Lucy opened up the flimsy box and pulled out a tiny cobalt blue bottle with a green and peach label. "You never called me after."

"Because it didn't end until well past midnight! I'll tell you later," she said, grinning. "I'm still in work mode right now."

"Fine."

"I brought some ylang-ylang for you."

"Thanks!" Lucy lifted some of the other little bottles out of the box and checked the labels. The rest were the usual lavender, sandalwood, peppermint, jasmine, and vanilla.

Athena took out a bottle that was missing its seal, opened it, and held it to Lucy's nose. "This is my newest scent, tuberose."

She inhaled deeply. It was refreshingly sweet without being sickly so. Floral, yet subtle. "Smells wonderful!"

"Keep that for yourself. I'll have more at the Expo."

"Ugh. I don't think the Universe wants me to go this year."

"Why, what happened?" Athena asked.

Lucy had been so wound up about meeting Thomas and fretting about whether he liked her or not, that she'd forgotten all about the expo. "They moved me to some godforsaken corner with no traffic, so I have to get new flyers done and on Saturday I've got this stupid … ugh, enough." She took a deep breath and exhaled sharply. "I'm *trying* to be less negative, I am. But it's hard, when random bad things keep happening to me."

"Oh, what is it now?" Athena came around the counter to hug her. The scent of herbal cigarette smoke blended with strawberry shampoo filled her nostrils.

"It's dumb," Lucy said.

"Spill the beans, lady. Something's been bugging you all week."

"Fine. When was the last time you heard of anyone being asked to do a séance?"

"A séance? Ooh, how Victorian."

"I'm serious. This guy came in the other day complaining about a poltergeist. He says it almost threw him down the stairs!"

Athena snorted. "What, it didn't suck him into the TV?"

"I know, totally out of some horror movie, so I told him I wanted to do a consultation visit first. It's just as well. A couple of his friends were treating it like a joke!"

"Maybe they're planning a prank on someone?"

"Then why not let me in on it?"

"To make it seem more realistic? You could always ask him." Athena threw up her hands, silver bangles jingling on her wrists.

"Yeah, yeah," Lucy said. "Normally I would've said no, but I can't afford to turn any business down right now."

Athena narrowed her eyes. "He better be cute."

"Oh, he is! He's absolutely gorgeous, incredibly smart, and I love his style," Lucy gushed like a burst pipe. So much for not wanting to jinx it. She'd never been able to fool Athena anyway.

"He's really quirky, totally my type and—oh, my God." She stared out the window, stunned. Thomas was right outside, gazing at the sign for her hours. "Speak of the Devil."

Before Lucy could duck down, Athena gripped her shoulder with fingers like grappling hooks. "That is one beautiful man."

He remained outside, staring in the window. Lucy wondered what had caught his attention, since she hadn't put that much in there to look at. As he glanced up at her sign, then at the door, her stomach twisted in knots. Yet he didn't come in. Instead, he pulled his phone out of his pocket and wandered off.

"Go!" Athena shoved Lucy out into the middle of her store. "Go out and say 'hi' to him!"

"I can't!" Lucy's feet took root in the floorboards. She was as relieved as she was disappointed he hadn't come in. "I'll look too desperate if I rush up to him now."

"This is how you sabotage yourself, sweetie. You're so afraid of looking like an idiot in front of men you like, that you leave no impression on them at all."

No, Lucy thought, *a bad impression is always worse.*

Athena picked up her box and gave Lucy a hug with her free arm. "I have to finish my rounds. Call me later," she said and let herself out of the store.

Lucy went back behind her counter and pulled out some plastic bags full of knitting, something she'd been meaning to work on more. Since business in the store was slow, she figured she could start making and selling items online. She'd even come up with what she thought was a cute name on Etsy, *The Kitty Brat*. She'd considered *I Love Lucy*, but it was already taken, along with a dozen or so variants. On top of that, she'd always hated the TV show anyway. She pulled out a ball of wool, dyed various different shades of blue, and set it on the counter.

The bells on her door jingled again. Thomas slipped inside, cringing at the noise he'd just made. "Hello." He came up to her, smiling. "I was in the neighborhood, so I thought I'd drop by."

Lucy visualized giving herself a hard kick in the butt, and smiled back. "What were you doing here?" *Lame*, she thought.

He had a plastic bag in one of his hands, with clothing of some sort inside. "A new Thai place opened up, so a bunch of us from work went to check out their lunch menu. It wasn't bad. Seems to be the thing these days. Thai, Vietnamese, Korean. Yet they're all run by Chinese people. And sushi is on the menu."

Lucy giggled. If she was too nervous to speak, she could still be an audience for him.

"They only ever have that 'sri-ratcha' or however you

pronounce it. I prefer *sambal oelek*, or chili flakes in oil. Of course half the time it's at least a decade old, even if the restaurant's only been open a few months."

She giggled again. "I like spicy food too."

He bit his bottom lip and quirked his eyebrows. "I like the endorphin rush."

Lucy didn't want to think about food; her stomach was doing somersaults. His steady gaze didn't help either. "I thought I saw you outside earlier," she said. So long as she was in salesperson mode, she'd be okay. "Were you checking out something in the display case?"

"Not really. I didn't want to come in while you had a customer, so I waited around for them to leave. They were taking ages, so I thought I'd go into another shop until they were gone." He glanced at her needles prodding the wool and put his bag on the counter next to it. He pulled out a grey-blue vintage sweater with a wide shawl collar. The buttons were made from slices of wood.

Lucy stroked the fabric. "It's so soft."

He looked pleased with himself. "I think there's either cashmere or angora in the blend. It was the buttons I really liked, though. I got it at that shop a few doors down." He put the sweater back and pulled out a pair of black leather ankle boots, similar to the pair he was wearing. "Got these too, only ten dollars. They're in perfect condition, see?"

"They're nice," she said.

His phone rang. He took it out of his pocket, checked the screen, and put it back without answering it. "Work. I've been bunking off since lunch. Better get back, I suppose." He picked up his bag and said, "See you Saturday, then?"

"Looking forward to it!" Lucy grinned and waved as he left, then let out a deep breath. She watched him smiling to himself as he passed by her front window. Maybe he did like her.

Then it struck her, like a slap across her face. His thing for footwear and vintage jackets and the baroque silver rings he wore. Hair that looked messy in a calculated way, tousled just so, and his taste in luxury fabrics.

It would even explain how he could afford such a beautiful old house on his own. It was so clean, immaculate. It must also be why he was single. How could she have missed it before? A lead blanket of disappointment weighed on her shoulders as it sank in. He was gay. He had to be.

*   *   *

Thomas slipped into the jail cell of a conference room just as Dave was passing around a set of notes to Isaac, the Executive Producer and four others seated at the long oval table. There were no windows to outside, no décor, just a taupe carpet and grey walls and unpleasant halogen track lighting overhead.

"We had fantastic traffic from the river rock episode," Dave said. "On the day of upload, we got over thirty-thousand hits."

The Executive Producer perused his copy and nodded, then frowned. "Wasn't as high as that one in May. What happened?"

Dave riffled through his papers. Thomas slid into the seat next to him and whispered, "The magnetic bracelet salesman."

"Oh, that's why. We were too nice!" Dave said. The Producer stared at him, waiting, and he added, "See, people love it when these scammers get taken down in a big way. Humiliated live on TV, their bullshit staring them right in the face. With all their customers looking on."

"Sounds like the direction we should be pursuing, then."

Thomas gazed up at the blank wall above their heads, wondering why he'd raced back to the office so fast. Lucy's shop had been so cozy and relaxed. On her home turf, she seemed so much more at ease as well. He could have come up with some ridiculous excuse about why he'd missed the production meeting. They always believed him.

"Already on it," Dave said, reaching into his briefcase. He took out a bundle of dark blue and white flyers and tossed them onto the middle of the table. They were flyers for the Psychic Expo.

The Producer picked one up and tapped it on the table. "I thought you were doing some kind of séance."

"We're filming it tomorrow." Dave opened up one of the flyers and spread out the map of exhibitors. "But we're going to do the big exposé in her booth, which is practically in the center of the whole auditorium. A two-part episode."

Thomas shifted uncomfortably in his seat as the Producer flipped to the back of the flyer and checked out Lucy's photo.

"Nice looking girl!" he said. "This was your pick, Tom?"

Thomas nodded absently. When Dave had caught him staring at her that first weekend of Canal Fest, instead of saying he thought she was cute like any normal person would, he mentioned she'd be a great candidate for their show. Really, he'd just been thinking up an excuse to go talk to her. "I don't know why we always need to expose random people the same way. It's a bit too predictable, isn't it?"

"People like predictable. That is why movies have happy endings." The Producer donned a smug expression like a new bespoke suit and resumed tapping the edge of the flyer on the table.

"This is our plan." Dave shaped his hands to create a frame in the air and said, "We film the séance, catch her tricks, and at this expo, we show her how we figured it all out. Live on camera, in front of hundreds of people!"

"This thing needs to go viral in time to renew our ad contract," the Producer said. "The séance will be this Tuesday and the exposé the next. Think you'll get it?"

"Oh, we'll get it, all right," Dave said.

Everyone grinned at each other in a self-congratulatory way except for Thomas, who sulked at the photo of Lucy. She looked so harmless. And yet ... They'd have to be living on Mars to think footage of someone writhing in a chair or making the windows rattle had any chance of going viral. Knowing Dave, he'd use a shot of Jenn's cleavage for the thumbnail image and that would be the extent of it.

CHAPTER TEN

Lucy stood at the counter inside a hole-in-the-wall print shop that still treated email like a novelty. A clerk came out carrying a cardboard box and set it down on the counter. Lucy studied the sample flyer taped to the top, making sure the new location had been highlighted exactly the way she'd asked. Everything looked okay. The Expo organizers were the ones being billed. Good.

"Lucy?" A silver-haired woman tapped her shoulder.

"Shirley!" Lucy turned around to give her a hug. "How are you, it's been ages!"

"I've been better."

Lucy looked at her quizzically.

"This stupid show," Shirley said. "These guys contacted me a few months ago and told me they were doing research for a documentary on astral energy. They warned me they were skeptical, but were keeping an open mind and wanted to present both sides of the argument. So I went into the theories of Faraday and Tesla, and loaned them some books on the subject."

"It sounds really interesting!"

Shirley grunted. "I spent three days explaining everything to their TV crew and even allowed them to view a private therapy session I only do three times a year!"

The cashier nudged Shirley's arm and handed her a slip of paper. Shirley nodded in thanks. "Afterward, they went and edited everything down to five minutes, cutting it to make me look like a total fraud. Thank God for my clients. They're disgusted with these guys."

"Why would they do such a thing?" Lucy picked her box up off the counter. It was much heavier than she expected and now she had to walk six blocks with it.

"It's all good, hon." Shirley opened the door for her. "My clients have been so incredibly supportive. They were the ones telling *me* how much I give to them, and what value they get from my sessions. The funny thing is, while these guys thought they were outing me, I've been getting dozens more calls for new business! I know I shouldn't be upset, but ... you know how it is."

"What channel is it on?" Lucy waited for Shirley to limp out the door of the printer shop. Her knee was bandaged and Lucy remembered she'd mentioned getting surgery on it.

"No channel, it's on the internet. I should have realized it at the time because they never had a release form for me to sign. Like I said, I'm *trying* not to let myself get upset by it."

"I don't blame you. I'd be furious!"

"They'll probably be at the Expo, so keep an eye out for them. I'm not the only person who's been burned by them." Shirley unlocked the back passenger door to her car, an old VW, and gestured for Lucy to set her box on the seat. "Need a ride? I know it's only a few blocks, but the road's pretty bad these days."

"Thanks, I'd love one," Lucy said, climbing in. Shirley had a catering business on the side and the car smelled like fresh-baked cookies and cake.

"I forget the name of the show, but it shouldn't be too hard to find. Google my name and you'll find it." Shirley then muttered something unintelligible under her breath, still in the habit of never swearing in front of her even two decades later.

*   *   *

With Dave spotting him, Thomas stepped onto an upper rung of the folding ladder he'd placed in the middle of his library. Thank God, it was Friday. Even better, for once the cheap bastards agreed that setting up the cameras and so on offsite counted as work time.

"You okay up there?" Dave gripped one side of the ladder and planted his feet onto the carpet.

"I'm fine." Thomas braced his knee against the topmost rung and fastened a camera to the overhead chandelier. As he eyed the round table below, the room below swelled. Heights gave him vertigo, which he always forgot until it was too late.

He felt better as he looked up again and concentrated on

adjusting the camera, tilting it more towards the bookshelf.

Dave squinted and said, "Too much, move it back a little."

"It all seems so utterly pointless." He sighed and nudged the camera to the left, not caring what it may end up capturing. If Dave and Alistair thought this had a chance of going viral, they were smoking better drugs than he'd ever tried.

He climbed down the ladder and let out another deep sigh, glad to be on solid ground again. "Apart from the odd blip, we've been losing traffic for months. It's getting so I can scarcely make all the pie charts look good anymore. We need to do something different, completely different."

"Tom, it's fraud. This costs the consumer millions—billions! It's not just a show, it's a public service."

"So? No worse than spending on designer clothes, or drinking your face off every night. Why not do a show on over-priced real estate or luxury brands? Think a five-hundred dollar handbag will make you look like a roaring success when the rest of your outfit screams 'people of Wal-Mart'? Or that river stone woman. Not her, but the ones who go to her retreats and what-not. These people go around being all 'spiritual' yet drive an eighty-thousand dollar car! You should be targeting *them*!"

Dave took out his phone, opened the video of Mrs. Torres at Canal Fest, and held the screen up to him. "She's a fake. Conning little old ladies and bereaved widows. Look! Don't let that cute smile fool you. These people are sociopaths."

A camera had been concealed in a brooch on Marcia's mum's black scarf. In the upper left corner of the screen, Lucy was squinting out through her partly opened eye, mouthing the name *Matthew*. He handed it back, keeping his face impassive. The sooner they were finished, the better.

"We're helping people accept reality, not live in some dream world fantasy where they can avoid dealing with their lives!"

"Perhaps they don't want to. Why should they? Life can be horrible sometimes. That goes back to my point about alcohol."

"You're saying you believe in all this shit?"

"Of course not! But why should I care what other people

believe? They're not forcing anybody!"

Dave grabbed his toolbox and crouched down next to a cabinet by the entrance. He was about to drill straight into the middle of a panel of dark wainscoting when Thomas grabbed his arm. "Don't drill into the wood! Christ—that's hundred-year-old mahogany!"

Dave drilled a tiny hole into the white plaster just above. "Look. This show is how you can afford the upkeep on this fancy house. Capiche?"

Dave brushed dust away from the hole. Thomas picked up a tiny spy camera from a case on the round table and tossed it onto the carpet next to him. What a bloody idiot, was all he could think. Dave secured the camera into the hole and got up again.

"I'm almost done." Dave carried the ladder over to the set of shelves between the round table and a window that looked out onto his neglected back yard. Thistles were spreading like wildfire.

Thomas gripped the ladder and Dave climbed up, clutching a wooden soldier in one hand. He balanced the statuette on the top shelf and tilted the head down so that the camera inside was aimed at the round table. "Hey, you could always leave this one in the bedroom next time you and Jenn, you know."

Thomas scowled. "She left me ages ago."

"She's single again! Clinging to him for dear life, but expect a call soon, is all I'll say."

Thomas laughed, trying not to shake the ladder while Dave clambered back down. "You just made my day."

Dave shook his head. "Make her get tests done first."

"I'm not stupid!"

"Yes you are. Never mind. Did we put any beneath that table yet?" Dave crawled underneath and peered up at the joints.

"So you're saying Steve dumped *her*?" he asked, glad for a topic suiting his spiteful mood and hoping he'd continue.

"Late last night." Dave fumbled around on the carpet and Thomas kicked a package of blue tack over to him that had been lying on the floor nearby.

"Oh, cosmic justice." He crouched and handed Dave a camera to stick into the blue tack. "There really is such a thing."

"Whatever. I give you two weeks, tops."

Thomas couldn't wait for Dave to be out of here so he could call Jeremy and Marcia. So much for Steve being her *Soul Mate*. He got back up, collapsed the ladder, and carried it towards the doorway. "Are you done with this?"

"Yeah, I'm done."

He took the ladder outside, down the steps of his porch, and propped it against the van. Steve had dumped Jenn. After wooing her for how long? He couldn't wait to hear Marcia's reaction.

When he came back into the library, Dave was still fiddling under the table. "Damned thing isn't sticking!"

He set the package of blue tack on the table and handed Dave a roll of electrical tape.

"You're all quiet now. Why wait? May as well call her up."

"There is no fucking way I'm getting back with her," Thomas said, feeling giddy. In the past, he'd gone back to her at the snap of her fingers. This time, he couldn't wait to blow her off.

Dave bumped the table as he stood up again. He wagged two fingers in Thomas's face. "Two weeks."

"Nope. I'm older and wiser now."

"Yeah, and how many times have I heard that over the past what, five, six years? Let me guess." Dave put his fingers to each side of his head. "I'm tuning in my psychic powers here. There will be some crisis and Jenn will beg you to meet up with her at one of your old haunts."

Thomas bit his bottom lip, amused by Dave's routine for once. "Not a chance."

"Yeah, right. She'll pick where you like to go. She'll wear something so low-cut you can almost see her nipples. She'll be sniveling and will have already ordered a glass of wine for you. She'll compose herself while you drink your first glass, and she'll rant about whatever catastrophe she's just had to deal with."

The last thing he wanted to do was admit he was interested in Lucy, who seemed to be the polar opposite of Jenn. She was nearly as attractive in her own way, but also shy, quiet, and most importantly, not a lying cheating bitch. If a little fortune telling and New Age woo was the extent of her annoying traits, he could manage. "I don't care anymore."

"A little small talk, and at your second glass of wine, she'll apologize profusely for whatever nasty things she said about you. She'll take it all back. Then she'll be crying again, about how Steve was such a jerk and you're so much better and how she made the biggest mistake of her life and–"

The wooden soldier toppled off the shelf, landing with a *crack!* by their feet. The body lay splayed while the head rolled under the table. Dave and Thomas stared at it, exchanged a glance like a pair of cats sizing each other up, and continued their argument.

"Like I said: two weeks, tops."

"Enough. I don't give a fuck." Thomas backed away as Dave stepped closer. Yes, he'd gone back to Jenn before, several times before, no need to rub it in his face.

"She'll bawl and take your hands and make you look into her big beautiful eyes, knowing that third glass you're drinking is actually your fourth since you downed one before meeting up with her. By this time you're a little drunk and–"

"My tolerance is way higher than that!"

"Whatever. By your fourth glass, she'll have you staring into those big beautiful eyes of hers, and then she'll start kissing you and the next day I'll be picking you up from her place."

Thomas paced around the library, fuming.

"Might as well call her up now and get it over with."

"Go fuck yourself." He stomped outside and sat on his front steps, pressing his fists into his cheeks even though he was well aware the pose made him look like a spoilt three-year-old.

Dave came out, carrying his tool box, and said, "You're only mad 'cause you know I'm right. See you tomorrow."

He glared off as Dave loaded his things into the van. Nobody ever took Thomas seriously when he was angry. Although he might swear, grimace, and say all sorts of horrible things, he rarely yelled and was never violent. He was also forgiving. After an outburst, he'd carry on as if nothing had ever happened. He rarely let anything faze him for long.

On top of that, even when he was furious, he never looked very angry. His face never turned red, no veins popped out of his neck or twitched uncontrollably. He looked more like a child who'd been scolded for trying to tattle on someone bullying him.

"Have a good night!" Dave called, waving from the truck.

"Whatever." He felt a sudden empathy for people who went postal, not that he'd ever do such a thing. His phone rang. He took it out of his pocket and checked the screen.

Bloody Jenn. He turned it off and lumbered back indoors. Hopefully, after Saturday he'd never have to see her again. He'd flirt with Lucy and with any luck, she'd respond in kind. All he had to do was figure out some way to sabotage this stupid séance without getting himself fired.

~ CHAPTER ELEVEN ~

Lucy sat in her living room, balancing her laptop on top of a coffee table atlas she'd placed across her knees. A warm breeze wafted in through the open window behind her, filling the room with a fresh floral scent. She'd yet to figure out what kind of tree or plant produced it and kept forgetting to ask Athena what she thought it might be. It was too late in the year for lilac.

An internet search of Shirley's name had brought up nothing so far about the show she'd mentioned, that had been edited to make her look like a fraud. Lucy thought for a moment, and tried a search using just her name, along with the word *debunk*.

Her chest tightened as a video appeared in the new set of results. The thumbnail for it showed Shirley hunkering down on the driveway of the retreat she occasionally held at a spa just outside of town. Lucy had once come along. Although most of Shirley's clients were on the yuppie side, they'd been nice, friendly people. They were positive, optimistic, and things always seemed to be going well for them. The older she got, the more she realized that attitude preceded good things happening to someone, but it didn't make changing her own any easier.

She hesitated and clicked the link. The screen went white. Bland electronic music piped through her speakers and a large, balding man with a greasy ponytail walked onto the screen. She rattled a button on her laptop to turn up the volume. "This is my partner, the Doubting Thomas."

Lucy gasped as Thomas walked onto the screen from the right and smiled for the camera. Ugh. He was as hot as ever, but the smug, condescending expression he wore made her want to put her fist through the screen.

She tried to freeze the image and instead scrolled the video ahead, just in time to hear him say, "I suppose that Mercedes energizes those rocks and holding them makes you feel as if you're riding in a brand new luxury car."

That asshole! She muted the volume and glared off into space, overwhelmed with the urge to hurl her laptop across the room. "What the hell."

Eyes tearing, she grabbed her purse and found the telephone number he'd written out for her. She picked up the handset of her vintage rotary phone and began dialing, starting with the area code. There was something cathartic about watching the clear little wheel spin back around after she turned each digit. With each turn, she grew more enraged.

"Hello, this is Thomas. Leave a–" Lucy slammed the receiver down. The phone's bell dinged, punctuating her fury. Something you could never do with a cordless, and definitely not with a three hundred dollar smart phone.

Seconds later, her phone rang; he must screen his calls. She steadied her nerves, readying herself to really give it to him. On the third ring she picked up and yelled, "What the hell do you think you–"

"Whoa, you all right?" It was Athena! Fuck.

"I'm so sorry!" A cold bucket of guilt doused her ire. "I thought it was Thomas calling back and I just want to strangle the living–"

"I'm coming over, right now. Stay put, I'll be there in five."

*   *   *

After telling Athena the entire story, Lucy paced furiously on the vintage linoleum floor in her kitchen. The yellow and orange flowers were annoyingly cheery. Athena stood guard by the stove. A box of Calming Tea sat on the counter nearby. "What a prick! To think I felt sorry for him, that he was suffering from delusions of all things!"

Athena grabbed the whistling kettle and poured water into a blue earthenware mug. "Here, sweetie." She held the tea to Lucy.

"Where does he get off setting people up like that?"

"You assume too much. This doesn't mean you're a target for the same thing." Athena set the cup back down on the counter.

"Of course I am! How did I not see this coming? He seemed like a great guy. Deep down." Lucy paced and fretted, and eyed a bottle of Shiraz next to her stove. She was planning to open it later tonight anyway.

"People see what they want to see. Including you."

"I know. When I first saw him, I thought he was cute, so of course he's a complete ass. It doesn't matter anyway, he's gay."

"What makes you think he's gay?"

"He's hot, he dresses cool, he's witty, smart, and single, and I liked him. Of course, he's gay. On top of that, he's a complete asshole!" Lucy kicked at one of her cupboards.

"You're being ridiculous!"

"Athena, you saw the video. These guys are sadists. Shirley, of all people." That was what bothered her the most.

"So what? Who even watches their lame *Youtube* show?"

Lucy stopped pacing and stood in the middle of her floor, letting out a deep, frustrated sigh. It wasn't just Thomas that upset her. This struck at the core of her beliefs about everything.

"It's just a dumb internet show," Athena said, as if she was trying to coax a kitten out of a tree. "Forget about it."

"I don't understand," Lucy said, her eyes stinging. "Do they just want everyone to believe in nothing? That when we die, we're gone as if we never existed to begin with, and that all there is, is nothing?" She again eyed her bottle of Shiraz waiting to be opened, and something clicked. Fuck him. She was going to get him good. She was going to own him. "You know what?"

Athena braced herself. She always did whenever Lucy came up with a new scheme. Usually because it was incredibly dumb. Not this time.

"I know what I'll do," Lucy said, her inner fire beginning to blaze once more. "They will get an atheist conversion!"

Athena again held the cup of calming tea to her, but Lucy was in rant mode, pacing and flailing her hands.

"I will say on camera that I make it all up off the top of my head, and I only do it for the—ha—easy money! There's no such thing as ghosts or angels, or unseen energy or any other supernatural phenomena." Raising her arms like Charlton Heston's Moses, she proclaimed, "There is no God!"

A thud echoed in a nearby wall, as if a transformer had just blown out. The room went dark. Lucy and Athena gawked around the kitchen, then at each other, stunned.

Athena rummaged in a kitchen drawer next to the fridge and drew out a candle and some matches. "Where's your flashlight?"

"That was so freaky!" Lucy held her hand to her chest and exhaled sharply, then burst out laughing. "I can't believe that just happened."

Athena lit the candle and said, "Let's head outside. You've created some bad energy in here, girl."

"I don't think I made the lights go out!" *Did I?*

"Of course not."

They climbed out of her kitchen window onto the landing of the metal fire escape. The lights of the neighboring buildings were out too. Farther away, the rest of the city was still lit, the sky incandescent from haze and freckled by a smattering of stars.

Lucy propped the window open with an empty mason jar, perched on one side of the sill and gazed up at the sky. It was warm out here, with a gentle breeze blowing. "Wow, you can really see the constellations tonight."

Athena took a joint out of her purse. She lit it, took a couple of drags, and settled next to Lucy on the windowsill.

"That was just a coincidence, wasn't it?"

"Relax, here." Athena held the smoke in her lungs while she handed her the joint. It smelled like a skunk ambling past.

She took a tiny drag, coughed and handed it back. For several minutes, they gazed out at the darkened neighborhood in silence. Candles began flickering in the windows of several houses across the alleyway. Soon, she could hear someone plucking and strumming a vaguely familiar melody on an acoustic guitar.

"What a beautiful night." Lucy felt calmer now; her storm had subsided. "Why do I get so wound up like that? You're right; it's just some internet video. Shirley even told me business was way up afterward, so the five people who watched it turned out to be more customers. Why did I let myself get so upset just now?"

"You're emotional. Right-brained." The real answer was

obvious to Athena, but she didn't feel like bringing Thomas up and risk ruining Lucy's ponderous frame of mind.

"I don't know what I really believe in sometimes, but this can't be all there is. Whenever I look at up the stars ... it's hard to explain." Lucy shifted her position a few times, trying to get comfortable. She stared out at the twinkling lights in the distance, deep in thought. Then the corners of her mouth curled up and her cheeks dimpled as a mischievous smile spread on her face.

Athena nudged her with her elbow. "What's up?"

"I figured out what I'm going to do about tomorrow night," Lucy said calmly. "I'm going to go through with it all anyway and then tell him there're no ghosts in his house. That's it."

Athena giggled, unsure if she believed her. Lucy had many ideas, but little follow through.

"At the end of the failed channeling, I'll tell him old houses settle and make strange sounds, drafts are coming in from all over, but I can't sense anything paranormal!" Lucy grinned and clasped Athena's knees. "They can't debunk me if I don't come up with anything for them to debunk. It's perfect!"

"Do it, then." Athena finished her joint and they clambered back into the kitchen. "We really have to do a cleansing in here."

Lucy stood in the middle of the floor, sensing residual esoteric grime covering every surface. She'd do a quick one for now. She fumbled around on the shelf above her fridge for the jar of dried sage and turned on the gas burner of her stove. "I'll be fine. I just have to get through tomorrow."

"You're actually going to do it?"

"May as well." Lucy lit the sage. A tiny flame erupted and flared out, leaving a smoldering orange glow that sizzled slowly down the branch. "I broke even the past month, but I have to think of the next one now. It'd be dumb to decline a couple of hundred bucks."

"You want to see him again," Athena said.

"It doesn't matter, he's gay. He has to be."

"Didn't sound like it to me! It sounded as if he was interested in you."

"Hardly. He just showed me stuff he bought; he didn't ask me about myself or anything."

"You're assuming things. For all you know, he was nervous too!" Athena sighed. "Quit thinking you can read people's minds. That's where the self-sabotage comes in."

"He did it to himself," said Lucy, her throat clenching. At least Athena wasn't mentioning that stupid love spell, which had resulted in the same thing as always: her being hooked on totally the wrong kind of guy. She slid open the drawer next to her stove and rummaged around for her wine bottle opener.

*   *   *

Thomas walked alone down the street in the general area of Lucy's shop, in a wandering mood. Dave's rant had made him even more determined that this time, he was going to ignore Jenn completely. Five years of his life he'd wasted on her, though if he counted the entire on-off relationship, it had been closer to eight. He'd been putting up with her crap since he was twenty-five.

Enough already. The previous few years of his life had been a write-off as well, though for different reasons. Now forty wasn't so far away. Jeremy and Dave were already there, balding, gaining weight, beginning to look old, bitter about everything they hadn't yet done in their lives.

He passed a brightly lit bookstore and stopped in front of the window. A psychedelic cover had caught his eye. He stared at the display, then at the blinking traffic light a block away, and walked into the shop.

"Appears to be a blackout down the road," Thomas said to the clerk bent over an opened crossword booklet. The clerk glanced up at him, nodded, and went back to his puzzle.

Thomas wandered through the aisles, scanning the titles. In the middle of the store, he spotted a two-dollar bin of DVDs. He already had enough crap movies he'd bought from similar clearance bins, garage sales or flea markets that he hadn't had a chance to watch yet. To avoid temptation, he headed further towards the back.

"Can I help you with anything?" the clerk called to him.

"I'm fine, thanks, just browsing."

The same book that had grabbed his attention in the window snagged him again. Sitting on the top shelf at the end of the aisle, large and brilliantly colored, beckoning him to look. In gold lettering, the title read *Sacred Geometry*. On the cover below the title was a gorgeously ornate Mandala in gold, black, orange, and red. Incorporated in the baroque design were circles of various sizes, squares, and in the center, a mustard-colored hexagram. It was almost hypnotic as he observed his attention shifting between the different shapes, then at all the surrounding patterns replicated in the whole.

He flipped through some of the pages inside, illustrated with images of the golden ratio as it appeared in seashells, flowers, and galaxies, then at graphics of Penrose tiles and yantra and Persian building facades. Even if the notion of magic math was complete rubbish, the photographs and artwork were beautiful. He took out his wallet and strode up to the cashier.

~ CHAPTER TWELVE ~

Lucy busied herself straightening the shelf behind the counter in her store, counting down the minutes until she closed for the day. Twenty more to go. Even with the construction going on, she did her best to keep regular hours. Two businesses on her block had already gone under. Neither of them had bothered staying open as often as they needed to at a time when every dollar counted. Today, she'd made almost sixty. Sixty more than she'd have had if she'd ducked out for the wrong five minutes.

She set her brown leather satchel next to the cash register. Time to get ready. She brought a glazed ceremonial bowl out from underneath her counter, which she wrapped in tissue and placed inside the case. Next, she packed her candles and incense. For now, she left her crystals and more specialized herbal concoctions in the antique medicine chest behind her counter.

Keeping an ear out for the door, she ducked into the back room to change. Athena said dressing to the nines would be the best way to spite Thomas. Look sexy. Then she'd know for sure whether he was gay or not, too. She opted for a black, long-sleeved top that was slightly see-through, with a lacy black bra underneath. Her black pencil skirt went perfectly with it. It had a long slit up the back that went past her knees, and her stockings were black and sheer. For shoes, she decided to go with a pair of vintage Mary Janes.

She considered straightening her hair, and then decided to use an anti-frizz lotion to tame the curls for once, instead of tying it back in a loose ponytail. The sickly sweet smell hovered around like department-store perfume, but it worked amazingly well. Her hair was silky and lustrous.

The bell at the front door jingled. Lucy poked her head between the strands of her beaded curtain. Athena entered, holding hands with a man who looked like a GQ model. He was well over six feet tall, muscular, and almost swayed as he came around the door into Lucy's shop. He had angular features, heavy brow, and dark, brooding eyes that lit up when he smiled.

"Come meet Derek!" Athena said. "This is my best friend, Lucy."

"Wow, you look nice!" he said in a baritone voice as Lucy emerged from the back. He sounded shocked, which distressed her more than it should have.

"I'll be on camera, so I figure I should look my best." Not that my best is that great, she thought, then cursed herself for allowing such negative thoughts to enter her brain. She was trying, she really was.

"For the cameras, eh." Derek grinned through perfect teeth.

"It's for some internet show," Lucy said, her nerves starting to veer out of control. Earlier she'd been able to put a brake to it, but their unexpected presence gave her the sensation of slipping across spilled ball bearings.

"We're on our way to the theater," Athena said, feigning a pretentious accent. "Harold Pinter's The Homecoming. I came in to wish you luck." She trotted up to Lucy and whispered, "Wish me luck too. Our third date and you know what that means!"

She returned to Derek's side, took his hand, and hunched her shoulders excitedly. "Hope it goes well tonight, sweetie!"

"Have fun, guys!" Lucy simpered while she rolled up a baggie of dried sage. She stuffed it into the bowl she'd already placed in the satchel. Hopefully, they'd take it as their cue to leave.

But no. Athena watched her put some more candles, sticks of incense and a bundle of chalk into the case, then went back up to her and whispered, "I hate doing this to you. Normally I'd say to call me later, but … I don't think tonight's going to be ending anytime soon, if you know what I mean."

"Don't worry about it," Lucy said. At worst, tonight would be over fast and she wouldn't need to talk to Athena about anything. She did have plenty of other friends, even if they forgot about her the way paired-up people often did. "Gord and Becky said they'd be at Lava later."

Athena hugged her again. "You're the best. However, if it's a case of wrong identity and you decide you still like him, be direct. Ask him out for a coffee or something. Promise?" She joined Derek again, who was waiting by the front door. After blowing a kiss to Lucy, the two of them left.

Lucy sighed a lonely sigh and began closing up her store. She locked up the entrance, shut off all the lights and gathered the rest of what she'd need for tonight. She put a box of wooden matches into her case and gawked around the darkened store, trying to think of anything she might be forgetting.

Of course, after getting so upset last night, then plotting her revenge, she'd totally forgotten to ask Athena for tips. Each session she'd previously visited was different from beginning to end and none of them had involved possible murder victims.

"Fuck it." She fetched her laptop. Since she had an hour to kill and was going to fake it all anyway, she may as well pull something off the internet. She set her laptop on the edge of the counter and began printing off whatever looked useful, periodically checking the window outside. If a customer wanted to come inside in the meantime, she may as well let them. Marcia and her husband weren't due for another forty-five minutes.

Four different sets of instructions ought to be enough. She skimmed through each of the pages. She recalled one more source she should check out again, which always had fantastic, in-depth articles. If only she could remember the name of it. She'd been reading an especially noteworthy one just the other day.

She opened her internet history and clicked to the next page. Tension surged in her chest as she spotted the link for *that* video. To torture herself, she again watched the clip of Thomas sneering at Shirley's meditation session. She should *not* be interested in him. She should hate him. Shirley had babysat her when she was a little kid. While they didn't talk as much anymore, she'd been like a second mother for a big part of her life.

She froze the image, shaking her head in disgust. Thomas was so full of himself, sauntering onto the screen, leaning against Skeptical Dave and mugging for the camera. Yet by the twinkle in his eye and the jocular tone, it was obvious he didn't take himself seriously. And those eyes, his smile, his cheekbones. If anything, he should be hosting a real television show, not some dumb Youtube channel. Why hadn't he gone further in his career? He had to be at least thirty and he sounded well educated.

A car horn beeped outside and her insides fluttered. A silver Honda had pulled up in front of her store. Marcia leaned out the front passenger window, waving. Shit, they were early. On top of that, nearly an hour had slipped by in seconds.

After checking through her list, she threw everything that had been on the surface of her counter into a pair of plastic bags, grabbed purse and her satchel, and hurried to the door. Out on the sidewalk, she set everything down by her feet and locked up, then peeked inside to make sure she'd turned off her laptop. Break-ins were rare in this neighborhood, but not unheard of. The sign in the window was already turned to *closed*; she'd forgotten to turn it around this morning. Oh well.

"Pardon the mess," Marcia said as she climbed out and pulled the front seat forward. The back was spotless apart from a package wrapped in a brown paper bag and an empty water bottle on the floor.

Lucy gave Jeremy a sheepish smile as she climbed in. Marcia handed Lucy her satchel and bags, waited for her to settle in and pushed the seat down again. "Let me know if you need me to move forward," Marcia said.

"It's okay, I have short legs." Lucy hugged the bags on her lap. She was thankful Marcia had a calming presence to counter Jeremy's dour, almost intimidating mien.

While Jeremy pulled out onto the graveled road, Marcia leaned between the two front seats and said to Lucy, "How was your day?"

"It was all right, thanks. How was yours?"

"It was good. Didn't do much. Some cleaning, some internet surfing." There was an elegance to Marcia that made her heavy brows, prominent nose, and bony features still appear feminine. Her eyes were fringed with long, thick lashes. She raised one eyebrow and said, "Are you ready for tonight?"

"I hope so," Lucy said. The car drove roughly over the roadway, lurching as they rolled up onto a ledge of newly laid asphalt. She sucked her breath in, trying to calm her nerves. "Thanks for offering me a ride!"

"No problem. Thomas said you didn't have a car and you're on the way for us." Marcia faced forward again while Jeremy steered the car around the various road barriers and yellow caterpillar trucks.

"They're still digging that up? Seems they've been working on here forever! We haven't gone down this stretch for months." She turned to Lucy again. "You must be so sick of it by now."

She nodded. "They say it's supposed to be finished soon."

"Oh well, what can you do. Hey, when it's all done, it'll look great!"

"I hope so." Lucy stared out the window and Jeremy turned the car to the left. She knew that was the right direction, but the bus always turned right and looped around first, so it still *felt* wrong. The silence in the car made her even tenser, so she leaned forward and asked Marcia, "How do you know Thomas?"

"I went to high school with him. He and his mom moved here halfway through grade ten. It was him who really pulled me out of my shell, I'd have to say."

"How do you mean?"

Marcia pursed her lips. "I was bookish and kind of weird as a kid."

"You were a *geek*. Admit it, Marsh." Jeremy chuckled.

"Yep, I was a geek." Marcia gave him a playful shove. "I got picked on a lot in middle school and just, really didn't know how to socialize, let's put it that way. At least my marks were good!"

"Yeah, I went through a phase like that too," Lucy mumbled. It was something she preferred not to tell anyone. At least in high school she'd been popular. Once the other kids heard she knew how to read palms, use Tarot cards and do other forms of divining, they'd come up to her and barrage her with questions.

"Anyway, Thomas had just moved here from Denmark and all the kids wanted to be his friend. All the girls, *loved* him."

"Why did he move here?"

"His mom. He had an uncle already over here, her brother, and." Marcia stopped, her eyes narrowing.

"So he's a mommy's boy?" Lucy asked and slapped her forehead. What made me say such an awful thing?

Jeremy's breath hissed in through his teeth and Lucy caught his eyes gleaming in the rear-view mirror.

"I'm sorry!" she said in the most self-flagellating tone she could muster. Then she remembered the video with Shirley and felt slightly less guilt.

"He is a little." She winced, though Jeremy nodded adamantly. "His dad was a jerk and she moved here to get away from him. Biggest asshole ever and his older sister is almost as bad."

"She's a fucking ..." Jeremy grumbled and shook his head.

"We had art classes together," Marcia said and Lucy was relieved the original conversation was back on track. "On his third day he came to my desk and sat down right next to me. I had this notebook of Edward Gorey-type drawings and he really liked them. Over the year he kept chatting with me, then introducing me to the other kids, getting me to wear cooler clothes—"

Jeremy snorted and again Marcia smacked his arm. "He even introduced me to the love of my life."

"Sounds like he's really sweet," Lucy said blandly. She still wanted to hate him.

"He is! He has his moments, but hey, everyone does."

"So he's been here since grade ten? What about his accent?"

"I think he hangs on to it," Marcia said. "He can be a little pretentious sometimes."

Lucy giggled. Then she looked out the window. They'd turned onto the two-lane highway that led down the hill, through the forest and up into Thomas's neighborhood. Her chest tightened.

"No, that was mean. And we love him." Marcia sighed. "He went back for a few years, too. It wasn't as if he was here the whole time."

Lucy found herself liking him again. With all her strength, she resisted asking Marcia whether he was gay. At least in front of

Jeremy. Maybe she wouldn't pull any fake stunts after all, she'd just take him aside and gently confront him about the internet show and … now she was mad again. Her heart quickened as they neared Thomas's house.

Marcia continued, "After high school, he went back to Denmark to study because it was a lot cheaper for him. Then he met some girl there, found a job he really liked … at the time it didn't seem as if he was planning to come back at all!"

Lucy wished he'd stayed there. Then she never would have met him and wouldn't be feeling this weird ache in her chest. She should have canceled the appointment tonight. Even when Marcia had called to arrange picking her up, she'd been tempted to say she already had a ride. Or felt sick. Then she would've still had the option of not showing up. At the sight of the iron gates, her stomach flip-flopped and she clutched the satchel on her lap.

Jeremy's car slowed and turned up the driveway. A black SUV and Thomas's Karmann Ghia were parked outside the house. Lucy noticed Marcia scanning the yard as if she expected to see yet another vehicle.

The porch light had been left on and the window in the upper part of the door glowed. Along the flowerbed in front, a line of solar garden lights flickered. Jeremy parked and said, "Ready?"

"As ready as I'll ever be," Lucy mumbled.

Marcia got out and pulled the seat forward for her. "Need help with anything?"

"I'm fine, thanks." She gathered the handles of the plastic bags in one hand, slung the strap of her purse around her body, gripped the satchel in her arm, and got out. Apart from the steady wheeze of cicadas, the front yard was deathly quiet. Traffic in the distance was barely a whisper.

Marcia hurried past Lucy up the flagstone walkway. "We're here!" she called out.

Jeremy escorted Lucy onto the porch and hammered the bronze doorknocker. "It's open!" came a female voice from inside.

Marcia barged in first, followed by Jeremy. The instant Lucy stepped into the entryway, panic flooded into her. The sensation was overpowering, like an electrical field zapping all around her. It wasn't just her own anxiety; someone else in here was equally on edge.

Thomas greeted her politely from the doorway to the library. He was quiet, impassive. She couldn't glean anything from him. Marcia seemed to sense it too, nodding only briefly at him as she slipped her shoes off. She then went to give Isaac a hug. Jenn and Steve sat behind him on the chaise lounge, also looking subdued.

"Come in!" Thomas said, herding everyone into the library. "Nice to see everybody so punctual."

Lucy hugged her satchel and the plastic bags to her chest as she waited for them all to sit at the round table. Jenn sat next to Steve. Again, she'd dressed in a slinky Lululemon outfit, revealing ample cleavage, though Lucy noticed she'd tied the sleeves of a sweatshirt around her thick waist. Her body wasn't so perfect after all. Isaac sat on the far side from her, a hint he didn't think much of her either.

Thomas sat on the other side of Jenn. Lucy set her things down by the foot of her chair. A white linen cloth shrouded the table. Although she smelled fresh bread in the house, it hadn't been put out anywhere that she could see. She placed her satchel on the table and took out her pillar candles, arranging five of them in the middle to form a circle.

Thomas took a remote device out of his shirt pocket and dimmed the lights on the chandelier. Out front, wheels turned on gravel, then brakes whined and an engine cut. Noticing no empty seats at the table, Lucy asked, "Is someone else supposed to be coming?"

Thomas eyed the others as he spoke. "There shouldn't be, though occasionally people use my driveway to turn around in."

"I keep telling you not to leave that gate open," Jenn said.

Lucy set several more candles on top of various tables and desks around the library and began lighting them. Watching her, Thomas asked, "Is there anything else you need?"

"Not that I can think of, thanks." In the faint, flickering glow, the library really did look the part of an old-fashioned séance now. Everyone at the table seemed tense and they kept squirming in their chairs. Lucy didn't want to say anything yet, but she sensed something else in the room with them.

Thomas sidled toward the hallway and said, "The bread should be cool by now. I did remember."

*   *   *

Out in the hall, Thomas locked the door to the library with a small iron key, which he placed deep in his pocket. As quietly as he could, he opened his front door and slipped outside.

He spotted Dave's white van parked under the low hanging branches of a droopy pine tree around the side of his house. Although the top of the vehicle was concealed, the wheels were still visible to anyone with sharp eyes.

He opened up the back doors and climbed inside. "You were supposed to get here half an hour ago!"

"I got delayed."

As usual, Dave didn't bother coming up with an excuse. It was always Thomas's fault if anything went wrong. Thankfully, Lucy was preoccupied setting up her candles and such. "You know, she didn't bring much with her."

"Spools of thread and wires don't take much room." Dave flipped on the monitors that covered each wall of the truck. The company they worked for had bought it from a local television station and the equipment was dated, but functional.

Thomas glanced up at a screen showing a view of his library from a camera Dave had set on top of the bookshelf. Lucy wafted incense around while everyone else fidgeted in their seats like schoolchildren on the last day of class before summer holidays. "How's everything coming along?"

"Works great!" Dave flipped a switch and the rest of the screens flickered on, showing the library and front hall from myriad angles.

Thomas peered into a surveillance screen that showed Lucy up close, lighting a stick of incense with a match. In her black top and pencil skirt, her figure was a near-perfect hourglass shape. He'd always assumed she was a bit frumpy, but it must have been because of the saggy cotton blouses and hippie skirts she always wore. "Find it a bit warm in here?"

"It is summer." Dave shrugged, looking annoyed.

"There's something odd about her, but I can't put my finger on what."

"You think she's the real deal?" Dave chuckled. "What do you bet while she's waving that stick around, her other hand is attaching wires behind all your knick knacks. With a single pull, she could knock them all out. Hope you put away the pricier ones."

"Nah. Even she called séances parlor tricks. And when she came in just now she seemed a bit, I dunno. Look. There is no way she's stringing anything around the way she circled back just now. She'd have tripped."

"So she'll writhe around and fake some voices instead. We'll run them through an oscillator. You'll see."

It was all he could do not to laugh out loud at the man. Even if he'd had zero interest in Lucy he'd still think this scheme was moronic. Shame she seemed to be so thin-skinned or she'd get a good laugh from it too.

He watched her through the camera lodged in the grandfather clock, wavering. One reason he'd gotten along so well with Jenn was that she was about as sensitive as a rhinoceros. He never had to walk on proverbial eggshells around her. Lucy, on the other hand … She'd finished setting up and was glaring towards the door to the library. She was short on patience too, apparently. Isaac rose out of his seat and ambled in front of the fireplace, making it a little *too* obvious he was checking for wires and strings.

Thomas felt as if he were watching two trains that were still miles apart, but destined to collide on the same track. "I better head back in."

~ CHAPTER THIRTEEN ~

Lucy lifted the ceremonial bowl out of her satchel, set it down in front of her on the large round table and took out the baggies she'd crammed inside of it. After dumping all the various herbs into the bowl, she took out a wooden pestle. She ground them to powder, taking care to leave one sprig of dried sage intact.

"What's all that stuff for?" Steve craned his head to peer inside of it, mouth hanging open, Neanderthal brow furrowed.

"Protection ritual," she said blandly. She laid the pestle against the bowl, setting it at an angle so it wouldn't roll. "You have to do one before initiating any contact with the other side."

"I see." He snorted, as if trying not to laugh at some joke only he thought was funny.

Lucy then caught Jenn and Isaac suppressing smirks. Just ignore them, she told herself, it'll be over soon. She lit another match and held it to the furry grayish green branch inside the bowl. The leaves fizzed and erupted into flames, plumes of grey smoke swirling out. Burnt cedar, chamomile, and sage filled the air.

Jenn crinkled her nose. "That stuff reeks."

"It's just some dried herbs and—"

"Do you have to use it?"

Lucy smothered the bowl with the base of her satchel. It felt like she was in a room full of three-year-olds who had to ask questions about *every little thing* for the sake of asking, not because they were interested in the answer.

She tossed her satchel onto the floor just as Thomas came back into the library. "Everything all right?"

"Where's the bread?" Lucy snapped.

"Oh, it's on the counter. Where I left it to cool." He froze at the entrance. "Want me to bring it in here? You'd said the smell would be enough."

"You know, I don't sense any bad entities," Lucy said, "so I really don't see the need to do the protection ritual and the bread will only attract them. Let's just skip it and go straight into the channeling, shall we?"

"Are you sure?"

She nodded. The others all looked at each other and shrugged. Thomas sat down and Lucy sucked in her breath, trying to stop her frayed nerves from unraveling. Originally, she'd planned to do the protection ritual and excuse herself so she could scan through the papers she'd printed off. Now, she'd have to wing it. "Okay everyone, we all need to join hands."

Jeremy and Marcia were already holding hands on top of the table. Lucy's anxiety spiked as Thomas locked his fingers into hers and began idly stroking the back of her hand with his thumb.

"Are we all ready?" she asked.

Everyone nodded.

"Okay, close your eyes." Lucy held her own eyes slightly open to ensure everyone else obeyed. To build tension, she allowed a few moments of silence before starting her routine. Not that it was necessary. The atmosphere in the library was so taut she felt as if she'd just interrupted a marital spat.

"Dear, departed one," Lucy said, "who was violently murdered in this house, we respectfully ask for you to honor us with your presence this evening."

Squinting out one eye, she glanced around at the others. They all still had their eyes shut tight, solemn expressions on their faces. The sight made her a little less self-conscious.

"Spirit from the other side, commune with us, and move among us," she said.

One of the candles in front of her fluttered. At first, she thought someone was blowing on it, but everyone's faces were still, their mouths closed.

"Dear—" Lucy had forgotten to ask Thomas the alleged murder victim's name. She hissed to him, "What's his name?"

Steve said, "Freddie," then he and Jenn nudged each other and snickered. Thomas shushed them. So much for the spooky atmosphere, she'd created. Back to her original plan.

"Dear Freddie." She shrugged, determined to play along. With luck, she'd be out of here in ten minutes. "We welcome your presence at our table. Commune with us and move among us."

More snickering.

"Cut it out!" Thomas hissed at Steve and Jenn.

Lucy yanked her hands away and glowered at him, fed up. Time to lay it on thick. "It is impossible for me to sense anything if no one's willing to take it seriously. Otherwise, why am I here?"

"Sorry," Thomas said. At least he looked chastened. Marcia and Jeremy were just sitting quietly across from her. The wheels in her mind spun. As much as she wanted to bolt, she'd be dumb not to milk this. The sixty bucks she made at the store today barely covered this week's groceries. Since she was charging hourly and had stupidly forgone the protection ritual, she was going to damn well stretch this out, make it worth her time.

Eyeballing Steve, she said, "As a medium, I need to be in a completely relaxed, passive state of mind in order to make contact. This means, no distractions."

"Sorry, nerves. It's a little spooky in here." Steve huddled his arms to his chest, pretending to shiver.

Lucy shot him a dirty look.

"Please, continue," Thomas said and gave Steve a hard kick under the table, while Marcia smiled encouragingly at her.

"Okay, everybody, breathe. In." Lucy inhaled deeply through her nose, counting to four, and held her breath.

The others, watching her, did the same. She counted to seven in her head and said, "And out." She made a whooshing sound as she exhaled out of her mouth to the count of eight.

Marcia and the rest *whooshed* in unison.

"Better?"

They all nodded, closed their eyes, and took each other's hands again. Her chest constricted and her mouth was parched. Nausea welled into her stomach. She felt hot, and her cheeks and neck burned. The candles in front of her blurred. She feared she was going to be sick. She bowed her head, her hands curled into fists on her lap. Something—she had no idea what—stopped her from saying or doing anything further. She sat, catatonic.

"Does anyone need a drink first?" Thomas asked as if he'd read her mind.

Lucy nodded, desperate for something to settle her stomach. "I'd like some tea, if you have any."

"I should have offered earlier. I've been a bit scattered today." He led her out of the library. She wobbled like a newborn calf behind him. "You sure you're okay? We don't have to go through with this if you aren't feeling well."

"I'll be fine," she said, trying to put on a brave face. "Do you have some fresh ginger?"

"Absolutely." Like the rest of his house, his kitchen was immaculate. The only things left unwashed were two cast iron frying pans on the stove. Even the light beige potholders and oven mitts hanging on a nearby hook were spotless.

She took a stool at the island in the middle and leaned next to the sink. The counter was unfinished wood and she spread her hands across the surface, concentrating on feeling the grain against her palms and fingertips, trying to ground herself.

He smiled sympathetically and set a steel kettle onto the stovetop to boil. While he grated a knob of ginger, she gawked at the bank of white cupboards surrounding his gas stove and exhaust fan. Everything was so clean. He was the opposite of her slovenly ex, for whom every stain and spill was conveniently invisible. Going by the bowl of shallots, foil-wrapped olive oil and half-empty bottles of various vinegars on the counter, he must cook at home often. Dinner parties, or for himself, she wondered.

The kettle whistled. He turned off the gas and held the mug up to her. "Is that enough?"

She peered into it. "Perfect. Thanks."

He filled the cup with freshly boiled water and set it on the counter. She noticed he washed the knife and grater right away, drying it with a dishtowel. "You really don't seem well tonight. If you don't want to go through with it, I'd be more than happy to still pay you for your time and—"

"I'll be fine." Lucy dissembled even though she suspected Thomas could see right through it. Part of her wanted to tell him outright that she knew what they were up to, but then she'd have to explain why she still came.

She sipped the tea, the ginger sharp and tangy on her tongue. He tenderly pushed a stray lock of her hair behind her ear. A quiet moment, where they just looked at each other, not yet ready to smile or speak. He didn't come across as if he was intentionally pulling some nasty prank on her, and not just because of his angelic face. If it really were all for the sake of some show, surely he wouldn't have invited idiots like Steve to participate.

"Do you find that stuff helps?" he asked.

She nodded and blew over the top of her mug.

"I should try it sometime."

She relaxed as he began massaging one of her shoulders. "I should apologize. I'm sorry it hasn't gone so well tonight. Listen, I have to confess something. This whole séance thing was all a stupid—"

Footsteps pattered in the hall toward them. Jenn stopped at the threshold of the kitchen and cleared her throat loudly. Simpering at Lucy, she said, "Are you guys coming back anytime soon? We're in the middle of holding a channeling session, remember? There's a ghost in there wanting to talk to you."

"Not now, Jenn," Thomas said.

Violent thudding erupted from the library. Jenn pressed herself against the doorframe as Thomas rushed past her. She cocked her head to one side, eyeing Lucy's see-through blouse. "You like him, don't you."

She stared into her cup and said, "None of your business."

Ignoring Lucy's non-verbal cues telling her to buzz off, Jenn came closer. She pulled the sides of her pink hoodie away from her waist and rubbed her belly. By the bulge protruding above her waistband, Lucy could tell she was pregnant, roughly four or five months along. "Just so you know Tom's my ex. A recent ex."

Lucy tried to keep her eyes fixed on the golden liquid in her mug, the pungent ginger stinging her nostrils. Her eyes burned. If only she could click her heels together and be home again.

"The second I want him back?" Jenn snapped her fingers. "Tom does whatever I want him to. He's my little puppy dog." She whimpered mockingly and skipped back out of the kitchen.

Lord, what a spiteful bitch. Lucy sucked her lips into her mouth and scrunched her eyes shut to stop them from tearing. She hadn't felt so humiliated since grade school; she had to get out of here. Athena was right. It was dumb to have even thought about going through with this.

More noises erupted from the library: thudding, banging, hysterical laughter, and scolding shouts. She finished the tea, left the cup on the counter, and crept back down the hall. From the threshold of the library door she watched, her eyes clouding. Steve flailed on the carpet, his legs and arms thrashing, while Jenn giggled like a teenager backstage at a boy band concert.

Thomas glared down and nudged Steve's thigh with his foot. The look on his face suggested the next nudge would be a good swift kick. "Enough, Steve."

Steve got up and brushed himself off, though there wasn't a speck of dust on his clothes. "I'm just having some fun. Everybody's too … too moody tonight, y'all need to lighten up!"

A strange energy surged in Lucy's body. She'd had the same sense once before, in fifth grade after a group of kids had been chucking snowballs at her. It had been a warm day after a major storm and the snow was good and wet, which made for perfect aim, including one that hit her square on her head. While they taunted her from the side of the road, she stood and glared at them, wishing to the Universe that they'd get their comeuppance. Seconds later a bus roared past, straight into a pool of melted slush, sending a salty, muddy wave crashing over all of them.

Watching Steve and Jenn doubled over in hysterics, she steeled herself. One thought exploded in her mind: *Fuck them all*. She cleared her throat and said in the most intimidating schoolmarm voice she could summon, "Everyone ready to continue?"

Thomas, Isaac, Steve and Jenn all stared at her, agape and horrified, as if she were a teacher who'd just caught them having sex on school property. Without saying another word, they settled into their chairs around the table.

Marcia and Jeremy looked at her expectantly. Avoiding eye contact, Lucy sat back down and pulled her chair closer to the table until the edge of it pressed against stomach. Screw them. They could have warned her. The ginger helped, but she still felt queasy. Thomas took her hand again; she wanted to slap it. In less than a minute she'd gone from thinking he was actually interested in her, to feeling like the biggest idiot in the world.

"Okay, let's start where we left off. Everyone, close your eyes." She pressed her feet flat on the carpet beneath her chair, trying to ground herself again. Game on. She'd go through the motions, conclude no ghosts or other entities lurked in the house, grab her check and be on her way. Every candle and stick of incense would go on the bill. Retail, not cost. She'd add a note at the end of the invoice that her rate involved a three-hour minimum. No. Make it four. Plus cab fare home.

Again, Thomas stroked the back of her hand with his thumb. "Sure you want to do this?" he whispered.

"Dear Freddie," Lucy said in a loud voice, "We welcome your presence at our table. Commune with us and move among us."

Whatever presence she'd sensed earlier was gone. Damn it. She'd love to freak out a couple of these assholes. She flashed her eyes at Jenn, who wore a self-satisfied expression on her face. The taunting voice still rang in her ears. *He's my little puppy dog.*

She tried to center herself so she could sound sincere, and spoke more slowly this time. "Repeat after me: Spirit from the other side, commune with us, and move among us."

"Spirit from the other side," everyone mumbled in a monotone chorus, "commune with us, and move among us."

Lucy caught Thomas eyeing Jenn. Gritting her teeth she said, "Oh, being from the spirit world, who dwells within this house. We request your presence tonight at our table."

"Oh, being from the spirit world," everyone repeated, sounding like bored monks, "who dwells within this house. We request your presence tonight at our table."

A breeze from outside fluttered the curtains, bringing in an oddly pungent scent. Lucy tensed. In the corner of her eye, shadows began spreading across the mantle of the fireplace. Her skin tingled and the air electrified like high-voltage fog. Maybe she shouldn't. She gazed ruefully at the materials for the protection ritual by her feet. Not too late yet. As Steve and Jenn elbowed each other, she continued, "Oh, spirit being, we welcome your presence here."

The wind in the room picked up and Marcia made a hissing sound as she drew in her breath. "Oh, spirit being, we welcome your presence here," the chorus of voices said, though it sounded as if others had joined in, too.

Lucy's eyes narrowed and she spotted a hole in the casing of a grandfather clock behind Jeremy's head. A small hole, but not too small for a camera. Her face contorted into a grimace. The breeze in the room strengthened and her hair billowed up around her head, glints of candlelight casting an orange halo around her. Goosebumps spread along her arms.

"Oh non-material entity, we call out to you tonight."

Dozens upon dozens of voices wailed, "Oh non-material entity, we call out to you tonight."

She shut her eyes tight. Energy coursed up through her feet, surging into her legs, her chest, exploding out the top of her head. A terrifying power, fury, concentrated within her. It pulsed through every vein in her body as she said, "Cross on over from the other side and appear before us! Oh, entity, show your presence in this room. Reveal yourself to us—*now!*"

Wind blasted in from all directions. The door to the front hall slammed shut and shuddered in its frame. Books and knickknacks flew off the shelves and curtains thrashed, knocking over lamps and side tables.

Lucy leapt out of her chair and flattened herself against the wall next to the bookshelf. Shadowy figures peeled away from her, swirling into the room. A heavy volume struck the back of the chair she'd been sitting on moments earlier. Thomas, Steve, Jenn, and Isaac ducked under the table while Jeremy sheltered Marcia in his arms.

The wind died down abruptly, leaving the room eerily silent.

One by one everyone returned to their seats and eyed each other. It was perfectly still now, like the aftermath of a tornado once the funnel cloud had lifted away. Books were spilled across the carpet. All the lamps, desks, and chairs had toppled.

Isaac gawked around at the mess, then at Lucy. She caught her anguished expression reflected in his oversized glasses.

"Holy shit," he said, gaping at her.

With some trepidation, Thomas, Jeremy, Marcia, and Isaac got up and went around the room to pick up the lamps, setting them back on their stands. Lucy sat with her shoulders hunched, frozen in shock. Never before had she seen anything like this. Her mind had to be playing tricks on her, or Thomas had rigged it all for dramatic effect. That had to be it. There was no way she could have done this herself.

"That was odd." Jenn watched Thomas replace a tall black vase to its spot between a sofa and two overturned Morris chairs.

As soon as he looked her way again, Lucy jerked her head toward the hallway outside.

*   *   *

Thomas's heart pounded in his chest as he ushered Lucy into the entryway and locked the door behind him. She hadn't moved from her seat when it began—he'd seen for himself she hadn't, no one had—and yet. Someone else must have followed her here. It hadn't occurred to him earlier she'd bring an accomplice.

His library was trashed. Yet her body quivered and by the blanched expression on her face, she looked as shocked as everyone else.

"What is going on here?" she asked, glaring up at him.

He gulped, speechless. Her reddening eyes flashed brilliant green, like the plumage of a tropical bird. He shook the image out of his head; his brain always did odd things whenever he was under pressure.

"Is this all some game? The shelves, the lamps falling over, books flying all over the place? Come on!"

"A game? You'd think I'd destroy my own library for a lark?"

"Then what happened just now?"

"How should I know? You were the one summoning things!"

She glowered at him and crammed her feet into her shoes.

"Wait." He grabbed her arm, which she immediately tore free. "You're saying you didn't do any of this?"

"How could I? Didn't you see what happened in there?"

Now was not a good time to suggest she may have arranged for someone else to help rig everything. She looked as though she was about to bawl. "Could have been an earthquake or something," he mumbled.

"An earthquake. In Western New York."

"It's not unheard of. Toronto had one a few years ago."

"And the wind?" She stared at him as if he was being an utter moron. Which he was. He could've been more forceful with Dave, stood up to him for once.

"I doubt you believe me, but I had absolutely nothing to do with any of that. I've no idea what happened. Two of the chairs that toppled are solid oak!"

She rolled her lips into her mouth and hung her head. Then the obvious popped into his mind. His fingers clenched. He went up to the nearest doorframe and pounded it once with the side of his fist. "Fucking Steve."

"He's a bit of a jerk, isn't he," Lucy said.

"Oh, you've no idea." Adrenaline flooded into his body. He stayed frozen by the front door; if he returned to the library and saw that smarmy bastard's face right now he'd want to strangle him. "Ignore anything coming out of Jenn's mouth too. She's a fucking cu–"

"I should go," Lucy said, her voice barely above a whisper.

"I'm really sorry." He wasn't at all sorry, apart from nearly saying the *c-* word. Part of him wanted to kill Steve, but it was the perfect out. The entire night had been sabotaged, exactly as he'd hoped, and none of it was his fault! The most Dave could do was blame him for inviting Steve, which he'd never do because they'd been friends for years.

Even better, Lucy didn't seem upset with *him* any longer.

"I managed to get my car running earlier, so I should be able to drive you home." Although he was ecstatic the night was now ruined, he didn't want her to leave. Everyone else, on the other hand, was welcome to go anytime.

"I'd rather go quietly," she said, jerking her head towards the library. "And not have to wait around."

He dropped his voice. "Want me to call a taxi for you?"

"It's okay; I've got my phone on me. I find they come faster if you just hail one that's passing by."

*   *   *

Thankfully no one paid attention to Lucy as she trailed him back into the library. They all seemed too preoccupied trying to figure out what had happened, examining all the windows, shelves and every nook and cranny around the fireplace. While Thomas returned to picking up scattered books and DVDs, she snatched up her things from around the table and stuffed them into her satchel.

Jenn put a single book back on the shelf, then stared at Lucy wrapping the bowl in tissue and bundling in the remaining herbs. "What about the candles?" She blew out the nearest one and held it out to Lucy, the wax dripping onto the tablecloth.

"Leave them; they're cheap." She was *not* going to let Jenn get under her skin. The sooner she was out of here, the better.

"Leaving so soon? We're just getting started!" Steve put his arm around her shoulder and she tried to shrug it off. "Stay, we'll have some drinks! Tom has more booze here than a—"

"Enough!" Thomas snarled at him.

Lucy caught Jenn watching smugly as the two men glared at each other, circling each other on the patch of carpet like a pair of wolves staking out their territory. The love triangle was as obvious as a novel about sparkly vampires and she wanted to slap herself for not clueing into it sooner.

"I have to go. Nice meeting everyone!" she said brightly through gritted teeth, a tone she'd perfected through years of customer service where every day brought a brand new type of idiot. She grabbed her satchel and purse, and marched out into the hallway.

Thomas chased after her and barricaded the front door while she sat on the bottom step of the staircase and buckled her shoes. Jenn lurked in the doorway of the library. That same smug expression was still painted on her face.

"You sure keep a short leash on your puppy dog all of a sudden," she mumbled. Whatever sick games the three of them played with each other, she wanted no part of it. She glared at him as she got back to her feet and slung the strap of her satchel over her head. "You're in my way."

"Wait. I didn't mean for this to end like this."

Her eyes darted to Jenn, then back to him. Surely, he wasn't *that* oblivious. "Have a nice life."

She pushed him out of her way and opened the door, went through and slammed it shut behind her. Outside, she stood on the front porch. She tugged a black pashmina out of a pocket of her satchel. Jenn and Thomas were arguing on the other side of the door, but she couldn't be bothered eavesdropping. What did it matter? She checked to make sure she had her phone, wallet, and keys on her.

Stomping down the porch steps, she tried to drown out the sounds of Jenn's laughter coming from somewhere in the library. Finally, she was out of there. Tears streamed down her cheeks and she scurried along the gravel driveway toward the main road. The Universe really did have it in for her. She hadn't even remembered to collect a check from him. The night had been a total disaster. If only she was the fraud those producers seemed to think she was. If only she was that competent.

~ CHAPTER FOURTEEN ~

Thomas jogged up to Steve, who was staring out the window that overlooked the front of his property. "What the fuck did you do in here?"

"Nothing! You and Dave were the ones rigging everything."

"Not like this!" Thomas tore the curtain aside and scanned all along the entire frame. Steve gawked around the library, blond brows knitted and jaw slack like a particularly stupid ape; Thomas could tell he wasn't lying.

On the far side of the room, Isaac investigated a second window. "How did she do that? Wires?"

"No idea." He joined Isaac's side, anguish giving way to astonishment. The lower pane was propped open by an old dictionary, exactly how he'd left it earlier in the afternoon.

He peered outside. A silver moon, nearing fullness, lit up the yard. He could see no fan or any type of machinery on the lawn or hidden among the tree branches. Nothing close by except flowerbeds and grass that needed mowing. He spread his hand against the mesh. Not even a whisper of a breeze came in now.

"What do you think could have done this?" Steve asked.

"Dunno." He stepped back and gazed up at the crown molding, looking for any wires or hooks. Perhaps she'd broken into his place earlier. That idea was even more idiotic than the idea that it had been a ... His mind went blank, as if a circuit had just blown.

"Air hose, maybe?" Steve asked.

"It would still need some sort of pump or motor and I don't remember hearing anything." He was too baffled to be annoyed with Steve any longer.

"I haven't found any wires or threads yet." Isaac stood on the far side of the round table, his head bobbing and craning from side to side as he checked all the surrounding shelves.

Jeremy bonked his head as he came out from under the table. "Nothing down there either, besides one of your little cameras."

Isaac tapped Thomas's shoulder and said, "Let's go see what Dave might have caught."

"Later." He just wanted everyone to leave, especially Jenn, who hadn't moved from the doorway to the library. She was still sulking and staring out into the front hall. Funny how Lucy's mood took such a dramatic u-turn after her appearance in the kitchen. No prizes for guessing what she'd said to her.

"Anyone else feel cold? I'm turning into a popsicle here." Marcia shivered and pulled her shawl around her throat. Jeremy put his arm around her and hugged her close.

Thomas stood still, and frowned. It was getting cold in here. A draught blew in from somewhere along the floor that he'd never felt before, even in the midst of a winter storm.

*   *   *

Dave lounged in a chair in the back of the white van and browsed through a Chinese takeout menu. He rarely monitored live footage closely once he knew everything was running smoothly. Usually he'd read or play solitaire, taking the odd glance at the screens to make sure none of them had gone dark. Tonight, all the cameras had been working perfectly, even if a few of them had lousy resolution. Just that one glitch when the computer system had spontaneously decided to reboot itself. No biggie.

The surrounding screens flickered, then steadied. Dark mist swirled and eddied throughout the inside of the house. He glanced around at the various indicator lights. The screens continued blinking off and on. He leaned forward and peered into the closest monitor. Mist spread in the captured images, enveloping each person assembling in the front hall. Smoke or vapor of some kind separated and drifted around Jeremy and Marcia's shadowy figures, following them as they went into the library to check for something and back out into the hallway.

"Goddamn cheap made-in-China junk." He tore off a sheet of paper towel. He wiped the screens, and then fiddled with various dials underneath. The fog still hung around. He took out his phone and checked the weather forecast. According to his app, it was still around seventy-four degrees, with only ten percent humidity.

Then again, measurements were taken at the airport. In the upper part of a valley like where Thomas lived, at this time of night, it could easily be much damper. He crawled into the front seat of the van and rolled down the window. The air outside was warm and dry, with only a light breeze wafting from the north. Maybe Tom had forgotten to turn that kettle off in the kitchen. That would explain it. That guy would forget his own pretty head if it wasn't stuck on his neck at all times.

*   *   *

Marcia sat on the chaise lounge and stuffed her feet into a pair of pointy-toed leather pumps. She smiled ruefully at Jeremy sitting next to her, then up at Thomas. "This little black duck is going home, right now. I am beat."

Steve tugged Jeremy's arm. "Come on guys, stay. We barely hang out anymore."

For a reason, Marcia thought. As much as she couldn't stand Jenn, she liked Steve even less. Although being tired was her excuse every time she felt like going home, this time she meant it. She was exhausted. Whatever caused that wind in the library had drained her to where all she wanted to do was curl up in bed and sleep for a week. She leaned against Jeremy and yawned. "I'm so tired. Don't know why, it just hit me all of a sudden."

"Ready?" Jeremy helped her stand and Thomas escorted them out onto the front porch.

Jeremy gave him a bear hug. Marcia kissed each of his cheeks and said, "I'm sorry tonight was a bust."

Thomas shrugged. Poor guy. Whenever there was a chance for him to screw things up, he did. In all the years she'd known him, he sabotaged himself, whether it be his job or his relationships, every chance he got.

"I'll call you tomorrow," he said. "Get home safe."

Marcia jerked her head in the direction of his library and said, "Though she looked pretty pissed when she left, I'm sure she'll be fine. I get the sense her memory's about as long as yours when it comes to people acting like jerks."

"Speaking of. I think Jenn had something to it," Thomas said, lowering his voice. "She can be such a bloody—"

"Jenn's as transparent as cellophane. She was obviously with Steve the whole night and the rest was the same stupid games she always plays. Go to Lucy's store tomorrow and explain. Promise?"

He nodded and Marcia hoped that he'd take her advice for once. She followed Jeremy down the steps. "Bye!"

"See ya!" Jeremy waved and got into the car.

Marcia climbed into the passenger side, shifted her seat back, and belted up. "I keep feeling as if I'm forgetting something."

"Let's get home. It's not like we never see the guy."

Gravel crunched under the wheels as Jeremy backed out of his spot. The car rolled slowly down the driveway. While he waited at the gate for oncoming traffic to pass, Marcia squeezed his hand. As much as she adored Thomas, she could never picture herself married to him; she'd bludgeon him.

"You okay?" he asked.

"I love you."

"Love you too." He kissed her and turned onto the road.

She leaned her head against the window and stared out into the shadows of the passing trees, as if the rest of the world was moving by and the car was still. Unease clung to her, prickling her skin like an old wool blanket. This stretch of road was always spooky and dark at night, reminding her of the woods belonging to the Wicked Witch of the East.

Up ahead she spotted a lonely Lucy trudging along the edge of the shoulder. A shawl of some kind was draped around her shoulders and with her form-fitting skirt, she looked as if she'd just emerged from an opera house or some other soirée. "Oh, jeez, Tom didn't call a taxi for her?"

Jeremy put his flashers on. He slowed the car while Marcia rolled down her window and leaned her head out. The poor girl was still upset over earlier. At any rate, she shouldn't be out by herself like this. "Lucy! Need a ride?"

Lucy sniffled, turned briefly to them, and shook her head. "I'm okay, thanks."

"Are you sure? We're pretty remote." Marcia stared out at the surrounding forest, almost expecting to spot a serial killer lurking among the fir and pine trees.

"Thanks, but I want to be alone right now." Lucy pushed up her sleeves and kept walking.

"Let her be." Jeremy put the car into neutral and rolled alongside at the pace she was walking.

Fearing Lucy might end up a headline on tomorrow's evening news, Marcia said, "Get home safe, okay?"

"I will."

"You have my number; call us if you change your mind or if anything happens. We'll come pick you up."

"Thanks."

Jeremy braked and put the gear back into drive, then called to her, "We'll drop by your store some time. Tom said you have good stuff in there."

Lucy nodded, still facing stonily ahead.

"Take care." Marcia rolled up the window. While Lucy made it obvious she wanted to be left alone, she hated leaving her like that.

Jeremy drove on and she watched Lucy's shrinking figure in her side mirror. "Poor girl, I think she had a crush on him. I'm just guessing, but–"

"He has to figure out his shit with Jenn first. You know he won't. He never does."

She groaned. "You know, I've never said this about anyone, even the kids that bullied me from kindergarten 'til the tenth grade. But you know what? I hate Jenn. With a passion. She's such a fucking skank, a cheap, stupid, useless whore and if it wasn't for her blonde hair and her giant fucking tits no guy would ever–"

"Whoa, Marcia!"

"And I hate Tom too! I hate him for putting up with her shit for half a fucking decade. All she does is play head games. How many years has she played him and Steve against each other? There are three billion other women out there, all of whom are a better catch if the two of them didn't think with their fucking dicks for once and—"

"Marcia, what the fuck? Put a lid on that potty mouth, holy shit!"

"You're one to—" She stopped herself. A sigh shuddered out of her chest and she wiped her eyes, her fingers slick with tears. It was as if someone else had taken over her. They were both silent as the car sped along the road, lit only by a gibbous moon stabbed by the tops of the passing trees.

"What got into you just now?"

"I don't know!" She stared out at the dark, two-lane road. That was creepy, beyond creepy. She felt as if she'd lost control of herself, skidded, and crashed into a wall. All she could do was watch and let it happen. Thank God only Jeremy had been around to witness the outburst. He'd nearly launched into a similar tirade, probably feeling similarly hijacked. "It just came out of me. It was so weird."

Jeremy rubbed her shoulder, keeping his eyes fixed ahead. At the bottom of the hill and around the bend, the faint glow of city lights appeared. He chuckled. "You should say that to his face sometime. I'd love to see it. He needs to hear it."

"I shouldn't have said anything," she said, still ashamed of all the terrible words she'd let loose. As much as she loved bashing Jenn, she always had a lingering sense the only person she ever hurt was herself. It was an ugly side she wished didn't even exist and so long as she stopped herself from saying nasty things, that side grew steadily smaller and smaller.

At the next red light, Jeremy slung his arm around her shoulder and pulled her closer. "Whatever. Everyone gets a little cranky when they're tired."

She hoped that's what it was, but she knew better. She'd felt possessed.

~ CHAPTER FIFTEEN ~

Thomas picked up the rest of the spilled books and knick-knacks, setting them into a corner for now. The stench of burnt wax filled the air as Isaac snuffed out the remaining candles. He tried to ignore Steve, who'd again dropped to the floor, spasming as if hooked up to electrodes. The idiot. Jenn watched on, giggling, which annoyed him even more. Another twit.

"Enough, already." He stood over Steve and kicked his calf, though not nearly as hard as he'd like. "It was a channeling, not a bloody exorcism. Thanks to you, we got some fantastic footage here. Fuckwit."

"Whatever, you'll find another psychic. Hey!"

He noticed one second too late to stop Steve from lunging at it. Lucy had left behind a white plastic bag, still underneath the chair. Thomas reached for it, saying, "Leave it."

"Relax!" Steve yanked it away, rummaged inside and pulled out several sheets of paper. "How to initiate contact with the other side and ... what the—she took this off the internet?"

Thomas snatched the sheets from him, fuming. He knew she was a fraud psychic but she'd dealt with enough tonight. The sooner Steve and Jenn left, the better. His temper was so frayed it was about to split apart at the seams and while he wasn't prone to violence, there was always a first.

"Come on, this shit's hilarious!" Steve laughed and Thomas's fists clenched even more. The man was pushing it.

Jenn tore one of the pages out of his fingers. Doing a hammed-up B-movie impression, she held her hand to her forehead, arched her back, and said, "Commune with us and move among us. Oh, entity, reveal yourself to us!"

"Hey, you can use this for your show," Steve said. "What else she got in here?"

"Let's call it a night, shall we? Out!" Thomas herded them towards the front hall. The sooner these idiots were gone, the better. Both of them were testing the outer limits of his patience tonight.

Steve took her arm. "You're right, he is no fun. We didn't even get any–" The heavy wood door of the library slammed shut in their faces.

Thomas jerked the handle. Locked.

Steve elbowed him aside and rattled it. "Lucy! This is lame. We know you're a fake, give it up!"

Thomas shoved him aside. "She left ages ago!"

"Damn, it's stuffy in here." Isaac grunted and heaved open the nearest window.

"Who shut it?" Thomas asked.

"I dunno. Not me."

Steve resumed pounding on the door and yelled, "Fine, we'll use another fake psychic instead. Open up!"

"Settle down! I have a key." He took the key out of his front pocket. No sooner had he put the key into the lock then the chandelier lights blinked spasmodically. The room went dark. "Bloody hell! Second one this week!"

Jenn slinked up to the front window and pulled one of the curtains open. "The lights down by the bus stop are still on."

Thomas watched Steve peek out the same window and put an arm around Jenn. He then slid his hand down onto her hips and began groping her rear end. Yet Dave said they'd broken up. Didn't look like it. He was not going to be provoked further.

Instead, he crouched and twisted the key in the lock, trying to get something inside to catch. It worked fine earlier.

"Calm down, Isaac," Steve said. "Just chill."

Thomas turned to see Isaac pacing around like a caged wolf. "Go fetch some candles will you, get some light in here?"

Isaac lit a large pillar candle with his cigarette lighter and said to Steve, "This is your fault, dumbass."

"How? You're the one who opened the window!"

"Opened windows cause blackouts now?"

"Enough! Shut up so I can concentrate." Summoning every last ounce of patience he had, he gently turned the key from side to side in the lock until the mechanism tumbled. He stood, stretched his cramped legs and opened the door.

"Finally!" Jenn strode out into the front hall and flicked the light switch. Nothing.

Isaac picked up a thick white candle and followed them. "Where's your circuit breaker?"

"Bet he still has knob and tube in this old place." Jenn stood by the front door, her arms folded across her ample chest.

Thomas eyed Isaac's flickering candle; wax was already dribbling down the side, threatening the carpet. "Anyone got a flashlight?

Jenn dug into her purse. She pulled out a key chain attached to a tiny LED flashlight and dangled it from her fingers. "Here. Need me to show you how to turn it on?"

Steve chuckled. "I never have that problem."

"That's not what she told me, pencil dick." Thomas snatched it from her and headed along the hallway to the basement door. Isaac trailed after him, clasping his hand to his mouth.

"What's so funny?" Thomas asked.

Isaac straightened his expression as if he'd just been caught playing with himself. "Nothing. It's nothing. Steve's a douche."

With scarcely a faint circle of light to see by, Thomas gripped the railing and took his time descending the narrow, wooden steps. At the bottom, he stepped onto the concrete floor of the basement, cold under his socked feet.

"Why did you invite them, anyway?" Isaac asked.

"Because I'm an idiot," he sighed. "I don't know. I must like to torment myself. And despite her legion faults, Jenn shows up when she says." The bulb on the tiny flashlight cast barely a spot on the floor. It was so dark in the dank, musty basement that the shadows seemed to come alive, shifting in his peripheral vision.

*   *   *

Jenn and Steve lingered in the foyer while Thomas and Isaac's footsteps echoed up from a vent in the wall beside them.

"What a waste of a night," she said, pacing in a tight circle.

Steve stared at her bemusedly. "Are you all right?"

"I'm fine."

"You don't look fine."

As a test, she sidled closer to him and he shifted away from her. Again, he was pulling this crap. Whenever Thomas was around, he was all lovey-dovey and the second he was out of sight, Steve treated her as if she was contagious. "It's a little awkward right now, that's all."

"No kidding. You should've said 'no' when he invited you. And maybe a few other times too? Back in a sec, gotta take a whiz." Using the flash on his phone to guide his way, he headed upstairs.

"Thanks for letting me know, douchebag." Her eyes burned. She slumped onto the chaise lounge. It was so pathetic how she clung on to him, no matter how he treated her. Before getting pregnant, she'd had so many chances to kick his ass to the curb.

Then there was Tom. Another douche. Both men needed a new set of brakes between their brains and their mouths, though at least Steve wasn't so negative. Most of the time. With Tom, there was nothing on the planet he couldn't find fault with. But then Tom held down a steady job, had his shit together.

She shuddered and stared around the dark hallway. This old house always creeped her out and tonight it was worse than ever. Footsteps echoed toward her from inside the library. She clasped her hands to her belly, already in the habit of protecting her baby at the first hint of any threat. Her heart raced and she hissed, "Who's in there! Isaac?"

The footsteps stopped. She picked up the white pillar candle, not that it would help if anyone came at her. At most, she could splatter wax in their eyes.

"Jenn!" a disembodied voice echoed. Dave. Of course. She'd forgotten he was outside, watching from that white truck that looked like a freakin' pedo-van.

"You asshole!" she yelled, assuming microphones had been set up in the hallway. "You freaked the shit out of me! Happy?"

"Why don't you come in here and see for yourself, Jenn?"

"What, scared, little girl," another voice taunted.

She barged into the library. No one. Her skin tingled as she craned her head around the other side of the door. The white sheers fluttered gently, glowing from moonlight streaming in through the windows.

"I'm out here, Jenn," the voice whispered from what sounded like the other side of the glass.

She jumped, her heart pounding so hard she felt it was about to explode. Doing her best to keep her voice steady, she said, "I'm aware of the invention of microphones and speakers. Fuck you, Dave!"

Fear fuelled her rage. She set the candle back down on the floor and stormed outside, down the front steps and across the side lawn toward the van. Seething, she threw both back doors open. Dave was leaning back in his chair pretending he was sound asleep, his mouth hanging open. Mother. Fucker.

"Dave! Wake up!" Jenn climbed up and shoved him as hard as she could.

The front legs of his chair slammed onto the floor of the van and he pitched upright. "What!"

"You're supposed to be watching everything!"

He blinked and gawked around at the surveillance screens as if his eyes were still trying to focus. "Why is it all dark in there?"

What the … He wasn't faking. He'd been out cold. "I don't know! Come help!"

"What do you want me to do?"

"I thought you were an engineer!" She groaned, jumped out of the van, and slammed the doors shut again. He could be such a retard. Then she reminded herself she needed to keep calm. For the baby. She'd always been moody, but surging hormones sent her skidding like a car hitting a patch of black ice on the road.

I am so done, she thought. If Steve tried to pull anything more, she'd insist on crashing here for the night, hinting she and Tom would be sleeping in the same bed. He'd *have* to drive her home. She stomped back up the porch steps, making as much noise as she could, and flung the front door open.

No Steve. She took a couple of steps up the staircase. She eyed the darkness beyond the railing that ran along the second floor landing. There was no freakin' way she was going up there by herself. Cupping her hands around her mouth, she called up to him. "Steve!" No answer. "*Steve!*"

*   *   *

Isaac pointed Jenn's flashlight at the breaker box while Thomas checked all the switches. None of them had been tripped. Trying to be patient, he flicked each of them back and forth, and then tried the main switch. Nothing. "Guess I'll have to call an electrician tomorrow unless Dave can sort it out."

Isaac gasped at a muffled banging above their heads. "What was that?"

What is that fuckwit up to now? Thomas slammed the breaker box shut. The two of them rushed through the nearly pitch-black basement and back up the stairs.

Jenn was pacing around the entryway, her face frozen in a snarl. Somewhere above, feet stomped, then what sounded like a fist pounding on a wall, followed by a thud. Her eyes were tearing and she was cradling her belly, stroking it, with both her hands.

"What's going on?" Thomas asked.

"Steve being Steve." She kicked the foot of the staircase post and said, "He went to the bathroom ten minutes ago and hasn't come back down yet. What's he doing up there, jerking off?"

Above, footsteps thundered from room to room like a cat on a crazy midnight romp. "That fuckwit, I'll get him!" With visions of hauling Steve out the front door by his scruff, Thomas marched up the stairs. The little man did not know when to quit. Isaac followed him, still holding Jenn's flashlight.

The upper landing was empty. Steve must be watching from one of the bedrooms, since all the noises had stopped. He sucked in his breath and listened out for the slightest creak. Nothing. He peered over the banister and watched Jenn sitting on the chaise lounge below, shivering. She got up, fetched a candle from the library, and began creeping up the stairs. She joined them on the minstrel's gallery, hunching her shoulders and staring around.

Grunts and some sort of scratching on floorboards came from the attic above.

"What's that?" she asked, nearly jumping out of her skin.

She seemed genuinely scared, but in case she was up to her old tricks, he ignored her and hissed to Isaac, "Let's check the back set of stairs in that closet at the end of the hall. I don't think Steve knows about it."

"Ew!" Isaac stared at his palm. Blood was smeared all over his fingers.

"Where'd that come from?" He then spotted a streak of some dark, viscous substance on the railing. He wouldn't put it past Steve to go too far for a prank, and yet …

"Oh my God, did you cut it?" Jenn grabbed Isaac's wrist to examine his hand. She ran her index finger along the rail and held it up to Thomas. The blood looked fresh.

"It's not mine," Isaac said.

She backed away and held her hand to her mouth as if she were about to be sick. Thomas dashed into a nearby room, where a bronze lamp sat in one corner. He hefted it. Good and heavy. After making sure there was no light bulb in it, he removed the lampshade and set it down on the desk. Coiling the wire around the base, he came back out into the hallway.

He and Isaac approached the closet door at the far end like a pair of policemen cornering a suspect. The floor above creaked. Communicating only with head jerks and hand signals, Thomas held up the base of the lamp and Isaac flung the door open. The wooden steps, steep like rungs of a ladder, were carpeted in a thick layer of dust.

Isaac climbed up, shining the flashlight ahead of him. Thomas clutched the railing with one hand and carried the lamp base in the other as he followed. A dot of light flickered and flashed across the rafters high above.

He froze on the top step. "You have a lot of junk up here."

"Just find Steve." Thomas sighed, tension rising in his chest.

"Let's go back downstairs; this is creeping me out," Jenn whined.

Now was not the time to tease her. He tugged the leg of Isaac's jeans and said, "You'll be all right up here?"

"Yeah. Probably best if I find him anyway."

True enough. He passed the bronze lamp base up to Isaac and stepped back down. He reached the bottom and he stared up, watching Isaac's feet disappear into the darkness. Isaac's voice echoed against the rafters as he called for Steve.

"Let's go!" Jenn hissed, clinging to Thomas's arm. They skulked down the hallway towards the main set of stairs. Malevolence hung in the surrounding air, sticking on everything like residue from cigarette smoke.

"I'm sorry I brought Steve," she whispered, "but he didn't want me coming here without him. We're not even going out anymore and—"

"Not now, Jenn. I'd said I needed two more people." He eyed their ragged shadows thrown by the flickering candlelight. He was too spooked to be annoyed with her and he wanted her to be quiet in case someone was trying to sneak up on them. He stared at the railing as they passed. The blood was gone now. Of course it was, it was likely never there to begin with. All three of them were letting themselves get worked up over nothing.

Either that, or Lucy did have an accomplice, one who was still in the house. He shuddered at the thought and tried to dismiss it.

"Can I explain one thing to you? It'll take two seconds," she said, stepping slowly back down the stairs.

"Go on." He followed a few paces behind.

"When I told Steve I was expecting, he refused to believe he's the dad and—" Jenn shrieked, the candle flew out of her hands and she slid down the steps. She grabbed a post under the railing, landing hard on her side. Melted wax splattered on her like thick white blood. She gritted her teeth as she tried to prop herself up.

"Ah, fuck!"

He crouched next to her, his heart racing at the thought of what could have just happened. In some alternate universe, she was lying dead at the foot of his stairs. "Are you all right?"

She stared up at him, her doe eyes tearing from pain. She lay sprawled, breathing rapidly. The knuckles of her hand turned white as she clung to a balustrade.

"Are you hurt?" When she shook her head, he cradled her in his arms, taking in the scent of her herbal shampoo.

"I'm a little stunned, is all." Her legs wobbled and she gripped the railing hand over hand as she descended. He helped her limp down the steps, thankful her fall hadn't been worse.

Once they were on the main floor again, she slumped onto the chaise lounge. She leaned back against the wall and shifted sideways until her head was no longer bumping against the wooden trim along the bottom of the banister.

"You sure you're not hurt? You don't look too well."

She stretched out and lay her head on the armrest at the far end. "Just where I landed on my thigh. I'll be fine." She rubbed the side of her body on which she'd fallen. All the color had drained from her face. In the darkness, her eyes glistened like wet stones.

He listened out. It was quiet, then the floorboards above creaked faintly. He wasn't sure whether Jenn wanted to be alone or not, so he said, "I should go back up and check on Isaac. All right if I leave you here?"

"Don't bother. Dumbass is hiding somewhere, I know it. What do you bet he smeared that blood. Watch."

She did want company. He dug into the pockets of a couple of jackets hanging from a rack of iron hooks beside her. "Have you seen my phone anywhere?"

"Here, use mine." Jenn took her phone out of her hoodie pocket and handed it to him.

He fiddled with it, annoyed, and not just because she had to put pink glitter on nearly everything she owned. No matter what he swiped or pressed, the screen did nothing. "How do you turn this thing on?"

Jenn snatched it back. "You need to push the right buttons."

It was so hard for her to be pleasant, no matter how helpful he attempted to be. "I know exactly what buttons to push with you. Don't try me."

She swiped the screen a couple of times with her finger, then hammered a button on the side of the phone. "What the—I just charged it!"

She glared up at him as if her eyes could burn right through him. It was the sort of glare that made him wonder why he ever bothered with her, one that stung deeper than he cared to admit.

"What?"

"This was the dumbest idea ever! This whole holding a fake séance so that you can out some fake psychic. Everyone knows already!"

"If your boyfriend didn't have to be such a dick all the time we'd have–"

"He's not my boyfriend."

He smiled wryly and said, "I know. He's your karma."

Jenn gaped at him.

Since she was uninjured, he could be spiteful to her again and God, it felt good. "Believe me, nothing makes me happier than seeing him treat you exactly how you were with me. Really, I should thank him. He took the bullet for me. He's stuck with you forever, while I am free from you at last."

Dave opened the front door and paused at the threshold. Even Skeptical Dave could sense something wasn't right. "What's going on? Where's Isaac?"

"Never mind." Jenn swung her leg over the side of the chaise lounge, trying to kick at Thomas.

He stepped out of her reach and leaned against a far wall. As soon as Steve and Isaac came back, he'd send the lot of them home. He should have earlier, the second Marcia and Jeremy were gone.

Dave flicked the light switch on and off a couple of times. "What happened to the–"

"I told you—we don't know!" Jenn sat up and stamped her feet on the floor.

"I'll get my toolbox." Dave headed back out the door and down the front steps.

Jenn went to the base of the stairs again and hobbled up the first couple of the steps. "Where are they?"

"Fine, I'll go look for them," Thomas said. Anything to get away from her.

"Don't leave me alone down here!"

Sometimes, Jenn was twenty-eight going on three. "Dave's just outside. You'll be fine."

"I hate Dave! I'm sure all they're doing is jerking around up there. Stay and keep me company."

"Then settle down and quit being so bloody obnoxious." He kept his foot on the lowest step and listened. Upstairs it was quiet. Too quiet. If Steve had been pulling a prank, he would have done something more dramatic by now. Or gotten bored and come back down. The man couldn't go without attention for more than a minute.

"For fuck sakes, Steve, get your arse back down here. You too, Isaac, this isn't funny, this is boring. You're both boring and predictable!" he called up and kicked at the much-abused banister post. Even though he stubbed his toe, he felt better. Though not as good as it would feel kicking Steve.

~ CHAPTER SIXTEEN ~

Lucy was finally back in her neighborhood, her feet throbbing and swollen from the three-mile hike. The buildings cast unwelcoming shadows as she trudged the remaining blocks home. In the yellowish light of the streetlamps, the brick walk-ups she passed were so dingy and dilapidated. Cracks had spread in the white stucco along the side of one low-rise, looking like a photographic negative of a spider web. Chunks had fallen onto the empty lot next to it. Weeds sprouted out of the cracked asphalt.

She found it depressing how little upkeep there was in this area, an area that could be beautiful if it weren't for all the lazy absentee landlords. Only vestiges of former grandeur remained among the splintered fish scale shingles and paint peeling off once-ornate trim. Someday in the not-too-distant future, it would be replaced by boxy luxury condominiums. While her neighbors groaned and grumbled about the new chain coffee shop that had moved in, the owners kept the exterior spotless.

Two more blocks to go. She took her phone out of her purse, brought up Athena's name, and pressed the call button. No answer. She didn't bother leaving a message. While she hadn't been expecting Athena to pick up, what with her third date and all, she'd held out the faint hope her best friend would have just known how badly things had gone earlier tonight.

She glanced inside a trendy wine bar filled with contented couples nestled around each table. She felt lonelier than she'd ever felt before in her life. Even the waitress and busboy were paired up in their matching white shirts and black pants.

The sight of her own darkened storefront depressed her even more. Without any lights on, it looked as empty as the rest of her life. Keys in hand, she unlocked the door next to her store's entrance, which led into a grimy stairwell she kept forgetting to clean. Never mind clean, she needed to replace the World War II era linoleum. Another thing for she didn't have money. Besides her and her guests, only the two tenants living in an apartment above her store ever saw the staircase anyway, and all of them were used to it.

She lumbered up to the top floor, playing over the last few days in her mind. Athena was right. She'd had at least three chances to ask Thomas out for a coffee and she'd blown every single one of them. Not that it mattered. If he was going to be a father, he counted as taken anyway.

She stepped into her empty apartment and locked the door behind her. She tossed her satchel onto the velvet sofa and opened her half-empty bottle of Shiraz. While pouring the dark red wine into a tumbler, she glanced at her satchel and frowned.

Something was missing.

She set the bottle on her coffee table, opened the case and rummaged around inside. She'd left the candles and incense but they were cheap. She was billing for them anyway. She still had her bowl, pestle, and an extra sachet of herbs, as well as the crystal ball she'd brought as a backup.

"Damn it," she mumbled, racking her brain for what she might possibly have forgotten.

*   *   *

Thomas sat on the far end of the chaise lounge by the foot of the staircase. He rested his elbows on his knees, staring at the wall in front of him. Jenn sulked on the opposite end, peeling a strip of candle wax off her wrist. Underneath, her skin looked inflamed. Neither of them had said a word to each other for the past ten minutes, nor had Isaac or Steve emerged from wherever they were hiding.

Jenn slung her legs up and prodded his thigh with her toes.

"Get your feet off the furniture," he said, his patience wearing thinner than cheap paint. "What are you, five?"

"I have to keep my legs elevated. Doctor's orders."

"Then take your bloody shoes off. You know my rules."

Footsteps thundered down the stairs behind them. "Holy shit!"

Isaac flew out the front door. Thomas swung around to the

bottom of the stairs and stared up, seeing nothing. He got up and went out the front door. Steve and Isaac stood on the walkway outside.

"What was that?" Isaac backed away, gawking up towards the top of the house. Steve doubled over, howling, his face red.

Thomas was too drained to care what prank Steve may have pulled. So long as he left. He ambled out onto the front porch and stared at him impassively.

Jenn limped past him, hobbled down the steps, and swatted Steve's arm. "Where were you?"

Ignoring her, Steve slapped Isaac's shoulder. "Dude, it was nothing! I was just messing around!"

"You were already out here!" Isaac said. "I saw some–"

"A ghost? Woo-oo!"

"Both of you! Enough!" Thomas stood in front of his doorway, fully intending to block anyone trying to get back inside.

"I'm serious," Isaac said, flailing his arms. "I saw something up there!"

Jenn glared at Steve and swatted him again. "I said where the hell were you?"

"Just fooling around, having a little fun." Steve grabbed her hand and said, "Come on, let's get outta here." He pulled her towards his SUV, oblivious to her sprained ankle.

Thomas said to Isaac, "Are you going with them or waiting for Dave?"

Isaac stayed on the circular flagstone as if someone had glued his feet to it. "That was so weird. You should have seen it."

"Whatever."

Thomas went back inside just as Dave was coming up from the basement. Panting, he set his toolbox by Thomas's feet and said, "Breaker switch. It should be fine now."

"We checked already," Isaac yelled from outside. "It wasn't the breaker!"

Dave switched on the hall and porch lights. "Works now!"

"Thank you," Thomas said, not caring why his power had been out, so long as it was fixed and everyone went home.

Isaac sidled towards the white van. "Can we get going?"

"Yeah, sure." Dave lugged his toolbox to the truck. He set it down on the ground while he fished out his keys. Thomas watched on from the walkway. Although he wanted to go back in, it was rude not to see them off. Especially on a night when the weather was decent.

Isaac scrambled into the van through the back doors. Dave climbed into the driver's seat. The engine rumbled to life and Dave backed out from under the branches. Thomas waved from the edge of his driveway.

Once Dave had turned around, Isaac poked his head out the window like a dog putting its face into the wind. "Sure you'll be okay here tonight?"

"I'm fine," he said, thinking, please just go already. Further, down his driveway, the red taillights of Steve's SUV bobbed and disappeared into the night. Two down, two to go.

Dave leaned around Isaac. "You coming in tomorrow?"

"If I have to," he sighed. On a fucking Sunday. Whatever happened to weekends?

"Noon by the latest."

By the earliest, he thought and went back indoors. After making sure the deadbolt was turned, he crouched and began picking up all the bits of wax Jenn had flung off from her clothes. What a useless night. He knew it would be. He'd *told* Dave as much. Even a dim bulb like Steve thought outing a fake fortune teller as planned was a stupid idea. He'd seen her shop enough to know people weren't exactly beating down her door to spend their hard-earned savings.

He fetched an upholstery brush from the closet and swept the rest of the wax off the chaise lounge. The red brocade fabric was covered in white flecks like freshly shed dandruff. "Bloody Jenn," he mumbled, scooping sticky flakes into his palm. Looking at her, never a single hair out of place, you'd never guess what an absolute pig she could be.

Footsteps creaked along the floorboards above.

"Who's there?" Thomas rose to his feet. He peered out the

window next to the front door. No sign of Dave's van or Steve's SUV. Perhaps he was right and Lucy was still somewhere inside. Or she'd left an accomplice. Isaac said he'd seen something upstairs and he wasn't the sort to make things up. He cursed himself for not checking thoroughly while everyone else was still here, yet he couldn't imagine her doing any such thing.

He went into the kitchen and dumped the wax into a trashcan. Out the corner of his eye, a shadow flashed and he heard the door to the library slam shut. His heart hammered in his chest and sweat dribbled down his spine. He pulled the largest knife out of the wooden block next to his sink and crept along the hallway.

"Lucy?" he called through the library door, though it couldn't have been her. He peered through the keyhole and then pressed his ear against the wooden paneling above.

"Thomas," a voice whispered, breath warm against his neck.

He whirled around, slashing the knife into the air. The hall was empty. His chest heaved as he caught his breath. He held the knife straight out in his fist and pressed his back against the wall. Everything went quiet again.

His eyes caught sight of a camera Dave had installed over his front door. It was possible Dave had rigged speakers inside his house and was pulling some sort of prank. Possible, but unlikely. Pranks required far more of a sense of humor than Dave had ever shown.

Stress does funny things to a person, he thought. His mind must be playing tricks and if he went to bed, everything would be back to normal in the morning. He stormed into the kitchen and stabbed the knife back into its slot in the wooden block. Outside the window, another shadow flashed past in his peripheral vision. His fingers were still gripping the knife handle. He let go.

To calm himself, he switched on an old radio he kept on the table in his breakfast nook. Static blared through the speaker. He turned the knob slowly, trying to tune in a channel. Some music might help. Late night programming was better anyway. Layers of voices came through over the buzzes and hisses. He pulled out the antenna and pressed the tip of the extended rod against the window. The sight of his glowing reflection calmed him, tricking a primitive part of his brain into thinking another person was here with him, keeping him safe.

The radio went quiet. Then a female voice came through the speaker, babbling in some strange language. A chill settled on his skin as the voice became clearer and more coherent. It sounded like his mother. "Just bread and cheese," she said. "And maybe some bananas. I'm still not keeping—"

"I know, I heard you this morning. Just take what the doctor gave you, he didn't prescribe them at random, you know. They actually work," Thomas's uncle said.

What the fuck. He heard footsteps shuffling behind him and started, disoriented. He gaped up at the butter yellow walls, walls he'd painted over nearly two years ago. They should be off-white.

"Need anything Thomas? I'm off to the shops for half an hour."

"No, thank you." Thomas froze at the sound of his own voice coming out of his mouth. The front door shut, the deadbolt shunted, and he was back in the present. He remembered that conversation now. An hour and a half later, police would arrive at that same door; a pickup truck had run a red light and slammed straight into his uncle's car.

Thomas shut the radio off. His chest ached and his throat clenched as he relived that awful moment. The last time he'd seen his uncle, he was stepping out the front door to the shops and that was it. Forever. Within six months, his mum would be gone too. He'd lived by himself here ever since, apart from when Jenn used to stay over. Normally he could block out the aching loneliness, but not tonight.

He spun out of his chair and headed straight for the cupboard where he kept all his liquor. He rarely drank anymore but after all that had gone on earlier, he needed something strong to take the edge off.

~ CHAPTER SEVENTEEN ~

Lucy lay wide-awake in bed. Three glasses of wine had failed to make her even the slightest bit drowsy. Unfortunately, a fourth, especially on an empty stomach, would guarantee a hangover. Maybe she should close the store and get a job. Have things like weekends and holidays and sick days once more. If only she could afford a part-time employee. One who showed up on time. Didn't steal.

She tossed and turned, then rolled flat on her back. Her skin felt hot and clammy. A warm breeze blew in from her window and her hair tickled her face, tormenting her.

Thomas had caressed her cheek so tenderly earlier that evening, stroked the back of her hand with his thumb, and then Jenn barged into the scene like a putrid, festering blob. Perfect-looking Jenn with that it-girl smirk on her face.

She grabbed a tissue from a box on her bedside table and daubed the corners of her eyes. At first, she'd assumed Steve was Jenn's boyfriend. Looking back, all night he'd kept his distance from her, staying just close enough to keep an eye on her.

That love spell.

This time, she'd really meant it. Yet it hadn't worked; it hadn't done a thing. The Universe had teased her, dangling the most gorgeous, fascinating man she'd ever met right in her face, only to yank him away as soon as he appeared to be in reach. A depressed sigh shuddered from deep inside her chest.

The Universe didn't play games.

It didn't care enough to play games. Why would it? All that was out there was a cold and infinite vacuum, trillions of lifeless stars, and unfathomable depths of nothing in between. As Nabokov had once written, existence was but a brief crack of light between eternities of darkness. She felt that darkness closing in on her.

"He's right," she whispered to herself. He and Dave had probably rigged whatever had blasted through Thomas's library.

Or Steve had pulled an elaborate prank and she'd imagined the rest. Every hint of something more was simply a figment of her wishful-thinking mind.

She'd only believed in higher life forms, a guiding force, another realm, because she so dearly wanted to believe there was more to life than the painful here and now. That it didn't just end forever, all her memories and experiences gone as if they never existed. That she'd see her father again someday.

Her throat felt sore and raw. Belief her father was still looking down on her from somewhere had sustained her through her grief, as well as every other trial in her life. He wasn't. He was gone. Forever. Vanished like a spark from a fire.

"It is all just bullshit. Everything." She stared up at the ceiling, tears streaming down the sides of her face. Happy moments always had a fleeting, unreal quality to them. This darkness lurked behind each and every one, the underlying reality she spent her life trying not to face.

*   *   *

Thomas lay on his back in bed and clutched the covers around his throat. Normally he slept well, but not tonight. Several drams of whiskey had numbed the pain, at least. But as he drank alone in the library, the footsteps had returned. Along with the overwhelming sense of being watched, and not through the cameras set all around.

Almost nothing scared him, not even as a kid, yet he'd sat petrified as he chugged the remains of his glass. Then he'd raced straight up into his bed like a child traumatized from watching a scary movie. He didn't even brush his teeth, which he hadn't missed doing in years.

Not that he lacked deep-rooted fears. Embarrassment, coming across as weak. A criminal breaking in while he slept. Or an arsonist. This was different. It was if some being had invaded his house, was lurking, waiting to pounce, and there was nothing he could do to protect himself. Nothing. An unseen enemy waited in the shadows and no weapon existed that could fight it off.

Footsteps stalked the hallway outside his bedroom door and tromped up the back set of stairs and into the attic. At first, the steps sounded human. They were slow and deliberate, like a watchman doing rounds. He didn't dare get out of bed to check. His eyes darted around his room, which was lit by streams of moonlight coming in through the cracks of his wooden blinds.

The floor creaked in the hall outside again. Then, a quiet scratching on his door, followed by shuffling sounds, like of some animal dragging recently killed prey along the floorboards. He rolled more blankets up around his neck.

"It's all in my mind," he said, chiding himself aloud. For the first time in his life, he wasn't so sure.

~ CHAPTER EIGHTEEN ~

The next morning, Thomas poured coffee into a mug and slumped into the corner of his breakfast nook. Brilliant sunlight streamed in through the picture window. It had been a long, sleepless night. At dawn, he'd managed to doze off but still woke at his usual time. Long gone were the days of being able to sleep in past noon.

He sipped his coffee, grimaced at the bitterness exploding on his tongue, dashed to the sink, and spat it out. He dumped his mug, coffee grounds and curdled cream splattering around the drain. Yuck. He filled a glass with water and rinsed his mouth. A putrid taste lingered, like rotten cabbage or spoiled meat.

He went to the fridge and opened the container of cream. The expiry date was for two weeks from now. He sniffed it. Definitely off. He opened a fresh one and took a whiff, then a small sip. Sour and nasty. He opened his vegetable drawer and the stench nauseated him. Everything inside was rotten or moldy. Yellowed celery floated in a plastic bag of brownish, soupy goo. The power had been off for less than an hour, yet all his food looked and smelled as if it had been decomposing in there for weeks.

His cell phone bleeped. He picked it up from the counter and swiped the screen. A text from Dave, reminding him to come in to work this afternoon. Working Sundays was bad enough. Sundays without coffee was rancid icing on an already bitter cake.

After setting the kettle to boil, he put the coffee pot in his sink and began scouring black grunge from off the inside. Whatever had burnt onto the bottom of it, it was stuck like glue. The base of it didn't even appear as if it were made of glass any longer, more like cast iron.

His home phone rang. He rushed over to the console to pick it up and bumped his thigh hard against the corner of a chair.

"Ow!" He gritted his teeth and answered. "Hello?"

"Hey, it's me." Isaac.

"I'm not ready." Thomas groaned. "Tell Dave I'm running late today; I barely slept a wink last night."

"Is there anything weird going on for you this morning?"

"What do you mean?" Thomas sucked air in through his teeth as he rubbed his thigh. That was going to be one nasty bruise in a few hours.

"Strange stuff like things not working or dumb accidents or–"

"Of course not. Why would you ask such a–" His teakettle screamed from the stove. He forgot he'd turned it on.

"Nothing out of the ordinary?"

"I just banged into something. Haven't had any coffee yet, so I'm always a bit clumsy until–" The kettle vomited boiling water onto the stove, sending up hissing clouds of steam. "Aw, Christ. I have to go. Tell Dave I'll be late!"

He flung his phone onto the counter, turned the burner off, and grabbed a dishtowel. He'd been up less than half an hour. Already he wanted to go back to bed and stay there.

*   *   *

Jenn lived in a one-bedroom condominium with parquet flooring, beige walls, and cream floor-to-ceiling vertical blinds. It was all she'd been able to afford to buy at the time and although the place was small and in a building that needed fixing up, it was hers. Renting was for losers.

She woke to an empty bed, got up and went into the living room. She wondered if Steve was still crashed out on her leather sofa. He'd refused to come to bed with her saying he wasn't tired. She was the one who ended up unable to fall asleep. At some point later in the night, she'd gone out and covered his sleeping body with his favorite fleece animal print blanket. Not that he ever appreciated these gestures. She'd tried a few times to wake him and get him to join her. Nothing had worked.

The longer she lay in bed, the angrier she grew. She flung the covers off and threw on a robe. Mugs and dirty plates rattled on the coffee table as she stomped up to him and shoved his shoulder. "Why didn't you come to bed?"

He sat upright and scratched himself. "Should've gone home."

She groaned and went into the bathroom. Once the baby was

born, she'd definitely have to renovate. The sight of the pale blue walls, beige countertop, and sink all nauseated her, stained with memories of her constant morning sickness. More like morning, noon, and night sickness. Only for the past few weeks had she managed to go more than a few hours without puking. Supposedly, in the third trimester it came back with a vengeance.

She washed her hands, splashed water on her face and stared at herself in the mirror. She looked like crap. Dark shadows hung under her eyes. The skin on her normally perky cheeks sagged. Turning twenty-eight sucked. She brushed her hair and tied it back into a ponytail, then went to fix herself some breakfast.

The checkered floor of her windowless galley kitchen made her dizzy. So did the arborite countertop with its fake wood grain. Thankfully, she had lots of cupboard space and plenty of room for her supplements and vitamins. All the appliances were new. She had no idea how Tom could keep a gas stove in his house. Every time one of those burners sparked, she was sure it would explode on her, or fill the air with lethal poison.

She set her blender on the counter and plugged it in. She tossed in a banana and a scoop of plain yogurt. While pouring in a cup of orange juice, she yelled, "Steve! Want a smoothie?"

"Got any real food?"

Jenn huffed. Which was worse. Tom, who refused to touch anything except coffee before noon, or Steve, who insisted on a grease-laden egg, bacon and home fries spread each morning. Neither of them ate healthy. She set containers of blueberries and strawberries onto the counter and threw some from each into the blender. "Last chance, Steve!"

"Got any sausages? I don't know how you can eat that rabbit food all the time."

This morning, she had no patience for his bitching and moaning. She held the lid down and hit puree. The blender jackhammered on the counter and the clear plastic stopper flew off, splattering blueberry-strawberry-banana goo all over.

Steve charged into the kitchen and yanked the plug out from the wall. "What are you doing?"

Yogurt dripped from her forehead and down her nose, cold and slimy on her skin. Steve snorted and clapped his hand over his mouth.

"This isn't funny!"

"Sorry." His hand crept to the front pocket of his jeans, where he kept his phone.

"Don't even think about it," she said, pointedly eyeing a chef's knife she kept on a magnetic strip that ran along the backsplash.

He took his hand away.

"What did you do to my blender?"

"Nothing!" he said, throwing his hands up.

She grabbed a dishtowel that had been hanging on the handle of her oven door. She tossed it to Steve and snatched a roll of paper towels from the top of the fridge. "Help me clean instead of standing there gawking like you're missing a chromosome."

He wisely stooped and began mopping whitish globs up from the floor. "How did this happen? Lid not on tight enough?"

"I swear that thing was possessed," she said, her mouth quivering as she swabbed the counter with fistfuls of paper towel. It looked like a giant bird had crapped everywhere.

"I'm sorry, Jenn." He pecked the one clean patch of skin on her face. "Want me to throw this into the laundry hamper?"

"Thank you." She pushed the paper towels into her garbage can. The cupboards were still smeared but she could clean it more thoroughly later. "Wait on the couch. I'm going to hop into the shower."

It took ages for her to get the hot and cold settings right and the temperature kept changing on her. The second her hair was full of shampoo lather or conditioner, the water would scald or freeze. She swore Steve must be playing with the sink taps and yet each time she whipped open the shower curtain, there was no sign he'd been in here.

Her bathroom was thick with mist when she stepped out of the tub. She rubbed her scalp with a towel and wrapped it around her head in a makeshift turban. She took another towel from a nearby hook to dry the rest of her body.

The idiot box blared from the living room as some team scored a goal against some other team. Steve must still be here. He better be. She slipped into her clothes, a pale pink and black velvet tracksuit. Everything else she owned was too tight and she refused to buy those stupid flowery maternity dresses.

She winced in the fogged up mirror as she combed her damp hair. A vicious knot had formed underneath the back of her head. She'd forgotten to take out the elastic before going to bed and she cursed the way her baby fine hair matted.

In the mirror, a shadowy figure appeared behind her. She froze. Steve gave her a peck on the cheek and said, "See ya."

"I thought you wanted to go out for breakfast."

"I'm hungry right now. I can't wait the hour it's going to take you to get ready." He stole out again.

"Jerk," she muttered. He was getting on her nerves anyway. She picked at the knot of hair as if she was undoing a broken shoelace. The front door slammed shut. Fuming, she took out her hair dryer and plugged it in. She held it to the mirror to clear away enough condensation so she could see herself, and then held it against the side of her head. "Ouch!"

Strands of her hair tangled in the dryer intake. She turned it off and pulled them out, stinging her scalp. The dryer went on again, sucking more hair in and she clicked the button furiously. Panicked, she yanked the cord out from the wall. The dryer went off and the lights overhead flickered. Thankfully, the power stayed on. It better.

She slammed the hairdryer on her counter. A piece snapped off, flying behind the toilet. "God damn it, I hate this day!"

*   *   *

Lucy stumbled into her bathroom, trying to decide whether to bother opening the store. Ever since the road had been torn up, Sundays were the worst. The last time a customer had come in on a Sunday was three weeks ago and after well over an hour of browsing, they'd left without buying a single thing. Just promised to be back some other time. Then again, what else was she going to do today?

She braved her reflection in the mirror above her sink. Her smeared mascara and eyeliner gave her that smoky look makeup artists spent hours perfecting. She put a dollop of hand lotion onto a tissue and began daubing it off. Her eyes were googly enough; she didn't need anything to make them look bigger.

Makeup smeared on her tissue but refused to come off. Time for a proper face wash. She opened the cupboard next to her sink and an avalanche of toiletries spilled out. Boxes of tissue, makeup, shampoo samples, pill bottles, packages of cotton, aromatherapy vials, and jars of bath salts and tubes of moisturizer tumbled out as if someone had dumped a pharmacy shelf onto her. A bottle of conditioner landed square on the top of her foot. "Ow!"

She winced in pain and squatted down to rub her toes. Senses piqued, she froze. A presence was in the room with her. She could feel it, deep in her bones.

She stood again. She leapt onto the nearest bare spot of floor and hurried into the kitchen where she kept her supply of herbs and matches. She lit the biggest twig of sage she could find and blew it out. It flared orange, and a steady stream of smoke smoldered. She went up to the nearest windowsill and shook ashes onto the ledge. Careful not to let the stick go out, she waved it slowly around in circles, making sure to spread smoke around the entire room.

After cleansing the kitchen, she walked around her living room, wafting smoke with the solemnity of a priest. She went counter-clockwise, waving the stick into each corner, under the furniture, around the windowsills and above the bookshelves. She stopped every so often to collect the ashes into a saucer. More important than the ritual, was the headspace it put her into. She always felt so calm and relaxed afterward.

She set the remaining stub on a wooden incense burner and lit a fat black candle. That should absorb any residual negative energy. Taking one more branch of sage, she set it aflame and took it into her bedroom. Once she'd cleansed her entire apartment with the smoke, the place was bathed in a sweet, acrid scent. Her mother used to perform this once a month and her dad would sit in the kitchen reading the newspaper, occasionally glancing up and chuckling at her. Yet never with a hint of malice or scorn. Maybe it was this tangible reminder of happier times that put her into a better mental space.

Starting at her front door, she rubbed ashes on the frame of each doorway and window. She then stood in the middle of the living room, on a spot where sunlight streamed in through her parted curtains. Now, to bring positive energy inside.

She closed her eyes. She concentrated on her bare feet, feeling the sun-warmed wool of the carpet beneath her toes. Then she grew aware of her bare calves, the heat of the sun radiating onto her skin. She breathed in and out, slowly and with deliberation, visualizing an inner fire that the sun had sparked within her. First, an ember. With each breath, the flame grew larger and brighter. Soon the sun's radiance bathed her body and flooded the room, then the entire building with a form of energy that was neither heat nor visible light, making her feel amazingly at peace.

She opened her eyes again. The dark, troublesome presence was gone. Spreading her arms straight out from her sides, she basked in the positive energy.

Then memories of the previous night came back, like someone dumping a load of rocks onto her.

*   *   *

Thomas kicked a towel around the floor to mop up water that had spilled from the teakettle. It was a tiny pot and yet it seemed as though gallons had flowed out from it. Finally, the kitchen was clean, apart from inside the fridge. He debated on whether to head to the studio or get that over with first.

His phone rang. Probably Dave, wondering where he was and when he was coming in. Already he was half an hour late. He picked up the handset and was about to answer when he caught sight of the call display. Jenn.

He set the phone on the counter.

It stopped ringing for a few seconds and started again. Jenn was the sort who would keep trying until he turned off his phone, unplugged it from the wall, or answered it. To spite her, he usually waited until the fifth or sixth attempt. Today the ringing was only adding to his growing pile of things that were irritating the hell out of him.

After picking up, he let out an audible sigh and said, "Now's not a good time." He was about to hang up when he heard a loud sniffling on the other end.

"I'm having the day from hell. Not a single thing has gone right and I've been out of bed for less than an hour."

He looked down at the towel he'd been using. It dripped with smelly brown sludge. He'd only used it to clean water up. He grimaced and flung it into the sink. "Join the club."

"I'm already a platinum member. Can I come over?"

"Where's Steve?

"He went home after dropping me off."

"What, he didn't spend the night with you?" He looked around at his disaster of a kitchen. Either he was losing his marbles, or the more he cleaned, the filthier it got.

"No. He didn't stay overnight with me. I slept alone. Happy?"

Actually, he didn't care either way. "What do you want, Jenn? I'm on my way out the door."

"Can we meet up?"

"I have to go into the studio."

"On a Sunday?"

"I go in when I'm told to go in. You know that. I haven't had a proper weekend in ten years." For once, he was glad he'd been called into work. Any excuse to avoid her, and his job was the one thing that always stopped her from pushing. "Our deadline is Tuesday and thanks to your idiot boyfriend, we have nothing."

"I keep telling you, he's not my boyfriend anymore."

"Didn't look like it to me." He gazed outside. It was brilliantly sunny, and the trees swayed gently in the breeze. It was the perfect day for a walk outdoors, or puttering about in the garden. There was always something he'd rather be doing than whatever he currently had to do. Including talking to Jenn.

"How about afterward?"

"I have no idea when we'll be finished. It's up to Dave." Everything was always up to Dave.

"What about later tonight?"

"We'll see," he said and hung up. Thinking, *no.*

He hurried upstairs to get changed. With any luck, he could convince Jeremy to drive him to the studio; otherwise, the next bus came in ten minutes.

*   *   *

Marcia held her left hand under the running faucet, blood gushing out of a gash across the back of her thumb. The ghoulish side of her enjoyed watching the water turn pink as it swirled around the stainless steel basin, in spite of the agony.

Jeremy rushed up to her with sterile bandages and a dark dishtowel. "Water doesn't do anything. You have to apply pressure to it!"

"I had to clean it first."

Jeremy took her hand, patted it dry, led her into the mudroom, and made her sit down on a bench they kept next to the back door. Wrapping her hand tightly in the gauze, he said, "We're going to the hospital."

"I'll be fine. It wasn't that big of a cut."

"What the hell did you do?"

"I don't know! It just slipped!" She nodded in the direction of the knife and cantaloupe on a cutting board next to the sink. Blood smeared the rind of the half-cut fruit. More blood splattered on the cutting board and counter top, looking like a bottle of runny ketchup had exploded over it. "I guess that thing isn't Kosher anymore."

Jeremy snorted, shook his head, and led her outside. "We're going."

"Why? It's just a cut!"

"You're in shock, or you wouldn't be getting in the car right now."

Marcia gawked around. She was inside the car; she hadn't

been aware they'd left the house. "Yeah, but if I was in shock, wouldn't I be not talking to you right now?"

Jeremy pulled the handle next to her seat and pushed the backrest down. "You're getting it checked out, end of story. Now lie down and keep your hand on your chest."

~ CHAPTER NINETEEN ~

Dave sat in the editing suite watching the footage he'd recorded last night. There wasn't much. A power surge in his van had knocked out three minutes' worth of feed. Longer than he'd thought and at the worst moment possible. By the time it came back online, Tom's library was trashed. Nobody he called could explain how it had happened. Even so, not much he could have done while the system rebooted.

Worse, both Tom and Isaac were late. Right when he could use a second set of eyes. He leaned closer to the largest screen in the middle of his console, scrolling forward to ten seconds before everything went blank for him. As Lucy mouthed "Oh entity", he froze the frame. This was the third time he'd done it, and the third time that same thing had happened. Right as she mouthed those words, a spot appeared above the table like a puff of smoke. It was in this frame but not the previous one.

Coincidences like these always pissed him off. Maybe Tom wasn't making lame excuses and she had brought an accomplice along. He took out a tissue and rubbed the screen. The smudge stayed put. He scrolled back a couple of frames. Lucy's hands grasped Tom and Jeremy's hands tightly. In another screen, which showed feed from the camera he'd stuck under the table, he rolled the video forward until the times were in sync. Lucy's feet were firmly planted on the carpet. They didn't budge. The candles on the table were nowhere near the spot where the puff originated.

It drove him nuts. He flicked on a third screen and found the footage from the camera he'd placed in the grandfather clock. He missed having Isaac here to do the more tedious stuff for him. Tom would too, though not without bitching first.

After several minutes of fiddling, he got it to the same time as the other videos. Lucy stared straight out. She knew the camera was there; he could tell by her scowl. He rolled the video forward and the same tiny cloud appeared, as if from nothing. The candle flames danced on each side as if taunting him.

If she had some object in her mouth, he couldn't see it. Even so, the originating point of the cloud was too high. Her face had been tilted down after that glance at the clock, and she didn't appear to be exhaling. He forwarded the video frame by frame. The puff of smoke grew denser and expanded. He let the video play at half speed and the dark cloud swirled around the middle of the table.

The door clicked open, startling Dave. Isaac entered.

"Jeez! What took you so long?"

"Weird morning." Isaac rolled a chair next to Dave's and sat. "My car wouldn't start, and it's brand new. Then a neighbor checked it out and everything was fine. I looked like a friggin' idiot. Then on the highway, the engine cut all of a sudden. I had to roll to a stop by the—"

"Yeah, yeah, you can fill me in later." Dave leaned around him and looked out into the corridor. "Where's Tom? Weren't you supposed to pick him up?"

"He wasn't ready when I called him. Said he overslept." Isaac peered into the screen directly in front of Dave.

"How is he going to get here, then?"

"Bus? Pretty sure the bus runs on Sundays."

"I should have got his lazy butt out of bed myself." Dave replayed the video. Dark, swirling mist enveloped each person at the table. It exploded around the entire room and dissipated.

"What was that?"

"Ambient humidity. See it all the time." Dave wound the video faster, skipping over the part where the cameras had failed.

Both men watched as Steve goofed frantically in the video, Lucy flew out of the house, then Marcia and her husband tottered out as if they were in an old silent film. Tom and the remaining guests raced around the room and the lights flickered off.

"Wish I'd caught that earlier. I fixed the circuit-breaker, but didn't think to check and see if she'd messed with the wiring."

"We looked and there was nothing wrong!"

"Whatever, I'm the engineer, not you." Dave opened the file for the next camera. Surely, one angle he'd covered would show how Lucy made that cloud appear. Like a dog with a soup bone, he was damned if he was going to let go.

*　　　*　　　*

After jingling Tibetan bells in each corner, Lucy wafted a stick of burning sage all around the inside of her store. She didn't sense anything in here, but performed a thorough cleansing ritual just in case. The top of her foot still throbbed from the bottle falling on it earlier. Pain stabbed with each step she took.

She finished smudging ashes around the front of the store and snuffed the stick out. Time for some crystal energy work. She crawled beneath her counter and groped around inside the display case for the chunks of amethyst and black tourmaline she kept for personal use. At the sound of footsteps shuffling outside, she lifted her head.

Thomas came up to the front door. She kept her head down, pretending she hadn't seen him, wishing she hadn't unlocked the store yet. He slipped inside, careful not to let the bells jingle. He hesitated by the entrance but as Lucy kept low, he let the door slam shut behind him.

She stood and stared coldly at him.

He held up a plastic bag. "You forgot this last night. I'm on my way to work, but the connecting bus isn't for another fifteen minutes, so I thought I'd pop by."

All the stuff she'd printed off those internet sites last minute was in that bag. If Thomas had wanted to point a gun at her to blast away any credibility in her career, she may as well have loaded the ammunition herself.

"Don't worry, I didn't snoop or anything, just thought you might want it back."

She kept staring at him, her mind racing so fast she couldn't catch up to any single thought.

"I also came here to apologize."

"For what?" she blurted, harsher than she intended.

He gulped. He didn't seem sure of what he was apologizing for either. He came closer, holding the bag out to her to as if it contained meat for a starving lion. "Last night was ... Steve. He's not even my friend, he–"

"Jenn's your friend." Her stomach somersaulted. She folded her arms and cocked her head to one side.

"She's my ex-girlfriend. Okay?"

"Are you sure?" Going by the way he hesitated answering, she sensed he wasn't.

"You did say to invite people who are successful and so on. I don't know that many well enough to invite to my house. Especially last minute."

"Even a doubting Thomas should have figured exes bring a bad vibe to–"

"It's not what you think," he protested, his voice growing strained. "We were only ever off and on anyway and–"

"But she's carrying your baby."

His eyes bugged out and his jaw fell open. "That lying—Jenn's a fucking—what a, she's a–" he floundered and approached the counter, defiant. "I'm not the one responsible for that! That is all Steve's doing!"

Seeing the hurt in his dark blue eyes, she saw exactly what Jenn meant. He was her little puppy, her plaything to put on a shelf when she didn't want him around. The second she did, he'd be right back at her side.

"She did me a favor when she left me for him, okay? She's a shallow, materialistic princess who brings out the absolute worst in people. I need someone who will ..."

"Who'll what?" she sneered.

He recoiled and shrugged. "Well you're the psychic. Send me a bill for last night; I'll make sure it gets paid." He tossed the bag onto the counter, turned around and marched out of the store.

Just like with every other man in her life, the second she spotted a vulnerable spot, she stuck a knife into it. Athena was right. She'd never gotten over Pete. She was still angry with him and she took it out on every new man she met. She fretted behind the counter, then raced to the door, opened it and peered out. She looked up the street in both directions; he was long gone.

She came back inside her store, eying the Tarot cards in her window display. The Tower card was one of the cards laid out in a spread she thought she'd arranged at random on top of the black velvet shawl. She picked up the card and gazed at the orange and yellow flames blazing out of the broken stone turret.

"Step right up, ladies, and gentlemen. Come see Madame Zharakova, self-sabotager extraordinaire. Guaranteed to totally fuck up her life, or your money back."

She took the card, shoved it absent-mindedly into a pocket of her red cardigan, and went back behind the counter. As she went to sit on her stool, it slid out from under her, sending her sprawling on top of it. She bashed her chin against the edge of the seat. Her arm was pinned between her body and two of the legs. Something sharp dug into her right thigh. Stunned, she took her time lifting off. Nothing broken, thankfully. She just hurt in several different places.

~ CHAPTER TWENTY ~

Thomas paused outside the door of the editing studio. Such a beautiful sunny afternoon to waste inside some basement hole, but since the day had started so badly already, there was no point trying to save it now. He nudged the door open. Dave and Isaac were bickering in front of the editing suite like a long-married couple who'd sooner kill each other than go their separate ways. Similar to his parents before they'd split.

"I'm telling you, it's lens flare," Dave said. "I've seen it hundreds of times."

Thomas chuckled to himself. Dave's answer for any oddity appearing in a photograph was lens flare. At least the people claiming to see ghosts and angels were more creative.

"Lens flare, my ass. Look!" Isaac forwarded the video to footage of a spherical object that warped the surrounding air as it flew past. "See, lens flare doesn't—"

"I've examined years' worth of this exact same stuff okay? You were in diapers when I was working my first camera."

"That doesn't mean I'm blind! I know what I see!"

Thomas snorted as he suppressed a laugh.

Dave wheeled his chair around, eyes lighting up. "Hey, will you look who decided to make an appearance today!"

Thomas glowered and grabbed a seat of his own, joining them in front of the bank of screens. "I had an emergency to deal with."

"Yeah, yeah," Dave said.

"I'm serious! My fridge conked out on me this morning."

"Tom, help me out here." Isaac scrolled the video back to the source of his and Dave's argument. "What is this?"

"Lens flare," Thomas said, still glaring at Dave.

"You didn't look!"

"There is nothing to see."

"Exactly," Dave said. "All we've got is some wind knocking everything over."

Isaac pounded the desk. "Dude, the windows were closed. I checked right afterward!"

"Doesn't mean she didn't rig anything," Dave said. "She could have set it all up while she was waving that incense stick around. It would have taken her all of two seconds to gather up whatever evidence again while you guys were busy putting the furniture and stuff back."

Thomas rolled his seat backwards, away from them, and they resumed arguing. Isaac groaned. "Both me and Steve searched every single object that might have made those lamps and books fall over. If she set up anything, she's a better magician than both you guys put together."

"Ha, ha. Real funny," Dave said. "Just because you forgot to check thoroughly before she left, doesn't mean there was nothing there."

"She wasn't around for long enough to have set up any contraption," Thomas said, "unless she's able to shift the time-space continuum. I was next to her the entire time."

"She could have grabbed everything on her way out," Dave said.

"She ran out pretty fast," said Isaac. "She didn't even—oh! That bag! She forgot a bag full of papers she'd pulled off the internet! We can use that!"

Thomas sighed. No point in lying. "I returned it to her on my way here."

"What? That stuff was dynamite!"

"Why bother." He rubbed his face with his hand, wishing he'd had more sleep. "I doubt anything can be salvaged from last night at this point."

Just as Dave was about to berate him, a cell phone lying next to the keyboard rang. Thomas caught the name *Steve* on the glossy screen and rage flared in him. "If that's our Steve, tell him to get fucked. We'd have had plenty of footage if it weren't for him. Everything is his fault."

"Steve, what's up?" Dave said.

"I need a ride." Steve's voice was loud enough for Thomas to hear clearly as well. "My car got towed from outside of Jenn's condo and the lot they took it to is out in the middle of nowhere."

Thomas's blood boiled. That lying bitch. Steve *had* spent the night with her.

"Where are you now?" Dave asked.

"At the bank on Pine and Fourth. They only take cash; it's like a hundred bucks or something."

Dave nodded to Thomas and said, "We're kinda busy right now. There's not a whole lot of material to work with and–"

"Come on, Dave, it'll take half an hour, tops!"

"All right, already. But in exchange, *you* are our new fake psychic."

"Awesome! Thanks, bud—aw, for Chrissakes!"

Dave straightened in his seat. "What?"

"Can I borrow a hundred and twenty from you? The machine just ate my card."

"I'll be there in ten."

Thomas and Isaac eyed each other and smirked. With bated breath, they watched Dave pocket his phone. "We'll have to come back to this tomorrow."

*   *   *

Thomas slumped into the shotgun seat of the white van. The afternoon sun blazed through the windshield and he regretted wearing a long-sleeved black shirt. Dave leaned on the steering wheel, groaning. "Alastair's texted me and I managed to get our deadline pushed back two more days. What are we going to do between now and Thursday?"

"Get Lucy back in," Isaac said, leaning into the window on Thomas's side.

"No," Thomas said.

"Why not? Shouldn't be too hard to convince her. Show her the footage, say it's haunting your house worse than ever and you need her to help get rid of it. You could even guilt trip her over summoning it to begin with if you have trouble getting her to come," Dave said.

"I said, 'no'. Didn't you hear me?" Lucy would never be stupid enough to believe a ruse like that anyway. She'd known what they were up to; the only question was when, exactly, she'd figured it out.

Dave cursed as he struggled to get the engine started. "Still want a job tomorrow?"

"You're going to fire me if I don't cooperate in this, this farce? Go ahead." Thomas folded his arms across his chest, ready to explode from the rage coursing through his body. He could always walk the six miles or so to get home.

"I'll drop you downtown," Dave said, for once having the sense to back off. "Later, Isaac."

Thomas rolled his lips into his mouth and bowed his face so Dave wouldn't see him trying to suppress a triumphant smile. Never before had he dared Dave to fire him, not directly. His first round with him was a knockout.

Isaac leapt backwards and said, "I smell something acrid. Anyone else smell it?"

Thomas caught the check engine light coming on the same moment Dave spotted it. He was used to all sorts of stupid little things going wrong in a day, but this was getting ridiculous.

"It's just the oxygen sensor," Dave said. "I keep forgetting to replace it. Isaac, that smell? It's called engine exhaust."

~ CHAPTER TWENTY-ONE ~

Lucy pulled out a drawer at the bottom of her display counter, sat on her stool, and rested her feet on top of it. For the tenth time in the space of a few minutes, she glanced at the antique clock hanging on the wall beside her cash register. Two hours and forty-five minutes to go until she closed for the day.

"Why am I even here," she said aloud to the only company she had in her store. Herself. At least when she was with Pete, he kept her company. They'd play cards, read to each other, or one of them could mind the store while the other cooked a hot, fresh lunch. They'd had so much in common. It almost compensated for the amounts he stole from the till to feed his pot habit and whatever other substances he "experimented" with.

After Thomas had left, eight people had passed by on the street outside. Not one person had come in. The sky was brilliantly sunny. Normally she would have had dozens of customers by now. So long as the streets and sidewalks were torn up, the only ones who went along it were her own neighbors.

On top of that, Athena still hadn't returned her call. Sure, she had other friends, but they were always too busy to sit and chat on the phone, never mind pop into her store for a visit. They had even less time to hear her whine about her life. Now it seemed her best friend had joined their side.

A familiar car slowed outside her window. She sat upright and tensed. The silver Honda steered around an orange pylon and rolled to a stop right in front. Marcia climbed out of the passenger side and bumped the door shut with her hip. Her left hand was wrapped in bandages if she were an apprentice mummy.

All day Lucy had been bored and desperate for company and now she dreaded the idea of anyone coming inside for a chat. The bells above her door jingled. She stared blankly, her stomach churning, as Marcia nudged her way in.

"Hi." Lucy got off her stool, her mind spinning about what

might have prompted this visit. Had Thomas sent her? And why, to patch things up, or because he needed to sucker her one more time for his stupid internet show?

Marcia said nothing as she approached the counter. Her lips were pursed and her body was stiff like she was angry about something and still figuring out how to articulate it.

"What happened to your hand?" Lucy asked, trying to look and sound concerned. Marcia didn't appear to be in that much pain, nor did she have a glazed look of someone loaded up on meds.

"I cut it." Marcia shrugged.

There was an awkward silence. If she'd been faking an injury, surely she would have come up with a story explaining it. "Are you okay?" Lucy asked.

"You might think I'm insane, but all day it's as if something's been screwing with me. I don't know how else to explain it. My house is full of gremlins. So. I need to do one of those cleaning ritual things. Jeremy thinks it's stupid and pointless, but right now, I'm willing to try *anything*." She leaned closer and dropped her voice. "Between you and me, I think he is too, he's just too much of a stubborn ass to admit it. Even if it is all just in our heads, these rituals clear all the crap out of there, too, right?"

Lucy felt the blood drain from her face and she braced herself against the glass counter. Marcia's distress radiated into her body like heat from a raging fire and she realized she'd been blocking it until now.

"It's my fault. Last night after we left, I'd had enough of Jenn pissing me off so I went on this tirade, cursing her every which way to Sunday. Things always go haywire when I do that. And lately, her moods have been driving me insane."

"Hormones can do that. Though usually by the second trimester, they—"

"She's pregnant?" Marcia's dark eyes nearly bugged out of her head.

"I'm sorry, I thought you knew."

"I had no idea," she said in a quiet, faraway voice.

"How long have you been trying for?" Lucy blurted, covering

her mouth. Too late. Sometimes she hated how quickly she picked up on the subtlest cues and ran with them at full speed.

Marcia's eyes watered and she clasped her hands together on top of the counter. "How did you know," she whispered, her eyes fixed on her blanched fingers.

"I've always been able to read people's body language," she said in a soothing voice. "Other things, I just pick up on. Sometimes it's a lucky guess. One of my friends is going through the same thing. They're on their third round of IVF and again it's not looking good. I know it's tough."

Marcia nodded and her hands relaxed. One other thing Lucy had observed was that Marcia did not like to talk about her own problems. "Thomas is the dad?" she asked, her eyes still fixed on the glass countertop.

"Looks like it," Lucy said, again doubts about him clouding her mind and her senses.

"I can't believe he didn't tell me."

"He tried to tell me it wasn't his, but I don't know."

Marcia stared straight at her and said, "Jenn is such a fucking skank that I'll bet she doesn't know who the—" She threw up her hands and said, "Never mind, shouldn't slut-shame, her sex life is none of my business."

Lucy fought off the urge to stoke Marcia's hostility against Jenn, secretly pleased she wasn't the only one who found her so loathsome, wasn't alone in her struggle against hateful thoughts or the ensuing guilt over them. She lifted her tray of stones and crystals out from under the glass counter. "What sort of cleansing do you think you need?"

Marcia plucked an olive green chunk of jade from the box. "I'm always drawn to anything green. Don't know why, just like the color, I guess. At least this shade. Lime or yellow-green? Meh."

"It's a relaxing color, and relieves stress." Just in time Lucy stopped herself from pointing out green was also the color for fertility. Thankfully Marcia was as easily distracted as a toddler.

"So what do you do for a living?"

"I'm in advertising." She sighed and examined a darker green stone from Lucy's box. "Thomas thinks I'm a sell-out but hey, it brings home the bacon. Better than being broke."

Lucy stood glumly, watching her pick through the assorted crystals. At some point she was going to have to work on getting Thomas out of her mind, though she wasn't sure she wanted to.

Marcia gulped. "So how do you manage to guess all these things about people? I'm assuming you don't literally read anyone's mind."

"It's hard to describe, but sometimes I can feel other people's emotions as if they're my own."

Marcia nodded, plucking out more green stones and examining them one by one. "Empaths. People often think I'm one. Maybe it's how I dress, or something. I'm not. I'm actually kinda clueless most of the time."

"You know, I've never liked the term. There are all these weird connotations with it. Just because you are not as tuned in to others, doesn't make you selfish, and people who are, aren't necessarily any better than you."

The corners of Marcia's mouth twitched. "How so?"

"Most con-artists and psychopaths are great at reading people. That is how they take advantage of them."

"I hadn't thought of it like that. Huh." She seemed satisfied and took out a smoky quartz piece, turning it in her fingers.

"It also doesn't relay the confusion I get. It's bad enough sorting through what *I* feel, and then someone else comes near me and suddenly I'm angry, depressed, or agitated. For no reason. And then, even when I look at them and can see it's not me, that feeling stays so long as I'm in close proximity to them."

"But you can block it, can't you?"

"Not always. This is why I'm not that social sometimes. I can't stand crowds or big parties and I always need time alone so I can center myself. Otherwise it can get pretty overwhelming."

"Thomas is like that too, though he'd never admit that's why." She covered her mouth with her bandaged hand. "Sorry."

"Was I that obvious?" Lucy cringed.

"Even I'd clued into that! Everyone did except him. But then, he's so dumb sometimes."

Lucy giggled.

"Oh he totally is." Marcia's mood brightened like the sun burning through a dense fog. "I can say it because he's one of my best friends, but he's single for a reason. He's not that hung up on Jenn, either. Trust me. He has issues. His house is in move in condition, but *he* is definitely a fixer-upper."

Lucy giggled again.

"Meanwhile, Jenn? If she was a house, they'd board up the doors and windows and there'd be a notice from the city nailed to the front of it."

Lucy doubled over laughing and caught sight of Jeremy pacing outside her front window. If she wanted to get the lowdown on Thomas, she'd better be quick. "How serious were they?"

"Not very." Marcia shrugged. "They've always been off and on. Lots of stupid drama, fights, constant breaking up, and getting back again. He's pretty even-tempered; it was mostly her."

Just like he'd said. Maybe he was telling the truth about everything else as well.

"Jenn cheats like crazy and Thomas is super picky. He'd date a lot of girls and then dump them over the absolute dumbest thing. His mom was really flighty, so that could be why. Don't get me wrong, she was a nice woman, but flighty."

Lucy's heart sank. By the sound of it, Thomas wouldn't settle for less than a supermodel. He sure seemed to tolerate personality flaws. "So why did he keep going back to Jenn?"

"She's easy," Marcia said. "I don't mean she spreads her legs at the jingle of a belt buckle. It's more that I don't think either of them really cared where they stood with each other. It was emotionally easy."

Lucy furrowed her brow. For someone who saw herself as clued out, Marcia was quite insightful. Then she caught Jeremy pacing in tighter and tighter circles outside her store window, growing more agitated. "How do you mean?"

"You don't have to worry about getting abandoned by someone if you don't care much about them to begin with."

Lucy leaned forward. This could easily apply to her as well.

"His problem is, he doesn't know what he wants. With anything. But then when I saw how he was talking to you the other day, I could tell he—"

The bells above the doorway jingled noisily and Jeremy barged inside. "What's taking so long? Did you ask her yet about the—"

"I totally forgot." Marcia kissed Jeremy's cheek. "Sorry, got distracted. Chattin' away here."

"How could you forget?"

"Forget what?" Lucy asked, growing tense.

"All the damned morning." Jeremy threw his bear arms by his sides. "It's like our house is possessed by demons or something. The water pipe for our bathroom sink blew up and flooded our basement, the coffee maker literally had a meltdown, and neither of our cats would come out from under the couch. When I tried, one of them scratched the hell out of me, and then her hand." Jeremy grabbed Marcia's wrist and hoisted up her arm.

Lucy stared, frozen, guilt trickling in.

Marcia leaned her elbow on the counter. "Yeah, we're not sure exactly what happened last night, but something did. I'd be more disturbed by it if I wasn't wigged out on opiates right now."

The protection ritual. She knew better than to omit doing one, but at the time, she hadn't planned to try to contact anything. She fetched a pouch of dried herbs from the display case. She set it on the counter, turned around and took out some sticks of incense, a book on energy cleansing, and some Tibetan bells from one of the shelves above.

"Here, on the house."

Marcia took out her wallet. "At least let me pay cost."

"The bells were not even a buck and I grow the sage and other herbs myself. It's just the book that—"

Marcia pushed the book back. "I have my own thing I do. I was actually wondering if you have those Chinese coins? The ones with the square in the middle. I can't find what I did with mine."

"Oh, sure," Lucy said, scanning through the glass of her counter top. She thought she kept a box of them on the shelf next to a case of birthstone rings.

"There." Jeremy rapped halfway down the front of the cabinet with his knuckles. "Second shelf."

Lucy brought the box out and said, "Help yourself."

Marcia took out six bronze coins and slid a couple of one-dollar bills toward Lucy. She pushed them back.

"Is that everything?" Jeremy asked.

"For now." Marcia returned her eel skin wallet to her purse. She left the cash on the counter.

"Let's get you home," he said, trying to hustle her out. "That was a deep cut."

"Take care," Lucy said. "Say hi to Thomas for me."

Marcia paused halfway out the door and said, "I'll see if I can drag him back in here one of these days. If it's okay by you. See you later."

They both waved as they left the store. Lucy smiled ruefully and watched them climb into Jeremy's car. She hoped Marcia was right and Thomas hadn't been lying to her. He *had* tried to apologize. If she were smart, she'd do her best not to speculate on his reasons until she heard him out. Her chance with him might not be over yet.

~ CHAPTER TWENTY-TWO ~

Dave dropped Thomas off downtown on his way to pick up Steve. He could just ignore Jenn's text and continue home, or he could try to see if he could catch Lucy in a better mood. The wine bar was closer, as well as safer for his bruised ego. The sun was just beginning to set as he walked in. This had been his favorite hangout back when he and Jenn were together, with brick walls covered in large, moody black and white photographs of various buildings in Prague. The quiet jazz music and scents of fresh coffee did nothing to settle his nerves, though.

Jenn was perched on a stool in front of a counter that ran the length of the front window. He was of half a mind to turn around and walk back out, except that she was sniffling and gazing at the street outside. He couldn't leave her alone in such a state. Yet as he ambled up to her, Dave's taunting droned in his head.

"Thanks for coming," she said, a smile twitching across her lips. "I've had such a shitty day. I had some cramping and bleeding earlier, but the doctors assured me the baby is fine. They told me I need to avoid stress because of what it does to my hormones."

The waitress refilled Jenn's water glass and set a glass of red wine down in front of Thomas. He swallowed nearly half of it in one gulp. Out of the corner of his eye, he watched her stroke her rounded belly, intense pain rising in his chest. Every close family member of his was gone and having his own child was the only way he'd ever ... he forced those thoughts out of his head.

"I miss having wine with you here," she said. "I miss having wine period."

"About last night." Thomas glanced at her, then back out the window where it was easier to summon his anger against her. "*What* did you say to Lucy?"

"Why does it matter? I keep telling you, it's over with me and Steve."

For once, he didn't try to hide his bitterness. "It's over for us, too. It has been for a while.”

“It doesn’t have to be.” She turned his stool to face her and put her hands on his knees.

His head bowed, her swollen cleavage was still in his line of sight. He looked up into her dewy eyes. They were the warmest shade of green with flecks of brown and gold. When he first met her, he could lose himself in them.

“I made such a huge mistake,” she said.

He faced away from her again; those eyes made him sick to look at now. “Several huge mistakes, Jenn. Not just one.”

“I know. You were the one who wanted to settle down, and it was me who kept pushing you away.”

“Kind of you to notice.”

She sighed, flustered. “You know what I mean. I was only twenty when I met you. I hadn’t had that many boyfriends and I needed to know what else was out there. Some of our differences are major and we both have divorced parents. I needed to be sure I was making the right choice.”

“Good for you. I asked you once and you said ‘no’. I’ll not ask a second time.”

“Come on.” Jenn took his hand and stroked his palm with her fingers. “Aren’t you bored, Tom? Bored of bars, bored of the singles scene.”

“I’m bored with everything.” He yanked his hand away and took another gulp from his glass. “Including my drama with you.”

They sat, glaring out onto the street. He wondered why he wasn’t leaving, why he’d bothered showing up. Seriously. Saying *no* to her shouldn’t be that difficult.

Jenn wriggled on her stool. “It’s so hot in here,” she whined as she took off her velour hoodie and tied the arms of it around her waist. Again, his eyes fell to her cleavage. Her pink and black athletic top barely covered the top of her bra. Exactly as Dave had predicted. A waitress approached their table with an expectant look on her face and he waved her off.

“We had a lot of fun times together.” Jenn brushed his calf with the side of her foot.

He drained his glass and eyed the exit, suppressing the urge to bolt out without saying another word. She took his hand and locked his fingers into hers. He made no attempt to pull away.

"We didn't always fight. Lately I've missed you like crazy. It took being around some total dumbasses like Steve to appreciate how smart you are. Not just smart, *brilliant*. You know all these things and you read, you're good at figuring stuff out; I've missed that so much. All the conversations we used to have. All the guys I've met since are so boring. As for Steve, he can be such a retard. All he does is work out, drink with his buddies, and watch TV. That's it. He never wants to do anything or go anywhere."

Thomas missed sleeping next to a warm body more than anything else. He also hated being alone in his big old house, with only the memories of his late mother and uncle for depressing company.

"I mean it. I miss you, and I'm sorry I took you for granted."

For once, she looked sincere. "I miss you too. Sometimes."

She was the only one who knew how to chip away at the fortress walls he continuously erected. The only one who made the effort to break through them. The only one who cared enough to. When it suited her, he reminded himself.

She squeezed his fingers again and pushed one of her knees between his thighs. Then she put her mouth close to his ear. She said in a soft voice that always sent chills into him, "You're still the best lover I ever had. The way you used to start off, all nice and slow. Then you'd kiss me around the side of my neck and along my shoulders. The way you'd go down on me."

He sucked in his breath as she spread her palm on his thigh. Her fingers inched up, making parts of him tingle. Her lips brushed against his and the tip of her tongue pushed into his mouth. A shadow flickered past the front window and she stiffened. He pulled away and caught her staring at something outside, but missed what it might have been. A guilty look flashed across her face.

"We shouldn't be doing this," he said, wondering if Steve or some other ex had just driven by. "Not 'til you've sorted things out with you-know-who."

She wiped her eyes with a paper napkin. "You'd be such an amazing dad. I know you would be, I've seen how you are around kids, they love you. And I know you've always wanted your own."

Whenever her eyes teared up, they turned the most enchanting green, the shade of moss in a misty Danish forest. Years ago, he'd taken her through one after his grandmother's funeral. They'd walked alone in the woods for hours, neither of them saying a word. He did miss that part of their life together. Shame it had been so rare.

"Steve's been such an asshole about everything. He dumped me as soon as he found out, telling me to get rid of it or put it up for adoption. I can't! I should have never left you." She shook as she bawled, and he cradled her in his arms.

"You'll be fine," he said, his walls eroding more quickly now, melting into a sea of churning emotions.

"I'm going to be all alone!" She rubbed her eyes on the sleeve of her hoodie. "And I have no clue what I'm doing."

He hated to see her hurting. Or anyone, for that matter. He pushed a stray lock of her hair behind her ear that had come loose from her ponytail. "I'm sure you'll be a great mum. You're too hard on yourself. And you never know, once it's born Steve might come around."

She shook her head, her cheeks slick from tears. "He hates kids. He's made that more than clear."

"Loads of people can't stand kids, but still like their own. I'm sure he's in denial and as you get further along he'll–"

"I should have never left you." She threw her arms around his shoulders. "I still love you. I'll always love you."

They kissed and he sank into her embrace. Never before had she blurted it, as if shouting from a rooftop for the world to hear.

"I know I've treated you like shit and you didn't deserve it," she said. "If we got back together, we could be a family. Steve wants nothing to do with me anymore and I'm sick to death of his games."

"What if he changes his mind?"

"I can't go on like this. It's killing me." A sigh shuddered out of her chest. "My whole life has to be more stable, it's not just about me anymore. I have to make a choice and stick with it."

He let her hug him again. Her kiss was deliciously soft, tasting of strawberry lip-gloss.

Something within her froze and he opened his eyes.

This time he caught what she was staring at. Lucy stood on the far side of the road, her eyes wide, her face pale. She stared back at them, too, and bolted. Then Thomas caught the smirk on Jenn's face, which quickly vanished as if she'd tucked it behind her back.

"You bloody bitch," he hissed and ran out of the wine bar. Lucy was already halfway down the block. "Lucy!" He stood in the middle of the sidewalk and called after her, "Lucy!"

She was gone. Right then, he knew. He was truly over Jenn. If he hadn't been, he wouldn't have torn out of her arms like that. He wouldn't have cared what Lucy saw. Had Jenn been playing him like an expert violinist yet again? Until today, she'd expressed no interest in going back to him whatsoever, so why now. He stood there, the world's biggest fool.

He ambled back inside and glared at her. "Tired of games, hm? What was that, then? I know you saw her."

Jenn fumed and swiveled from side to side on her stool.

"You don't want me, but you don't want me with anyone else either, is that it? That's always when you took me back before, whenever I'd met someone new. I'll always be nothing more than your backup plan. A toy you take from your shelf whenever you're bored with all of your other toys."

"That's not true!" She folded her arms across her chest.

"I'm done." He felt like an idiot for ever having trusted her. How many times would this happen, before he finally came to his senses? No wonder Marcia and Jeremy had refused to take his calls the last time he went back to her. It never changed.

"What do you want me to do? Come crawling on my knees for you? If that's what you want from me, I will. On my knees. Prostrating."

"What were you even looking at her for? If you were so caught up in the moment, so overwhelmed with passion, how'd you even notice her? She was across the road; she wasn't rapping on the window outside, trying to get our attention."

Jenn glared up at him again. Nausea welled into his throat as he looked at her face, red and screwed up. Even if she wasn't playing games, enough was enough. All she ever offered was a fantasy life. One that kept him from living a real one. "You know what? I'm going to say something to you now that I should have said years ago. Stay out of my life. For good."

Fixing his gaze straight ahead, he strode out the door of the cafe. He wished he could feel proud for standing up for himself for once, but he didn't. Obviously, she was in a desperate state, trying to cling on to whatever rock she could and he'd always been that for her, had enjoyed the role of protector and savior that she needed him to play. He'd always welcomed her back in the past and cast his bitterness aside, so why wouldn't she expect it now?

The sun was sinking behind the low-rise buildings, casting long shadows over the bus stop. Who was he fooling? Tomorrow he'd be calling to apologize to her, or later this evening once he'd had more time to mull things over. Dave would have his laugh, so be it. Tonight he felt like wallowing, mourning the last hope for any alternative, salvaging what little was left of his pride.

Once Jenn was a mum, she might become less intolerable though so far, he hadn't seen much sign of it. If he were of a more superstitious bent, he'd be speculating about how Lucy's odd ritual was buggering up his life. Jenn had been completely out of the picture until the afternoon he made that phone call, asking her to help out with his show. He was short two people and she was always happy to volunteer. Perhaps a buried part of him was unable to give her up.

More likely, he was a glutton for punishment.

Even with the evening sun blazing on the horizon, setting the clouds aflame with streaks of gold and copper, an oppressive gloom like winter fog surrounded him.

~ CHAPTER TWENTY-THREE ~

Lucy slumped into her velvet sofa and Athena took the easy chair. Both of them were quiet while Lucy spooned heavenly hash ice cream straight from the tub into her mouth. After the fifth or sixth spoonful, Athena said, "I'm so sorry, sweetie, but you already knew nothing good would come of this, and you went through with it anyway. This is where the self-sabotage comes in. You always get hung up on the wrong guy. And by doing that, you're never open for the right one."

"Obviously he isn't gay after all. I've seen proof of that now. Thank you, Universe!" Lucy shoveled another spoonful of ice cream into her mouth. She barely tasted it. "I am such an idiot!"

"Yes, you are an idiot."

Lucy shot her a dirty look.

"Come on, he's been a complete jerk toward you."

"He's actually a really sweet guy."

"You've hung out alone with him what, once, twice, for all of five minutes. Anybody can pretend to be absolutely *wonderful* in small enough doses."

"When my stomach was upset, he was genuinely worried about me. He has this nurturing side I've never seen in a man before. On top of that, I got the sense he didn't want to go through with the séance. He kept asking me, 'are you sure you want to do this?' According to the credits, 'Skeptical Dave' writes and produces the show. He just shows up and reads a few lines from a script."

Athena shook her head. There was an eye roll in there somewhere, Lucy could tell even if she couldn't see it.

"That day in my store when he was showing me all the stuff he bought, he was like a little boy showing off his Star Wars collection. It was so cute. He has this whole side that—"

"He's back with her again. You saw them. What more of a clue do you need?"

Lucy shoveled another spoonful in her mouth.

"Lucy."

Her eyes stung as she left the spoon dangling between her lips, the cold metal pressing against the roof of her mouth. She hated when Athena got like this because she was always right.

"You're seeing things that aren't there. Remember that video?" Athena grabbed the ice cream tub from her and yanked the spoon out of her mouth. She shoved the container back into the freezer and tossed the spoon into the sink.

"What are you doing?" Lucy asked, tensing.

Athena stormed back into the living room and snatched up her clutch, on a mission. Those usually ended in a disaster even worse than anything Lucy ever attempted.

"Someone I've wanted you to meet for ages." She took out her phone and fired off a text message. "The only reason I hadn't sooner is because you'd complain he's too short. Maybe for once, you won't be so goddamn fussy."

"Huh?"

Athena grabbed Lucy's wrists and tried dragging her off the sofa. "We're going out. No more sinking in a mire of self-pity. There are tons of great guys out there. All you need to meet is one. And you can only do that if you go out once in a blue moon."

"I met one! It's just that he's–"

"–he's an asshole! You get hooked on men who aren't available so you can avoid meeting one who is. Admit it already, fear of commitment is your problem. You don't want to risk being dumped again. Abandoned. Like your father abandoned you."

"He didn't abandon me—he died!"

"It is still where that same complex comes from!"

"Nonsense!" Lucy threw herself back on her sofa. "Besides, you've seen Thomas, he's totally my type! He's smart, he's cute, he can be really sweet when he–"

"And he's not available. So get that brain in there to start looking for the next smart, cute and sweet only not a jerk this time. And not taken by some knocked-up Barbie doll, either."

"Fine." Lucy stomped her feet onto her knotted carpet, got up and grabbed her purse from the kitchen table. She hadn't been hearing things; Thomas had definitely called out to her, and she'd been too stupid and prideful to turn around and go back. Athena, of course, would hear none of it. She'd deride it as *insta-love*. This wasn't insta-love; this was insta-want-to-get-to-know-him-better.

Stupid love spell. Stupid tower card. Stupid pretending to contact some other realm for the sake of a couple of hundred bucks. At this rate, she was better off applying for a job at Burger King.

~ CHAPTER TWENTY-FOUR ~

Thomas sat alone in the dark at the round table in his library, in a mood for brooding and self-pity. A half glass of red wine sat next to him on the bare wooden surface. Ever since he'd come home, he'd gone through the motions of eating his dinner and tidying up as though he were a robot.

He rested his head on his folded arm and flicked a coin on the table. It was a novelty coin he sometimes used for magic tricks, roughly the size of a fifty-cent piece. He watched it spin in circles, pirouetting around the table. It wobbled and tipped onto its side. At the sound of someone knocking on the front door, he lifted his head. Another knock. He ignored it and flicked the coin again. A good one this time, spinning perfectly in one spot like a gyroscope.

An even more determined pounding at the door. "Open up Tom! I know you're home!" Marcia yelled.

"Go away," he muttered.

"I'm a big guy and that's a real expensive-looking door!" Jeremy called out.

Thomas groaned, slapped the coin down, and got up.

He flipped the deadbolt and opened the door to Marcia and Jeremy standing in front of him, furious. "What?"

Marcia stormed inside. "I've had it! Enough with this frigging … What happened to your lights?" She flipped the switch a couple of times.

"Lost power again. I tried to call an electrician, but couldn't get through. Joys of an old house. Everything's mucking up today."

Marcia hugged him. "I'm sorry hon. Us too, it's enough to drive a person insane. Good thing I'm already there." She took a seat at the round table while Jeremy lit some candles and said, "You were sitting here in the dark?"

"They only went out a few seconds ago." Thomas fetched two more glasses from the kitchen and returned, saying, "I was trying to find some matches for those candles when you knocked."

With her bandaged hand, she gripped her glass by the stem and plunked it onto the table in front of him. "Fill 'er up. It's been one of those."

Thomas tipped her glass, poured it a third full, and eyed her wrist. "What happened there?"

"Eight stitches. Wanna see?"

"No!" He made a face. The phone in his kitchen rang. He ignored it. After a few rings, the caller hung up. Then his cell phone rang. He ignored that too and poured a fuller glass of wine for Jeremy.

"Cheers," Jeremy said, not sounding at all cheery.

Just as Thomas was about to ask what sort of meds she was on and should she be drinking at all, Marcia's phone rang. She answered it, "Jenn!" and shrugged, looking at each him and Jeremy in turn. Jenn never called her. "Yeah, I'm–"

"Shh!" Thomas grabbed at her phone. "Hang up!"

Marcia leaned away from him. "Uh uh. May as well come on over, we're here too!"

Thomas glared at her and threw up his hands. Jeremy shook his head and whispered, "She really needs to clue in sometimes."

"We're sitting here in the dark, but yeah, it's turning into a little party," Marcia said.

Thomas drained his glass, cheap Pinot Noir burning his throat.

"May as well! See ya!" Marcia hung up.

Thomas bumped his head on his fists, aggravated.

"Steve's coming too, so you know."

"You're fucking kidding me!" He sat upright again and glared at her. God, she could be thick sometimes.

"Isaac's with them too," Marcia said. "Calm down, they were on their way here anyway."

He took a swig straight from the wine bottle and said, "I will *not* calm down."

"What was I supposed to do? She knew you were here and not picking up, you stubborn ass."

"She knows exactly why I wasn't picking up! And since when do you ever talk to her voluntarily?"

"Guys, cool it!" Jeremy pushed them apart and said to him, "Will you admit we've all been cursed because of last night?"

"There is no such thing as curses." Thomas got out from his chair and began pacing on the thick wool carpet. He'd been cursed his entire life; last night didn't make a whit of a difference there.

"Let's call Lucy and get her to straighten this out," she said.

"No!"

"Why not?"

Thomas stopped and stared at her, dumbfounded. "It's all in our heads. Stupid, annoying things happen all the time, it's only because ... you're making associations out of completely random happenings!"

"Oh, come on," Marcia said, pursing her lips as if she were trying to contain a tirade about to explode out of her mouth.

"Give it a rest, Marsh. You know how stubborn he is."

"I am not being stubborn!"

"What's happened to get you into such a bitchy mood, then?" Jeremy asked.

"Jenn insisted Steve is completely out of the picture now."

"So?" Marcia asked. "Don't tell me you believe her."

Thomas stiffened. There was nothing left of his pride anyway, he may as well tell them. "We might be getting back together. Jenn's pregnant and she'll need *someone* around to help with everything. Rather, the child will."

Her voice dropped an octave. "What?"

He sat again, rested his elbows on the table, and buried his face in his palms. "It's the right thing to do."

"You're not the dad," Jeremy said.

"Does it matter? That's not the child's fault."

"Don't," Marcia said. "You'll be miserable with her."

"I'm already miserable. What difference would it make?" He sighed, aware he was wallowing again, grateful neither of them called him on it for once.

*   *   *

Lava Lounge was an eclectic restaurant and bar Lucy and Athena had been coming to for nearly a decade. Middle Eastern-style lamps dangled from the ceiling between strands of Christmas lights. Wooden chairs were crammed around wrought iron tables topped with slabs of white marble. Tonight, the place was hopping. Scanning the crowd for anyone who resembled Thomas, Lucy trailed Athena to a table in the back corner.

A skinny guy with a shaved head looked up from his writing book and waved to them, grinning eagerly. He wore a tight burgundy turtleneck and loose blue jeans belted with a braided rope. A sack made from parti-colored fabric was slung over the back of his chair. This was not looking promising.

Athena hugged him and said, "Finally you guys get to meet! This is my best friend, Lucy."

"Hey." Lucy stood on the far side of the table and gave him a royal wave. There was something creepy about him, but she couldn't put her finger on what it was yet.

"Hi, nice to meet you. I'm Tad." Tad stood to greet her. They were the same height. He held out his hand to her. She shook it limply, pulled out the chair farthest from him, and sat. Out of the corner of her eye, she watched him, trying to figure out what it was that had immediately made her so uncomfortable. He wore an enrapt expression as if he was on something, or had just found a new religion. Either way, no thanks.

Athena took the seat in the middle. "Tad was in my gender studies class a couple of years ago. We hit it off right away."

Then why didn't you go for him, Lucy thought. She glanced at the book he kept on the table, on spiritual healing. It was one she herself had read a few months ago and she wondered if Athena had tipped him off about it.

"You've got very pretty eyes," he said, staring at Lucy's face as if he was peering through a microscope at her; she wished she could retract her head into her body like a turtle.

"Um, thanks." She scanned the rest of the tables. Everyone else in the place appeared to be happily paired off. And each and every guy was more attractive than Tad.

He tapped her shoulder and reached into his sack. "I brought this for you."

She tensed, unwrapping the rough, brown tissue paper to reveal a plush polar bear holding out a bouquet of red fabric flowers. "It's uh, it's cute! Thanks!" Definitely a creep.

"All the proceeds go to the Wildlife Protection Fund."

"Thank you." She set the bear on the table next to a vase of white carnations. To her relief, a waitress came up to their table and set down some menus.

"I'll have the usual," Athena said. "Shrimp Pad Thai."

Tad flattened his menu on the table and bent his head down as he pored over it. One of his knees bounced up and down, making the table shake. "I'll have the spinach ... it's vegan, right?"

The waitress nodded.

"I'll have the spinach fritters with mushrooms, and gluten free bread. Ooh! And no onions."

"Lucy doesn't like onions either," Athena said brightly.

"I love onions! Just not on my breath when I'm out somewhere." Tad held his hand to his mouth.

Lucy closed her menu and handed it to the waitress. "I'll have the burger and fries. The beef burger."

"Do you want no onions as well?" she asked, jotting down the order on a notepad.

"Um." Lucy glanced at Tad, then at Athena. "Could I get crushed garlic and feta cheese on it?"

The waitress nodded and took the menus. Tad stood and wrung his hands. "Back in a sec. Going to wash up. I always like to practice good hygiene, especially out in public."

"Thanks for sharing." Lucy watched him trot off toward the bathrooms. Even his bouncing gait grated her nerves. His sloped shoulders reminded her of a Dr. Seuss character.

While Athena texted on her cell phone, Lucy stared around the lounge, wishing Thomas would walk in through the doors. She'd apologize to him for being rude earlier. Crawling on her knees if she had to. Then she remembered catching sight of him kissing Jenn. Someone else had been calling for her and mishearing his voice was nothing more than wishful thinking. Her eyes stung and she blinked rapidly to get rid of any tears forming.

"So?" Athena returned her phone to her purse and nudged Lucy with her knee. "What do you think?"

She shrugged uncomfortably. "He seems nice."

"Lucy, he's perfect! He's like a gay guy only he's straight! And he definitely likes you."

"Gay but straight? What does that even mean?" She winced at the sight of the Polar bear he gave her. "There's something weird about him."

"He's nervous! It's been a while since he dated anyone and he doesn't get out that much. Like you, he's a homebody. Just get to know him more. Come on, you two have so much in common!"

"Like what?" she asked, though she didn't want to know. The idea of having anything in common with that dweeb repulsed her.

"He has his own Reiki business on the side. And the same experience with the psychic expo! At first, he had the perfect spot, and now he's relegated somewhere near the back because of the same stupid mistake they made."

"Hm." Great. Knowing her luck, his booth was going to be next to hers. Nor did she have a flyer on her to check.

"He's into all the bands you like, same taste in movies. Not only that, he's been to Russia! He also lost his father a few years ago. The two of you are so perfectly matched, it's crazy!"

"Marcia told me Thomas lost his mom to cancer," Lucy said weakly. She felt like even more of a loser than she'd ever thought possible. She had to be if someone like Tad was perfect for her. He was the anti-Thomas. He'd also been in the bathroom way longer than guys normally take if they'd gone for a leak. Eew.

"Listen," Athena whispered. "If he really liked you, he wouldn't have put you through what he did. He'd have told his boss or whatever to pick somebody else. Or if he did like you and still put you through all that, he's a moron."

"I know, but ..." After all he'd done, she still wanted to defend him, but couldn't think of anything that could justify it. She was the moron, not him.

"And that house of his! It sounds to me as if he rented a bed and breakfast or is house-sitting. How much of it have you seen?"

"Just the ground floor." That would explain the pathological tidiness. However, it didn't feel like a bed and breakfast. There weren't enough recent energy vibrations from other people in his house. Every room she went into felt like *him*. Of course, it was possible she was fooling herself. She fiddled with the spoon on her saucer.

"He's been playing you, sweetie."

"You don't know that! According to one of his oldest friends, he and that blonde were never serious."

"According to *her*. You said yourself that she hates her guts and didn't have clue about the pregnancy. For all you know, he's the one lying and this ex is telling the truth! And if he's to be a dad with somebody else, you don't belong in that picture anyway."

Lucy sulked, but Athena was right. That was what made it sting so much.

"You know, I wasn't crazy about Derek when we first hung out either. You have to keep an open mind!"

Easy to keep an open mind with a guy as hot as Derek, Lucy thought, watching Tad wend his way back to their table. The lurching spring in his walk alone made her cringe.

"Promise me you'll keep an open mind," Athena said. "Your own attitude is your biggest barrier to meeting someone."

"Fine." Lucy grimaced as Tad returned to his seat. This was going to be an extremely long night.

*   *   *

Jeremy slung his arm around the back of Marcia's chair and massaged her shoulder. Thomas stared broodingly into the flame of the thick white candle between them. Nobody had said a word for the past five minutes. Marcia had insisted Thomas try calling Lucy and he kept refusing to give her an answer as to why he couldn't, blurting out that he'd kissed Jenn at the cafe and she'd witnessed the entire thing. Yes, he was an idiot; surely, she knew that much about him by now.

Marcia was the first to break the silence. "Call her already."

"She hates me. Can't say I blame her. I hate me often enough."

"Quit being so damned Emo," Jeremy grunted.

Thomas took a swig from the wine bottle and held it up to the candlelight. Empty.

A car came up the driveway, the headlights sweeping through the front window like a lighthouse beacon.

"Thank God!" Marcia dashed out into the front hall. She bent down and switched on a couple of LED lanterns Thomas had set on the floor near the chaise lounge. She held one of them up as though she was about to guide everyone into the underworld.

Jeremy opened the front door and stood aside as Isaac, Jenn and Steve lumbered up the front steps. "Come on in."

"Or don't," he grumbled. All three glared at him. "What?"

"We need to talk," Isaac hissed, peeking in the library. "And not in this damned house."

"Ever since last night I've been dealing with the craziest shit," Jenn said.

Thomas ignored them and ambled into the kitchen. Although he should offer everyone drinks, he didn't want to encourage company. He fetched a bottle of Cabernet from a cupboard next to the fridge and found a corkscrew in his junk drawer.

As he came back into the lobby, Marcia was setting the lantern down. She picked up her purse from the chaise lounge and said, "Sounds like a plan! Lava's always good on Sundays. Let's go!" She gestured towards the front door to herd everyone out.

Thomas held up his bottle and said, "Have fun!"

Jeremy snatched it from him. "We're all going."

"No, we're not." Thomas planted his feet into the carpet. He had a dozen more bottles on hand if Jeremy took that one away.

"Let's go," Marcia said. Isaac, Steve, and Jenn headed outside.

Jeremy grabbed Thomas's arm, dragging him onto the mat where he kept his shoes. "I said, we're all going. You deaf?"

"All right!" Thomas crammed his feet into his black loafers, took the bottle from him, and went back into the kitchen. "Let me put this away first."

Jeremy followed. He took his time putting the bottle back in the cabinet and returning the corkscrew to the drawer. "Come on, already!"

"Why?" Thomas followed him back down to the front hall. "I was already out earlier."

"Just come," Jeremy growled, shoved Thomas out of his own front door and locked up behind him. Jenn and Steve climbed into the front of the black SUV. Marcia got into the rear passenger seat and shifted into the middle.

"Guys, I'll meet you at the gate! Gotta take a piss." Isaac trotted towards a cedar hedgerow.

"Use the lavatory! Here," Thomas said, fumbling in his pockets for his house keys. "For God's sakes, you're not some vagrant camping out."

"No way am I going back in there, not after what I saw last night!" Isaac stood in front of the hedge and unzipped his jeans.

"Isaac!"

"Get in already. He'll catch up," Jeremy said.

Thomas glowered at a trickling sound coming from the bushes. Bad enough when cats did their business in there. He climbed into the seat behind Jenn and slammed the door. The SUV rambled down the driveway, stopping at the gate.

"Why is it shut?" Thomas pushed between the front seats and stared out through the windshield. "How many times do I have to tell you never to—"

"I didn't know it *could* close! Hang on." Steve flipped his door handle. "What the ... Jenn, can you open on your side?"

She tried her own door, then the lock. "What the fuck."

Jeremy tried the back door, but it wouldn't budge either. "Steve, use your fob!"

Steve cradled the dangling keys in his palm and pressed his thumb hard on one of the buttons. He then tried to pull the silver stub in his door, but his fingers kept slipping.

"Let me try it," Thomas said.

"What's that smell?" Jenn sniffed and pressed the button to lower her window. Nothing. She held the button down, and then hammered it with her finger. "It reeks in here!"

"Yeah, what is that," Jeremy said, scowling. An acrid stench wafted inside the vehicle from the vents.

Thomas reached forward and jerked at her door handle repeatedly, then tried his own, slamming his body against it. "What kind of crap car do you drive, Steve?"

"One made in this century, unlike your shitbox." Steve's face reddened as he hammered all the buttons in his armrest.

"Mine doesn't need a computer programmer to repair it."

"This isn't a joke, let me out of here!" Jenn pushed against her own door, rattling the handle and pounding the window.

"Chill out!" Steve said.

"Unlock the goddamn doors. I can't breathe in here!"

Steve shut off the ignition, turned it on again. The windows and locks still refused to open. "What the hell?"

Thomas squeezed between the two front seats and reached for the keys. Steve swatted his arm away. "Here, let me—"

"Get lost, Tom, I know how to drive!"

"You can't even figure out your own bloody—" Smoke seeped into the SUV from the vents around the dashboard. Steve cut the engine again and smoke billowed into the vehicle.

Jenn covered her mouth and nose with her sleeve, her eyes watering as she glared at Steve.

"Press the trunk release," Thomas said, clambering into the very back of the SUV. "Useless fuck."

"I'm trying! It's not doing anything!"

He squeezed down and kicked at the bottom of the rear door.

"Quit it! You're going to break the latch." Steve hacked, smoke filling the truck.

"Better than suffocating!" Thomas kept kicking the door and the engine revved up. The SUV flew forward, then lurched to a stop and he slammed against the back seats. Rubbing his head, he sat up and yelled, "Damn you, Steve! You knew I was—"

Gravel sprayed up from the tires as the SUV spun backwards. He clung to Jeremy's headrest while the vehicle circled sharply, veered uphill, skidded into a sharp u-turn and halted, the rear bumper stopping inches from a giant oak tree. The engine roared and they flew forward again, racing down towards the fence.

Thomas climbed back into his seat and watched Steve grapple with the steering wheel. "What are you doing?"

"I'm trying to stop!"

Steve crushed the brake pedal with his foot. The truck fishtailed along the gravel driveway, crashing into the gate. Iron balusters shattered the windshield into glittering shards and a metal spike skewered in, just missing Jenn's throat. She stared wide-eyed at it and huddled against her the door. "Holy fuck."

The doors clicked to unlock. At first, each person stared at the handles and tentatively held their fingers to them as if they were expecting an electric shock. Marcia flung her door open. She and Jeremy clambered out. Thomas stumbled out on the opposite side, feeling disoriented.

Steve leapt out and skulked around to inspect the damage. The radiator hissed from inside the crumpled front end. Jeremy took a look from Jenn's side, and went to hug Marcia tightly. "Sorry buddy, looks like a write-off. No way it's drivable now."

"Guess we're not meant to go out tonight after all," Thomas sneered and strode back up the driveway.

Isaac raced up to him, panting. "I told you there's been all this weird stuff happening since last night!"

"No, Steve's just a shit driver," Thomas said, wondering what had been going through that man's pea-sized brain. Idiot couldn't tell the gas from the brake pedal.

"Fuck you!" Jenn trotted beside him and swatted his arm. "His SUV was frigging possessed like in that Carrie movie."

"Christine," Thomas said.

"Who cares? I almost got killed and you're being a know-it-all."

"Nobody made you come here tonight," Thomas said, fishing his keys out of his pocket.

"Tom, quit it," Jeremy said. "This had nothing to do with Steve's driving."

He sucked in his cheeks and marched up the stone walkway, wishing the ground would split open and swallow everyone behind him. He reached the foot of his front steps and balked. His house loomed up in front of him like a vampire's castle. Faces flickered in the windows. Shadows stretched around each side as though a giant hand from the depths of the forest had wrapped its fingers all around.

"You going in or what?" Jeremy said.

He gulped as he tried to move either of his feet forward. They were planted on the lawn. His chest heaved, but he couldn't slow his breathing. "What's everyone want to do now?"

"Go in and have a drink," Jeremy said. "I know I need one."

Jenn whimpered and Steve rocked her in his arms.

"Look at us!" He'd been losing it, the past day, or so. They all had been. He charged up his front steps. "I can't believe it! One single aborted séance and we're all spooked like little kids! It's pathetic!"

Thomas stopped in front of the door and his hand hovered above the knob. He reached for it and the air around it rippled.

"What's wrong, scared or something?" Steve said.

"Of course not," he said, paralyzed with fear.

Marcia took her phone and a card out of her purse. "Who are you calling?" Thomas asked.

"Someone I should have called hours ago since you're being such a stubborn ass."

Thomas leapt back down onto the walkway and began pacing around furiously. The way Jenn sank into Steve's arms, it was as if the two of them had never met up earlier.

Marcia kept out of his way and stood on the lawn. "Hi, it's Marcia. Listen, I'm really sorry if I woke you, but—"

Thomas's heart pounded at the sound of Lucy's voice. Marcia dodged away from him as he tried to snatch the phone from her.

"Things have been strange, to put it mildly. We're all at Thomas's house and if you get this message, please call me as soon as you can. Thanks."

"She didn't answer," Thomas said, stunned by the intensity of his disappointment. He felt bereft.

"Hold on," Marcia said, "I think that was the number for her store. You don't have her cell, do you?"

"Here," he said, handing her his own phone. "Look it up, but I doubt she'll answer if you use this to call her."

Marcia used her own phone to call the number and relief flooded into him. Closing his eyes, he prayed for her to pick up. If only he could go back to that other day, when they were alone in the library. In her presence, he'd felt so at ease. He'd had that same sense in her shop, that wonderful peace and calm.

*   *   *

Lucy felt more relaxed as the waitress cleared away the plates from their table, though bored. The evening had to end at some point. Athena grinned broadly, trying to get some sort of alchemy going while Tad droned about his chemical sensitivities and dietary obsessions.

"I tried to get Lucy into almond milk," Athena said. "Every flavor you could think of."

"As much as I love almonds, I don't want them in my tea. It's gross." Lucy craned her head around, trying to catch sight of their waitress. She could use a drink, something a lot stronger than tea.

"Almond milk is wonderful in Chai tea," Tad said.

"There is nothing wrong with good old-fashioned milk from a cow to go with good ole orange pekoe. Or cheese. I'd die without cheese!" Lucy felt guilty for being contrary, yet she couldn't stop herself. She did love cheese.

"I try to avoid all dairy products," he said. "There's so much exploitation of animals that goes on and I don't want to be a–"

"I lived on a farm until I was ten." She preferred to avoid the entire topic. Most of her friends were vegetarian. "Half those stories aren't remotely true. Cows just lie around in the grass most of the time and all of our chickens went wherever they felt like. This whole 'factory farming' is such sensationalist–"

"Oh, I have no problem with people eating meat so long as it's not being cooked in my house. I think you misunderstood what I was trying to say. For me, it's more of a personal choice that reflects higher spiritual values and–"

Mozart's *Rondo alla turca* trilled from Lucy's purse.

"Ooh, Sonata number eleven, right?" Tad asked.

"My phone!" Lucy dug in her purse and answered it without checking the caller. Saved by the bell. "Hello?"

Athena raised an eyebrow at her and she frowned.

"Hi, Lucy?" Marcia sounded stressed.

"Um, yeah," Lucy said, her stomach doing back flips.

"It's Marcia Lewis."

Both Tad and Athena stared at her. She hunched, pressed against the wall, and said, "Hi, what's up?"

"I'm at Thomas's. All of us are here and it sounds insane, but there is something inside his house. I have no clue what it is. We're all standing on his front lawn and none of us can go in."

"Why not?"

"I don't know, we're freaking out here! All day weird stuff has been happening to each of us and since we all got together again, it's gotten worse! We were in a car wreck just now so his gate's blocked off and—"

"Is everyone okay?" Her skin flushed and she felt sick in the pit of her stomach.

"We're fine," Marcia said and Lucy felt dizzy with relief. "We're all okay. Though Steve's SUV is toast."

"Have you called police?" She eyed Athena, hoping to convey the seriousness of her call. She wanted privacy and there was no way around either of them without forcing one of them to shift aside. Neither were about to volunteer.

"I doubt this is something police can handle. Besides."

Marcia's voice trailed off and Lucy heard a male voice in the background. She then heard Jenn saying something in a sarcastic tone, and, remembering that kiss, felt a dreadful sudden pain as if she'd fallen ten stories and landed on concrete.

"Look. You tell Thomas that if he needs my services, he can call me himself."

"Okay, I'll get him to—Tom—where are you going? Uh, hang on a sec," Marcia said. "Listen, I'll get him to call you back and—"

"Oh, sure! While you're at it, tell him I know all about his little

Internet show. Nice try, though, you almost had me fooled. Enjoy the rest of your night!" Lucy's hand shook as she switched off her phone and crammed it deep into her purse. She wanted to race into the bathrooms and collapse in a heap on the floor, but there were too many tables, chairs, and people crowding her path.

"You did it, you stood up for yourself!" Athena beamed at her.

Tad quietly applauded her and said, "You go, girl!"

"Good for you," Athena said. "I was terrified you were becoming a doormat for that asshole. Finally, you saw past the pretty face. I am so proud of you!"

While Athena clasped Lucy's shoulder, still grinning, her heart sank. There was no reason for her to have been so rude. Marcia's voice had sounded so strained, panicked, to a degree that was impossible to fake.

~ CHAPTER TWENTY-FIVE ~

Thomas stopped pacing and stood on the lawn, sick with tension. The air was humid and sticky, and as usual, he was overdressed in his long-sleeved shirt and black jeans. Marcia pocketed her phone, clenched her jaw, and said to him, "Fuck, she knew."

"Knew what?" he asked, though the answer was obvious. If only he could go back in time one week. Or a couple of days, even. Go back and do everything differently.

"The Debunkers, you moron. I warned you!" She lunged at him and he leapt back, flustered.

"I told you it was a stupid idea, that all these people run into each other at some point, that you never bother doing even the most basic research before you—"

"Marsh!" Jeremy pulled her away; she looked as though she was about to run Thomas into the side of the house.

"I can't believe you called me a moron!" He stomped up his front steps. The insult hurt mostly because of who it had come from. Anyone else and he wouldn't have cared.

Marcia followed him, arms flailing. "But you are sometimes! What were you thinking?"

"I wasn't."

Isaac mumbled to Jenn, "Dave would love to see this."

Jenn snorted and Thomas glared at them. "What's so funny? She was still a fake psychic, wasn't she? A con artist?"

Steve chuckled. "Come on, man, this is why I've been treating it like a joke from the get-go. You don't take it seriously yourself! And you're not half as smart as you think if a chick that stupid can see through you."

"Even in a coma I'd still be ten times as clever as you." Thomas eyed Jenn, leapt off the steps, and stood in front Steve. Something had taken over him, a fresh boldness, a need to say exactly what was on his mind. Enough social niceties, where had those ever gotten him? "So, Steven."

Steve poked at a dandelion with the toe of his running shoe; he likely knew what was coming next.

He again glanced at Jenn, whose smirk was gone from her face. This was going to be good. "Want to take bets on who the baby-daddy is? Guess it's fifty-fifty odds on the face of it. How's your math? Because mine's quite good. Let's see. Jenn and I last had sex on the eighteenth of–"

"You fucking jerk!" Jenn shoved him square in his chest. He staggered backwards and grabbed the balcony railing. She came after him and he gripped her wrists, hoisting them above her head.

"Let go of me!" she yelled, her face turning crimson.

"Three hours ago, you said you were done with Steve and then who do you bring here, *to my house*!" His arms quivered as he stretched her up to prevent her from being able to kick him. "Lucy wouldn't have freaked out last night if it wasn't for you feeding her a load of bollocks about carrying my–"

"What?" Jenn twisted her arms free and stepped back. "You knew she had the hots for you. The same chick you were going to set up to wreck her livelihood and ... Oh, my God. You like her too. And yet you ... How stupid are you?"

He turned and headed back up his front steps. "If you're such a saint, why isn't the father of your own child sticking around?"

"Fuck you!" She stormed up after him. Jeremy and Isaac each took one of her arms.

"Jenn." Jeremy led her back down and had her sit on an ornamental boulder. "Calm. Down."

"He is such a jerk." She sniffled, her eyes red. "No wonder he stuck with me, I'm the only one who'd put up with his shit."

"Look. It's Steve you should be ... mad at." Jeremy furrowed his brow and craned his head around.

Thomas scanned around the driveway and surrounding woods; Steve had vanished. Typical. He climbed up onto the railing of his balcony, gripped the post, and squinted at the gate far below. Steve's SUV was still there, though the end didn't appear to be crushed to the extent he remembered.

Jenn rose from the boulder and called, "Steve?"

"Maybe he went to get something from his truck?" Isaac said.

"He's not there," Thomas said, climbing back down. Feeling dizzy, he reeled and braced himself against the railing.

"Where'd he go?" Jenn dashed around the side of the house. "Steve!"

Thomas watched Jeremy chase after her. While Isaac and Marcia zigzagged across the lawn calling his name, Jenn returned and joined him on the porch.

"Forget it. I'll be your fake psychic. I've taken acting lessons, my dad has a vacant commercial property he can loan us, and I'll even sign up for that stupid expo."

"What's the point?" he asked, wondering why she was bringing this up now. "The show is about exposing real fake psychics, not fake, fake ones."

"Maybe you're the one with the problem. Just because you can't believe in anything, doesn't mean anyone else shouldn't."

Thomas began pacing again. Thankfully, Marcia came back, followed by Isaac.

"Any luck?" Jenn asked.

Marcia shook her head, resting her hands on her knees as she caught her breath. Why were they bothering; Steve was notorious for stupid pranks. The bushes on the far side of the driveway rustled and tree branches cracked. "No sign," Jeremy said, jogging back up to them. "I searched everywhere."

"Same," Isaac said.

Jeremy held a flashlight out to him and said, "Open your damned door already."

Thomas turned his key in the deadbolt. The door squealed open and his foot thumped. "That was me," he said at the sound of someone gasping behind him. "My toe nudged it."

Everyone meandered into the front hallway. Jenn and Isaac flinched as the door slammed shut behind them. "Air pressure differences," Thomas mumbled, trying to settle his own nerves.

The floors above creaked and moaned and Jeremy's flashlight cast crenellated shadows along the ceiling. Never before in his life had he felt so claustrophobic. He caught himself eyeing the walls to make sure they weren't closing in on him.

"Now, what?" Isaac asked.

"Let's go wait in the library," Jeremy said. "He'll eventually get bored and come find us."

"An excellent plan," Thomas said. That room was nice and big.

*　　　*　　　*

Lucy and Tad stood outside the door of the stairwell leading up to her apartment. It was only a little after ten, but she was so glad the night was over.

"Hey, you're the same height as me," Tad said, stretching his torso. As if this was a plus for him.

"Yeah, it's not often I wear flats." Lucy glanced at her feet. Because they still ached from walking home last night, she was wearing her patent leather slip-ons. Normally she would have worn her favorite pair of Mary Janes, the ones with red straps crossing the arches of her feet. Those added at least three inches to her height, at which point she'd tower over him.

"This Thursday Hartford Hall is holding a lecture on pyramids and ancient alien technology. Would you come with me?"

"That sounds great!" she said through gritted teeth. While she loved the idea of going to the lecture, she felt as if she was agreeing to a playdate with the dorkiest kid in school.

He stepped closer and held his arms around her sides, about to hug her. "Anyway."

She stood frozen, waiting for him to leave, but he seemed to be expecting her to invite him up. Great.

"Can I kiss you?"

She winced and shrugged awkwardly. It would sound so rude if she just said no and one kiss wouldn't kill her. "I guess."

He hugged her close and gave her a long, wet, sloppy kiss. She leaned back, but he kept kissing her, licking her lips and pushing his tongue deep into her mouth.

He pulled his face away, still holding her in his arms. She wiped her mouth with her sleeve. His eyes were closed as he smiled,

174

oblivious to her barely concealed revulsion. "So what do you feel like doing now?" he asked. "It's still early."

All she wanted to do was rinse her mouth out. "Um, I've had a long day and didn't sleep well last night. I'm really tired." *That* was why she found him creepy; he wouldn't take a single hint, no matter how obvious. Surely, he'd heard enough *anything but yes means no* in those women's studies classes.

He tried to kiss her mouth again and she turned her face away. "You're so beautiful. I can't wait to see you Thursday."

"Yeah, Thursday," she said, holding her words at the end of a long stick and wishing she could fling them into the storm drain.

"Unless you want to hook up before then. Tomorrow there's this–"

"Thursday's fine! Email me." Lucy patted his shoulders, cursing herself for not having the backbone to turn him down. If it weren't for him being a friend of Athena's, she'd have been much more abrupt. "Good night!"

He tried to hug her again and she slipped through the door, slammed it shut and thundered up the stairs. Everything about him made her skin feel like it was crawling with maggots.

*　　　　*　　　　*

Thomas sat between Jeremy and Jenn at the round table in the library, watching Isaac pace in tight circles as if waiting for a late prom date to show. Marcia crouched in front of one of the bookshelves. Most of the mess had been cleared up from yesterday, apart from books lying in stacks in each corner.

"I'm so bored!" Jenn pounded her fist on the table. As usual, she was being a childish dolt.

"Where'd Steve take off to?" Isaac asked, peering out the side window. "I don't remember him saying anything."

"Who cares," Thomas mumbled and finished his glass of wine. Four of them had gone through the entire bottle in no time.

One of the books Marcia had just shelved tumbled out onto her foot. She stepped back and shuddered. "Did you see that? I swear there's a weird ... a presence in here."

"A presence?" Thomas sneered. "The only presence I sense in here is telling me I need more wine."

He stood and Jenn grabbed his arm. "We almost got killed and all you can think about is getting drunk?"

"We panicked. That's all." He reeled, feeling tipsy. The second he'd stepped back inside his house, his foul mood had returned like a snowstorm in late spring. Jenn being here only made it worse. "You cannot expect me to tolerate your presence, and be sober at the same time."

"What should we do about Steve?" she asked.

"Fuck Steve. Oh wait, you already did." Thomas went around his chair, nearly knocking it over, and headed out into the hallway.

Jenn leapt up and yelled after him, "None of those doors would unlock, and the car just—you are such a cock-sucking–"

He stomped along the hallway, loudly to block out her voice, and into the kitchen. "Get a clue already. Just *go* away."

Everyone flocked after him like newly hatched chicks. He'd just have to endure, that was all. Eventually, they'd grow tired and go home. This night couldn't last forever.

Jeremy dragged a bar stool over to the island in the middle of the kitchen and helped Jenn up onto it, while Marcia poured her a glass of water. Bloody hypocrites, Thomas thought. If she only heard half of what they said about her the second she was out of earshot.

Jenn sipped from the tall glass and stared up at the creaking ceiling. "What's up there?"

"I've told you a million times; it's an old house. They settle." He found a fresh bottle of wine and steadied it on the counter next to her. Everyone was being stupid tonight.

"You'd think after more than a century it would be done by now," she said.

He peeled the metal foil off from around the cap and the edge slashed his finger. "Ugh! I hate when I—ow." He sucked on his finger, which stung worse than a paper cut.

Jeremy took the bottle and turned the corkscrew in. A single tug and the cork broke in half. "Oops. Sorry."

"All day!" He snatched the bottle back and tried to stab the corkscrew into what was left; it bounced off the lip of the bottle and slid, piercing his thumb. "Why can't I get this thing in?"

"Just push it in!" Jenn grabbed it from him.

"I thought you always liked a little foreplay first," he said, hoping to get on her nerves as much as she was grating on his.

She found a chopstick and stabbed it into the top of the bottle as if it were a voodoo doll made in his likeness. "Here!"

"Thank you," he said, bowing to her. "Would anybody else like some?"

Marcia, Jeremy, and Isaac grumbled that they would. He went over to the cupboard to fetch four glasses from the top shelf.

"Look out!" Marcia screamed.

He ducked and a knife stabbed into the wooden cupboard right where his head had just been. He crouched beneath the counter, staring up at the knife, then at his friends, then at Jenn, raw terror seeping into him.

Jenn looked up from her phone, her face glowing blue from the screen, which made the scene only more surreal. "I didn't touch it!"

He felt suddenly sober. An inner voice warned him if he didn't stop antagonizing people, the next knife wouldn't miss. As soon as he dared, he peered out the window into his yard, a swelling moon staring down like the eye of a wolf. No one.

"Let's try to find Steve," he said, getting back on his feet. The sooner he found that idiot, the sooner he could send the lot of them home. It would also give him something to do now that his pleasant buzz was gone.

"Thank you," Jenn said in a hushed voice, her eyes glistening. "He isn't picking up his phone or returning texts and his chest slammed pretty hard against that steering wheel. I can't believe the airbag didn't come out and he could have internal injuries."

"Come on." He helped her off her stool. Trying to reassure her, he added, "I'm sure he's fine. He's a sturdy lad."

"How about us three check the basement and back yard," Marcia said, nodding at Jeremy and Isaac.

"We'll check upstairs, okay?" he said to Jenn, still shaken. He took her arm and led her along the hall. He picked up one of the LED lanterns he'd set out, and up they went. At the top of the landing, they listened. They crept along the corridor. Together they checked each room they passed, including inside the tiny closets and behind any curtains or furniture.

At the rear staircase, he stopped. Despairingly and as free from malice as possible, he asked, "Jenn, why on Earth did you bring him here?"

She mashed one of her feet onto the polished floorboards. "I know, it was dumb. You say I only want you when someone else does, but that's exactly how he's been with me. So I wanted to do one final test. To see if he'd insist on coming with me, then to see how you'd react and to see if this Lucy was–"

"Stop doing this." He handed her the lantern and climbed a couple of ladder-steps.

"When you ran out on me like that, I had to–"

"Stop." He turned, wagging his index finger in her face and she closed her mouth. "No more games and no more lying. I know he stayed overnight last night."

"He crashed on the couch, okay? Ask him." That was entirely possible, though he didn't feel like dignifying it with an answer.

"Mind if I wait down here?"

"Do whatever you want," he said and climbed the rest of the rungs up into the attic. Find Steve, get them out of here.

The moon shone brightly in through the north-facing window. On the dusty wooden planks, a single trail of footprints circled around. Isaac probably left them earlier. Isaac, who'd seen *something* in here last night, yet refused to go into detail. Nor was he one to come up with stories.

All the boxes and crates and other junk were pressed against the walls and under the rafters on each side, giving him a clear view in all directions. He walked along the middle so he didn't have to crouch, and checked each of the dormers. Steve loved to play jokes on people and if he were hiding up here, he would've jumped out by now. He was nothing if not utterly predictable.

He climbed back down. "No sign of him."

"I'm so sick of his moronic pranks." She groaned and leaned against the wall, her head nudging the ornate gilt frame of a landscape painting. She lifted off and set it straight again. "I've had it with him."

"Welcome to my world," he said, sounding harsher than he'd intended. It was true, though. Feeling guilty, he slung his arm around her shoulder. They ambled back towards the main set of stairs. "He's a sperm donor, Jenn. Fathers stick around to raise their children. There's nothing wrong with giving up on him."

She nodded, knowing he was referring to his own father too.

"We'll go back down and search the basement," he said. "There's a crawl space beneath the porch and a few other nooks and crannies the others would easily miss."

"Mind if I go to the bathroom first?"

"I'll wait." He didn't want to chance anything after that incident with the knife, superstition or not. So far, being more pleasant to others seemed to be working for once. "There are matches and a candle on one of the shelves in there."

"Thanks," she said. He leaned against the long railing while she went in. From here, he had a bird's eye view of the corridor below, including the front entrance.

Now that he was alone, that same claustrophobic sense returned and the portraits hanging on the surrounding walls all seemed to stare straight at him. He strained his ears, trying to hear Jeremy or Marcia's voices coming from the kitchen or elsewhere, fighting the urge to call out to them.

At the sound of a violent thud on the other side of the bathroom door, his heart leapt into his chest. "Jenn! You okay?"

*   *   *

Lucy sat on her bed cross-legged and plunked the bag Thomas had returned onto her lap. He'd tied the handles together into a tight knot in an attempt to make it look as though he hadn't rummaged around inside. Maybe he hadn't. She kept making assumptions about him and so far, many of them turned out to be wrong. The more she thought about what she'd witnessed earlier, the more convinced she grew that Jenn had only started kissing him after spotting her first. Athena would tell her she was deluding herself.

She began prying apart the strands of white plastic. The phone on her bedside table rang and her stomach fluttered. The gap between each ring seemed like an eternity and she fought the urge to pick up the receiver. If it was Thomas, she wanted him to know she was still mad at him.

Her answering machine bleeped. She sat stiffly and a staticy male voice came through the speaker. "Hello, Lucy. Sorry if you're asleep already; I hope I'm not waking you up. I just wanted to let you know how much I enjoyed meeting you and I had a wonderful time tonight. Hope you sleep well. I'll see you Thursday, if not before then."

She tore the bag open, dumping the contents onto her bed. Her eyes stung and her heart sank down into her stomach. The phone rang again. She groaned, again ignoring it. This time, she knew it wouldn't be Thomas.

She was right. "Hello, Lucy, just one more thing. You forgot the bear I gave you in that restaurant, so I'll pick it up tomorrow and bring it with me on Thursday when I see you. Either that, or if I'm in the area, I'll bring it to your store. Good night! Kisses!"

"I hate my life!" She shook out the contents of the plastic bag, sending everything flying.

She cringed as the pages she'd printed off the internet fluttered across her mattress. Busted for being the fake he'd planned to expose. On a blank side of one of the pages, she spotted vaguely familiar handwriting. He'd left a note.

In black ink he'd written, "*I know ... and so do you. How about we start from scratch and pretend nothing happened. I really want to explain everything to you if you're willing to hear me out and I hope you'll understand. If you want. You have my number. Call me any time.—T.*"

She crumpled it and chucked it across her room. "Go to hell."

She flopped down on her bed and stared at the ball of paper on the floor. He probably just wanted to apologize to feel better about himself. Guilt did that to people and if she did go meet him, he would surely find some way to shift it onto her, or to someone else. It was human nature. Tears filled her eyes again. She curled up, pressing her cheek into her thick cotton blanket.

The universe was constantly teasing her. Guys like Thomas were the kind she always became hung up on, and they were never interested in her in return. No matter how smart they were, they always wanted their dumb blonde Barbie dolls with perfect bodies and perfect faces.

Part of her wanted to strangle Athena. She was supposed to be her best friend. Not once had she ever set Lucy up with even a halfway decent guy that she'd actually like. Not once. Athena never had problems meeting men and she kept all the good ones for herself, introducing only the rejects.

At least Athena was still her friend. The rest all disappeared as soon as they found their Prince Charming, no matter how "feminist" they'd proclaimed to be beforehand, and became "too busy" for any social plans that didn't involve other couples. Yet they, too, must have single friends. Single friends she suspected they were saving for someone better than she was and thinking about that stung just as deeply as her long, lonely nights.

Back when business was steady, she hadn't felt like such a failure elsewhere. She had plenty of money to go out, pursue hobbies. She'd never been one of those pathetic women who believed hooking up with the right man would fix everything else in her life. She knew better than that. Athena had always been the one chasing after men yet never finding Mr. Right, draining her psychic energy by falling for players. Lucy had quit that game years ago.

Women like her got dweebs like Tad. Not that there was anything that wrong with him. On paper, he had most of the traits she liked. He had an education, a decent job, a side business, was well read and reasonably intelligent. Inside her mind, something clicked. She tried to imagine Tad being the same personality-wise, only with Thomas's looks and style.

Style could always be changed. How could she be slamming

men for chasing after Barbie clones if she was being easily as shallow? Part of why she became hung up on Thomas so quickly was *because* he was so incredibly hot. She hadn't looked at Tad's facial features closely enough to see what potential the man had. At the very least, she should give him one more chance. And try, as Athena kept saying, to be more open-minded.

Unable to sleep and wanting to get out of her funk, she got out of bed. She put on her fuzzy leopard print robe and went into her living room. Some music might help. She rarely listened to late night radio and she was in the mood to discover a new artist or band. Just as she reached for the button on her amplifier, she heard a dripping in one of her walls.

That was odd. She sat up stiffly on the sofa, wondering if she'd heard right. It hadn't rained since Tuesday. She went into her kitchen, opened the window and stared all around. No trace of any eaves dripping. In the alley below, water pooled around the recessed back step. She'd been meaning to fill that area with gravel and kept forgetting.

She shut the window and sat, deliberating. A surveyor had done an assessment on the building not long after her dad had died. More than ten years ago now. She knew there were possible structural issues, ones she kept procrastinating dealing with.

Filled with dread, she crept down the back set of stairs. She rarely used them, since they were even grungier than her front stairwell, and so steep she often slipped on them. She gripped the rail tightly all the way down.

She reached the basement and yanked a chain to switch on the nearest light. The fluorescent tubes flickered and buzzed. The smell of must and damp earth seeped into her nostrils.

And there it was, on her left. A giant water stain on the whitewashed wall. To her dismay, she saw a long, jagged crack forming, wide enough to slip her fingers into.

She let out a despairing sigh and headed back upstairs. Time to call a contractor. She was terrified of how much this was bound to cost.

~ CHAPTER TWENTY-SIX ~

Steve peeked around the side of Thomas's house, watching Isaac and Jeremy head inside. His sides ached from trying his damndest not to laugh out loud. Three people had searched the whole back yard. Not one of them had thought to look where he'd stowed away, underneath the back balcony. Earlier Marcia had passed within two feet of him. He'd been tempted to jump out at her but wanted to wait. He had to get all of them. With any good gag, you only ever got one shot.

He loitered by the edge of the gravel driveway, trying to decide what next. All of them, even Thomas, were so spooked that he had to try *something*. He'd dealt with annoying BS all day too; shit happens. His SUV had gone psycho on him. Guy at the tow yard had messed with it. But Jenn damned Jenn, insisting on going to his place to confront him about that failed séance. Yeah, right.

No matter how much he tried to convince her it was all bullshit, she would not listen. Bad enough she lied about meeting him; he damn well wasn't going to trust her around him now. The second he brushed her off, she was back in Tom's arms. She wanted *him* to marry her? Whatever.

He crept up onto the veranda and peered in through the kitchen window. The door was locked, but an upstairs window was part open. He scanned the wall for a way up. One good thing about old houses, sturdy drainpipes.

He climbed up onto the railing and got a foothold on one of the metal braces holding the drainpipe close to the house. A smaller balcony jutted out from beneath a second-floor window, just within reach. He shimmied up and grabbed the railing with one hand, then gripped a spindle with the other. It broke free and he swung down. Just in time, he caught the main post in his other hand. His heart pounded as the rotted stick bounced off the steps below onto the concrete walkway. That would have hurt.

"Holy shit," he said to himself, adrenaline pumping in his body.

His hands burned as he hauled himself up and over the railing. Pain seared his right palm and the fleshy part of his fingers.

Safely on the upper balcony, he tried lifting the window. It refused to budge. Gritting his teeth, he hooked his fingers underneath the frame. He worked it up a further six inches or so, just wide enough for him to wriggle in through. He crawled into the darkened room and stood, waiting for his eyes to adjust. His hands felt like they were on fire.

The tiny room was some kind of guestroom. He saw a small bed on one side and a tiny chest of drawers on the other, neither of them good hiding places. He tiptoed across the dark carpet and went out into the hallway. Doing his best to avoid any creaking planks, he snuck along the landing. He could hear muffled voices coming from some nearby room. His heart thudded as he heard Jenn.

She was giggling. He could hardly make out a word except for his name a couple of times. Then he heard Tom's voice. Lower, even more muddy. His fists clenched. He was right, she wanted to see him again, needed a ride and all this crap about some shadow haunting her was a lame excuse.

The voices grew louder. Jenn was still giggling and now *Thomas* was laughing too. Steve inhaled deeply through his nose, stormed down the hallway, and flung the door open. Even in the darkness, he could tell no one was in here. Now that he was standing inside, the voices actually came from above, somewhere in the attic. Not caring anymore if anyone heard him or not, he found the back staircase and stomped up.

*   *   *

Jenn peered into the mirror and squeezed a pimple on her cheek. The first one she'd had since her teens. By the voices coming from outside in the hall, it sounded like Steve had returned and he and Thomas were arguing again. It was probably better if she waited a few minutes before going back out.

The bathroom was cramped, no bigger than a broom closet, and the sink was immediately next to the toilet. The place had a grannyish feel to it, with blue floral wallpaper above caramel-colored wainscoting. Ever since his mom had died, she'd bugged Thomas to redecorate, or at least knock out the wall between it and the room with the bath. It made no sense for them to be separate.

A quiet rapping echoed around her. "Just a minute! Jeez, I've been in here for like two seconds!" She took a step back and unclipped her hair, shaking it loose.

"Je-enn," a voice whispered from somewhere above.

"Fuck off, Steve."

"Hey," came Steve's voice from the other side of the door. "What are you doing in there?"

She'd been about to leave, and now she was going to take her sweet time. Fuck him. She began pinning her hair back up.

"Jenn," several voices called to her. She gazed up at the exhaust fan. "Jenn," they rasped. There were at least three or four voices, male and female. None of them sounded familiar.

"Uh, Steve?"

She caught her reflection in the mirrored cabinet above the sink. In the flickering candlelight, her skin looked haggard. Dark circles sagged under her eyes and deep grooves had formed between the sides of her nose and her cheeks, her face re-sculpted into someone decades older. She tried to relax her eyebrows, which were furrowed into a scowl.

Disembodied, unintelligible voices whispered from each direction, making the hairs on her arms prickle.

"Steve?" she called. No answer. "Tom?"

The voices grew louder, clearer, coming from all directions. She turned the faucet on full and the rushing water drowned them out. Her hands shook as she held them under the tap. The water turned ice cold and she leapt backwards, colliding into the door behind her. In the tiny white sink, blood mixed with water, swirling around the drain. More blood splattered onto the white faucet handles as she wrung her hands and grappled for a face towel hanging on a nearby rack.

"Where's your baby, Jenn," a voice taunted her.

She stared down and shrieked. The front of her pink shirt was stained and drenched. Thick liquid oozed out of the fabric and dripped onto the grey floor tiles. She pressed her fingers to her abdomen, warm and sticky, then felt something slimy between them. "Oh my God my baby what's happened to my baby?"

She screamed, out of her mind with terror. Thomas barged in and caught her in his arms. "What's going on in here?"

Her chest heaved and she cradled her still-swollen belly in her hands. The blood was gone. "Oh thank God," she whispered, dizzy from anxiety.

He wrapped his arms around her. "It's okay, it's okay, it's your mind playing tricks on you."

"I thought I'd lost it," she sniffled, tears streaming down her cheeks. She nestled her face into his soft, cotton shirt. The warmth of his body and the sound of his beating heart calmed her down.

He kissed her forehead. "Everything's going to be fine," he cooed in her ear, "I promise." He helped her out into the hallway. "If you want, tomorrow I'll take you to the–" A black figure flew at them and she shrieked, clinging to him like a newborn kitten.

"What's going on up there?" Jeremy called up from the bottom step, hand clasping the newel.

"Jenn fell and she's a bit rattled," Thomas said.

Her legs were unsteady beneath her; she wasn't sure she could make it down the stairs yet. "Can we sit?" she asked him.

He called over the railing to Jeremy, "We'll be down in a minute!" He helped her into the nearest guest bedroom, had her lie down on the daybed, and found an extra pillow for her. "You're not getting pains or anything, are you?"

She shook her head, thinking if only he could be like this all the time. He was so caring and attentive. When he wanted to be. He settled next to her on the mattress. He gazed at her and stroked her arm, and it tore her apart. He would make an awesome dad. But if she was going to settle down with him, she couldn't live with any what-ifs. Now that she was sure about him, he wasn't so sure of her anymore. "Thomas?"

"Hm," he said as if he'd been off somewhere else entirely.

She snuggled closer to him, her face inches from his. He let her take his hands, which she held between her own like they were both praying. Oh, why was this so hard, she thought.

"I need to know something."

"Anything," he said, hunching his shoulders.

Their noses were almost touching and so badly, she wanted to kiss him. "When you told me earlier that you loved me, did you mean it?"

He nodded. "I'd always meant it. There was a time when I'd have done anything for you."

There *was* a time. Yet the expression in his eyes didn't seem to be gazing into the past. She felt an ache in her heart and said, "I know there's no turning back the clock, but if you'd be willing to forgive me, I ..."

He closed his eyes tight, the way he always did whenever he wanted to disappear into himself. Maybe she could still reach him. If she didn't try, she'd regret it forever. She pressed her lips to his, her insides bursting as he yielded to her. Yet he wasn't in the moment. After lazily kissing her, he pulled away, frowned, and began fiddling with the string of her tracksuit jacket.

"I could sell my condo and move in here with you." That had always been a major sticking point. "With the money I make from it, plus my job, we wouldn't have to worry. You could even stay home with the kid if you wanted, and I could support all of us."

"Let me think about it," he said, not meeting her gaze.

"Enough thinking. What do you *feel*?"

"I don't know. I mean, if you're serious about wanting to get—"

"Hey, guys." Marcia appeared at the threshold, tapping her foot. Tom's omnipresent chaperone. She held out her phone to him. "We can't find Steve anywhere. We've looked."

"He's a grown man." Thomas propped himself up on his elbow, keeping his arm slung around her waist. "My guess, he called a taxi, went home, and isn't picking up so we don't realize what a self-centered prick he is being."

Jenn nodded adamantly and pulled away from him so it

wouldn't look as if she had any ulterior motive in front of The Chaperone. "Sounds like something he'd do."

"Just call her," Marcia said. *Lucy* appeared on the glowing screen. Jenn's heart sank as she watched him sit upright.

*   *   *

Lucy lay on her back in bed, slightly tipsy from the two glasses of wine she'd had at Lava. Part of her wanted to get up and have a third; that would put her to sleep for sure. But she was feeling lazy, and getting another glass would also mean opening a fresh bottle on a Sunday night, which she likely wouldn't touch again until at least Wednesday. By then, it would be off.

Thank goodness she'd decided to fetch her camera to take pictures of that crack. When she came back down to the basement, she realized she'd been seeing things. A hairline fracture in the thick paint, that was all. Her building wasn't about to collapse on her quite yet. Just as she began drifting off to sleep, the phone next to her bed rang like an alarm clock. She lifted the receiver and said, "Hello?"

"Hi, Lucy, it's—"

At the sound of a male voice, she hung up and returned the handset to its place.

"Why did I do that?" She sat upright, now wide-awake, and cursed herself. That was Thomas, not Tad calling. She yanked the cord of the lamp that sat on the table next to her bed. Her ceiling glowed red from the velvet shade.

Her eyes fell to Thomas's note, still crumpled in the corner of her room, then to her laptop, still propped open on her desk. Now that she was fully roused, her brain kicked into gear. Athena hadn't been selfish introducing her to Tad; she'd been desperate. Her best friend was always there to save her from herself, from making stupid decisions, or from being hung up on the wrong men. Even though she found Tad repulsive, they did have a lot in common.

He seemed nice. Dull, but nice. Thomas definitely wasn't nice. Even during the brief times they'd met, he'd been arrogant, complaining, and short-tempered. On top of that, she reminded herself, his whole intention had been to catch her on film and make her look like a fraud to thousands of people. She was insecure about that as it was. She even told new clients she excelled in cold-reading and not to stake any major decisions on the outcomes of her readings. She repeatedly explained she had no power to contact the dead. If she suspected a customer was mentally ill, she did her best to encourage them to seek professional help.

Already she spent most of her day gazing around her empty store, wondering what she was doing with her life. Crystal work and tarot cards weren't popular anymore and every flea market sold aromatherapy potions. Christians still thought her to be in league with the devil, while so-called social justice warriors came in only to lecture her about appropriating other cultures because she sold pewter and turquoise rings from Mexico.

As for her friends, whenever she'd asked them why they never set her up with anyone, all of them would respond the exact same way: *He's single for a reason. Trust me. You deserve better.* At which point, they'd launch into a story about how he's been dodging paying out child support for nearly a decade, blows his paycheck at the casino, or stalks his ex-girlfriend by parking outside her apartment building for hours on end.

She flung herself back down on her mattress. Her anger was simmering and she was ready to let it go full boil. She gasped as the phone rang again. She clenched her hands together to stop herself from picking up, and the answering machine clicked on.

"Lucy, I'm really sorry." Thomas's voice crackled through the speaker. "Sorry it's so late, although you had said you were a night owl. Listen. The entire Debunkers episode was a stupid idea from the get-go and I should've never gone along with it. I'm not going to shift blame to anyone else as much as I'd like to I–"

The answering machine cut off.

"Ugh! Go away!" She pulled her comforter over her head and curled her legs up to her chest. She knew what would come next anyway. It would still be his boss's fault, or Skeptical Dave's fault or his mom dying of cancer was something he treated as carte blanche to be an insufferable jerk to everyone. Anyone's fault but his own regardless of the words he used. Yet there'd been a hint of raw vulnerability in his voice that made her want to call him back. Buried inside, like a glittering jewel, she could see something beautiful in him, something she doubted even Jenn or any other woman had ever been able to dig out of him.

But *she* could.

She flopped onto her stomach, cursing herself. Again, she was being delusional. A thought floated into her brain that she quickly dismissed. She'd had this stupid crush since before the failed channeling and petty frustrations were an integral part of her daily life. Today being somehow worse was her imagination at play, nothing more. Yet her mood had definitely been worsening the past day or so. Trying to get herself into better spirits had been like climbing a mountain of scree; no sooner would she gain a foothold, she began sliding back down. That oppressive weight on her was how she felt in mid-January after months of no sun, not in peak summer. At this time of year, her spirits were normally at their highest, and almost nothing could bring her down. The same gloom had returned to her apartment as well. At this rate, none of her spells or rituals would vanquish it.

She rolled onto her back again and sighed. Even where she'd always thought she had a natural gift, of creating an atmosphere of peace and relaxation, she was turning into a total failure.

~ CHAPTER TWENTY-SEVEN ~

Thomas switched the phone off and handed it back to Marcia. She pocketed it and narrowed her eyes. "So what was that about?"

"She hung up on me." He felt numb. While he hadn't been expecting her to be instantly forgiving, he'd hoped she'd hear him out. It was only a little after eleven. In one of their online exchanges, he could have sworn she'd said she never went to bed before midnight.

He followed Marcia and Jenn back down the stairs to where Isaac and Jeremy were sitting on the chaise lounge. "Anyone heard from Steve, yet?" he asked.

Both of them shook their heads.

"I checked around his SUV and no sign of him," Isaac said. "He's not picking up his phone, either."

"Of course he won't," Jenn said. "I'll bet he took off on us and he's—"

Everyone jumped as Thomas's phone trilled. "Hello?" he answered. Sirens and horns blared out of his earpiece.

"Don't bother coming in tomorrow!" Dave shouted. "I'm almost there now and can see tons of smoke, flames, at least four trucks are there so far."

"You're kidding me!" Panic surged in him as Dave paused. Like being buffeted in an ocean storm, these waves were relentless.

"I have to go. Talk to you in the morning."

"I'm fucked," Thomas whispered. "I'm completely fucked." Stunned, he set down his phone. Something above creaked, then the windows rattled and the entire house shuddered. He opened the front door a crack; all the surrounding trees were still. He tried the light switch again; the power was still out.

"Come crash at our place tonight," Marcia said, taking his wrists. "It's not safe here."

"It's as safe here as anywhere else." He snatched his hands back and stuffed them under his armpits.

"He's right," Jeremy said. "Whatever this thing is, it follows us wherever we go so we might as well–"

"That's not what I said, there is *nothing*!" Thomas pushed the door wider and said, "Please—everyone—just go home already. I'm exhausted."

Marcia ripped off her bandages and thrust her hand in front of his face. He kept his eyes fixed on hers to avoid the stomach-churning sight of black threads encrusted with dried blood. "Eight stitches! I worked in kitchens until I graduated college. Since when am I ever clumsy with knives?"

"Everyone has accidents."

"Fine. Rot by yourself in here!" Marcia stomped out onto the porch, slamming the door behind her. Her footsteps thundered down the front steps and shuffled in the gravel, scattering stones like hail.

"Shouldn't you be going with her?" Thomas asked Jeremy, fighting the urge to chase after her and apologize.

He shook his head. "Let her cool off." He switched on his heavy-duty flashlight and said, "As for Steve, we'll go in pairs. Isaac and I will search the front and sides, you guys check out back."

Thomas knew what they were up to. So long as it was about Steve, Jeremy could keep his mind off worrying about Marcia. He helped Jenn up from the chaise lounge and led her along the hallway. In the kitchen, she paused at the back door. "Can you get me something to eat first? Just a piece of cheese or some fruit. Whatever's handy. I'm still rattled from earlier."

He opened the fridge, relieved everything inside was back to normal and glad he hadn't tossed everything this morning. While he rummaged in the cheese drawer, he had to remind himself not to offer any cold cuts to her. One of her hands clasped his waist and the other reached around and grabbed a block of cooking cheddar from one of the shelves.

"This'll do," she said, cutting a piece for herself and handing the rest back for him to wrap up again. "Thanks."

He took his time putting it away. She sighed behind him and he could tell she wanted to *talk*. There was nothing to talk about. Marcia had appeared just in time to save him from his own idiocy. Now was not the time to make any decisions about the future.

*   *   *

Steve searched every inch of the attic. Nobody was up here. When he first came in, he'd spotted what looked like two distinct sets of footprints on the dusty floorboards. Both were too big to be Jenn's, yet he'd definitely heard her voice. He crept up to a window that was open at one end, silver light shining in. He peered out at the moonlit back yard. In a shadow under one of the trees, he spotted Jenn being pulled along by her hand, her giggles carried up to him by the wind.

A rattling noise startled him. He looked down at a rope ladder unfurling beneath the windowsill. Without knowing why he was doing it, he climbed out, his hands still stinging from earlier. He clambered down the rungs. Once he was on the ground again, he looked back up at the house. The ladder was gone. "What the—"

Laughing voices came from the woods. He sprinted across the yard and caught a glimpse of Jenn peeking between a couple of tree trunks. Her teeth flashed at him. She turned and ran off, vanishing like that cat in Alice in Wonderland while her disembodied voice floated through the woods: "How do you figure he likes tasting his own medicine? Real funny taking off like that on me." From another direction, "We'll show him."

"You're absolutely right Jenn," Thomas said. "This *is* a lot of fun. You think he'll find us? I keep saying he's a bit stupid."

"Eh, fuck him," Jenn said. "I just want to see his face when you jump out at him."

Yeah, right. For *Thomas* to play a joke on someone, he'd have to take that stick out of his butt first. Steve traipsed along the trail, his tension amplifying the deeper he went into the forest. It smelled weird out here, like matches or burnt oil, not the usual nature smells of leaves and dirt and flowers and shit.

There was no way the two of them would team up to prank him. That was it. They didn't *want* him to follow them. They were trying to sneak away from Jeremy, Isaac, and Marcia—especially crazy Marcia—to be alone together. Plus, Tom called everyone stupid and could have easily been talking about Isaac.

He patted the pockets of his grey hoodie; sometimes he kept a spare bike light in one of them. Nope. With the moon out it was light enough anyway. Besides, the dark never scared him.

The voices quieted. For about fifty yards, he kept walking and all he heard was the wind blowing through tree branches high above. Holding his breath, he stopped and listened over the buzzing crickets. Weird how that sound came in waves, deafeningly loud and then quiet again.

Somewhere to his right, he heard a faint rustling and a couple of twigs crackled. He squinted, concentrating. Thomas's low voice came from that same direction. Barely above a whisper, he was saying, "Here's a good spot. Just lie down right there. Want my jacket?"

Steve crept toward the sounds and spotted a flash of light up ahead. Jenn must have that keychain with her. Another flash, like a lightening bug. In the dark woods, it was hard to see exactly where they were. He stayed put and watched the bright dot flit across branches and tree trunks, trying to figure out exactly where it was coming from.

"I'm sorry about earlier," Jenn said from somewhere to his left. In that same direction, he heard more rustling, like someone shuffling through or sitting down on dead leaves. Steve crept closer and heard her say, "When you stormed out like that, I thought you were gone forever."

"I'd never let you go, Jenn, you know that. I love you. And I can't wait to be a father for your child."

Every muscle in his arms constricted, curling his fingers into fists. That lying biatch; she swore up and down *Thomas* couldn't possibly be the dad. The timing was wrong. They'd *always* used condoms. His heart pounded as their voices hushed. He couldn't see them, but by the sucking sounds and hitching breaths, they were definitely fooling around. That was why she wanted to lure him here; she wanted to rub it in his face.

He'd show both of them. He found a rock and hefted it. Good and heavy. He charged through the low hanging branches, readying to pitch it straight at Tom's head. Going around each tree, he found nothing and no one. They had to be somewhere close. Now the voices came from the opposite direction. He raced back, only to lose sight of the path he'd been on. The voices and giggling stopped. He turned, stumbling over an exposed tree root, and continued along the trail.

Trees, endless trees. The trail took him in circles. Each time he thought he was about to come out of this forest, he came to the same little clearing with the two pine trees huddled together. Hearing a voice calling his name, he turned. A shadow swooped down at him. Pain exploded into the side of his skull and everything went dark.

~ CHAPTER TWENTY-EIGHT ~

Marcia struggled for nearly twenty minutes to haul the gate open wide enough to drive through. It seemed to be rusted into place and each jerk moved it barely an inch. Only now, as she was getting back into the car, did she notice the gate had no damage. Steve's SUV barely had a scratch. The windshield was still intact too; she could have sworn a metal spike had smashed through it. Oh, weird.

She climbed into the silver Honda and idled out until she was at the edge of the road. She tapped her fingers on the steering wheel. After burning off all that aggravation, she debated going back to the house, then thought better of it. Thomas was being too much of an ass for her to want to deal with and if she returned with that ditz still hanging around, all she'd do is blow up at him again. Looking left onto the empty road, she pulled out of the driveway, about to turn right. She stomped on the brake pedal and only afterward realized why.

A truck roared past, horn blaring. Her car shuddered from the suction of the wind that followed. She stared off after the truck, her heart racing. "Holy fuck," she whispered. Slowly, more cautiously, she continued turning out onto the road.

Branches of giant maple trees formed an adumbral canopy overhead, closing out the sky. Only her headlights lit her way, reflecting off cat's eyes buried in the road.

She turned sharply and descended into the gorge. An engine roared behind her, air brakes juddered and high beams blazed in her mirrors. A giant pickup truck loomed closer. The top of the front grill rose over the back of her car like a maw, baring fearsome steel teeth. She stared ahead at the double yellow line, trying to remember when the passing lane started.

The road kept turning and the truck kept tailgating. She pressed lightly on the brake, eying her speedometer as it fell from forty to thirty then to twenty miles an hour. The road straightened, but it was still pitch black beyond the glowing tunnel of her headlights. The truck behind her refused to pass.

"Fuck," she muttered, speeding up again.

No matter what speed she went, the truck kept within inches of her rear bumper. She patted the seat next to her, and then remembered she'd tossed her purse into the back. A chill spread in her as she passed a sign warning of deer crossing. This was a bad time of year for them.

The road kept winding steeply downhill. She pressed the brake pedal, keeping an eye on the truck behind her. By now, she should be seeing city lights. Thomas wasn't that far out of town. The narrow highway turned. She caught sight of a stone retaining wall on one side and a steep drop into the forest on the other. Where was she?

She tilted her rear view mirror and squinted, trying to see the driver's face, or if he had any passengers. The windshield was black. A whole group of men could be in there for all she knew. Keeping her wheel steady, she fumbled in the glove box for Jeremy's flashlight. It was good and heavy, the kind that could double as a baton. "Fuck!" she hissed and slammed the door shut. It wasn't there. She prayed the tire iron was still in the trunk.

Her throat clenched and she drove on, checking behind every few seconds. "Fuck where is that damn turn off!" Panic surged in her as she kept her eye out for mile markers. She saw none. She always turned right out of Thomas's place to get home and it was only a few minutes to the edge of town. Ten at most. The numbers on the odometer turned. She must have been driving for at least fifteen miles now.

"Calm down," she said aloud. "He isn't doing anything, apart from being an asshole tailgater."

His lights flickered as if he were trying to get her attention. She peered into the mirror, trying to get a glimpse of the driver's face or anything inside the cab. His engine roared.

"He's just some asshole," Marcia said, gripping her steering wheel. "An asshole seeing a woman driving by herself at night, who just likes to scare them because he hates women and can never get laid. There."

It didn't help. The same sick feeling welled higher in her chest as yet another turn in the road brought more darkness ahead. No road signs and no sign of the city. She *had* turned right, hadn't she? Besides, left would've taken her toward the interstate and she'd seen no signs for that either.

A deer leapt onto the road in front of her and she slammed the brakes. She braced for impact from behind as her wheels screeched on the pavement. The car lurched to a stop.

She stared around at the trees flanking each side of the road, then at the patch of bare asphalt illuminated by her headlights, where she'd been expecting to see a crumpled engine compartment and a tawny, mangled corpse. Her heart hammered in her chest. She rolled the window down and poked her head out, staring into the faint reddish glow cast by her taillights. No sign of any truck.

For several minutes, she sat catching her breath, shaking, her chest heaving, her mind spinning. She tried some breathing exercises a friend had taught her, inhaling slowly, holding it in, and only gradually releasing it again so her body would be saturated with oxygen. For nearly a minute, she kept at it, breathing, counting. Eventually, all the taut muscles in her body began loosening. As soon as her hands were steady enough to hold the wheel straight, she drove on.

*   *   *

Jeremy and Isaac aimed their flashlights inside Steve's empty SUV, which was now much closer to the big oak tree than the gate.

"See?" Isaac said. "I told you!"

"I swear we crashed into that gate." Jeremy scowled. "The whole windshield was smashed. And who moved it?"

"Weird night is all I can say." Isaac aimed his flashlight at the iron gate and a blurry dot lit each baluster as he swept it across.

"That is an understatement." Jeremy tried all the door handles. Locked. He squinted at the fence. They'd checked the whole surrounding area. There weren't that many good hiding places among Thomas's boulders and cedar shrubs. *If* Steve was hiding. He may have gone home, after all, still thinking it was wrecked.

Isaac knelt and peered under the truck.

"Let's head back to the house," Jeremy said. "Knowing him, as soon as we came out, he went in."

"Still think he's trying to pull something?"

"He's not one to let up. Ever." Jeremy strode ahead, forcing Isaac into a trot to keep up. Marcia storming off like that stressed him out more than he'd realized and it took everything he had not to bust into Steve's SUV, hotwire it and take off after her.

"How come Marcia got so mad?" Isaac said breathlessly.

Jeremy lumbered up the front steps of the house and pulled out his keys. "She hates Jenn."

"So? Most chicks hate her. Because most guys want to bang her."

He shook his head and unlocked the front door. "You always that clued out?"

"What, she sees Jenn and Tom getting back together?" Isaac laughed and pushed the door open. "Not gonna happen."

"Why's that?" Jeremy tried the light switch on instinct, knowing the power was still off, but forgetting until the lights failed to come on.

"Every production meeting this past week, he was barely there mentally. Right in front of the head honchos, he said she wasn't suitable, her business was failing, and that they should go after someone more well-known instead, and the rest of the time he sulked like he was in detention."

"Tom always sulks." Jeremy crept into the entryway and signaled for Isaac to keep his voice down.

"Oh yeah?" Isaac whispered. "Today, the whole time we were watching footage from last night, he couldn't take his eyes off of her. Trust me; I know when he likes a chick. And hey, she's pretty damn cute."

Jeremy was glad to avoid the entire subject of Marcia and her biological clock ticking down like a bomb set to go off. "We went out for drinks after that quote-unquote consultation visit and he didn't shut up about her the whole night. It drove me nuts."

"See?"

He opened the door to the formal dining room. He flashed his light around all the walls, still with that God-awful flock wallpaper on them, then under the table. "I dunno. Jen still has him wrapped around her finger so tight she may as well call him a wedding ring. I've never seen a man so pussy-whipped in my life."

Isaac shrugged. They came out of the dining room and headed upstairs. Jeremy shone the flashlight along the walls of the corridor and the columns of doorways. In both directions, the passageway disappeared into total darkness.

They must have stumbled into some part of the house he wasn't familiar with. He couldn't find the railing that ran along the second-floor landing. Instead, the corridor they found themselves in was lined with doors on both sides. For the life of him, he couldn't remember any other hallway leading off from the top of the stairs. This house was big, but not that big.

"This damned hallway just goes on and on!" He tried one door handle, then the next. "I could have sworn that–"

"Jeremy!" Marcia screamed.

Jeremy raced in the direction of her voice. Isaac's footsteps thudded after him.

"Jeremy! Help me!"

He stopped in front of a door where Marcia was sobbing on the other side. "I'm here, Marsh, it's okay! Open up!"

"Help me Jer, I'm trapped!" She sniffed and continued crying.

Isaac held the flashlight while Jeremy rattled the knob with both hands. "Marcia! Are you all right?"

She wailed incoherently.

"Hang on!" He slammed himself against the door and it shook in its hinges. He slammed into it again, and then kicked at the upper panels. Whatever wood they were made from, it was sturdy as concrete.

"They've got me, Jeremy. They're going to kill me!"

Desperate, he grabbed the flashlight and hammered the door with it, tore out pieces of wood with his bare hands and pushed his arm through the hole, shining the light inside. All he could see were patches of wallpaper showing ornate pink flowers intertwined with light green vines, and a pink carpet. "Marsh?"

He let the flashlight fall to the floor, reached lower, and unlocked the door from the inside. Apart from a couple of cardboard boxes, some old computer consoles, and a monitor, the room was empty.

He opened the closet, which was only a foot deep. It was empty too. Beyond the wall of the closet, Marcia sniffled and moaned. Isaac stooped for the flashlight.

"Check the next room!" Jeremy raced back out.

*   *   *

The air outside had grown chilly and Thomas regretted not grabbing a jacket when he'd had the chance. Clouds puffed in front of his face as he ambled along the trail, under the sort of brilliant silver moonlight one expected to see fairies dancing. In a better frame of mind, he would have enjoyed the walk, the smell of damp earth and fragrant summer flowers wafting around.

Jenn stumbled after him and took his hand. Whether she was actually scared or only pretending to be was anyone's guess, but for now, he let her hang onto him. Comforting her made him feel better without having to admit how on edge he was, too. As much as he tried to ignore it, he sensed someone following them.

"How big is your yard?" she asked, tripping again. "We've been going straight, haven't we?"

He slowed his pace. "We should be by the fence soon."

It seemed they'd been walking for miles. The woods at the very back were dense, but it was far too small an area to get lost in. He was never one to pay attention to public notices and possibly one of his neighbors had removed the fence temporarily. It had been at least a year since he'd ventured this far. Beyond the house behind his property, he wasn't sure what there was. A park of some sort? It was hard to remember now.

"We should start heading back," she said, stopping and tugging his wrist. "Before we get totally lost."

"You're the one who wanted to look for him," he said, stopping himself from adding that he didn't care either way and would be perfectly content going to bed and forgetting all about Steve. While he didn't wish anything bad on the man, he'd certainly be indifferent to anything bad happening to him.

They held hands and turned around, walking back more slowly. His legs and feet throbbed.

"Do you like that Lucy girl?" she asked.

"Why are you asking me now?" If only she could shut up for five minutes. She had to fill every moment with endless chatter, which had always irritated him. Before she could start coming up with her own guesses, he said, "I don't *know* her."

She put her arm around his waist and they followed the path, wending through the trees. At night, they all looked the same, dark silhouettes against the starry sky. Now that he thought about it, being lost wasn't so bad. It was quite beautiful. Directly above there were no clouds, making the various constellations easy to spot. About a year or so ago, he and Jenn had gone out for a long drive into the middle of nowhere and they had spent hours snuggling in her convertible gazing up at the stars. He gave her a squeeze. He was tempted to pull her aside and start kissing her.

"Lovely night," he said, slowing by a boulder.

"I have to pee," she whined, obliterating any romantic mood he'd felt with a single word. Just as well, he was getting stupid around her again. While his conscience said *yes*, his heart said, *don't even think of it, you blithering idiot.*

They passed an ancient tree he recognized, with gnarled roots rambling across the path. They weren't lost after all. "We'll be reaching the house in another minute or two."

"My bladder is smaller than a peanut these days. I'll be two seconds." She dropped his hand and dashed behind the giant, silvery trunk.

Somewhere to his left, a twig snapped. He held his breath in, listening. "Jenn?" No answer.

He heard nothing apart from trees whispering overhead, wheezing cicadas, and his own thudding heart. He shouldn't have let her out of his sight. He stormed into the thicket, calling her name and straining his ears. "Jenn, where are you?"

"Over here," came her voice from somewhere on his right.

"I can't see you yet, keep talking, and stay still," he said, trampling through knee-deep weeds and grass.

"My flashlight keeps cutting out; it's too dark to see my way back and oh my God, Thomas! Get help!"

He caught sight of her twisting figure and ran up to her. By the time he reached her, he found her sitting on the grass nesting Steve's bleeding head in her lap, her keychain with the flashlight looped around her fingers. "He won't wake up," she said, mascara-stained tears streaming down her cheeks.

Thomas crouched next to them and felt around his neck. Steve's pulse was somewhat normal but faint. He wasn't faking being unconscious. "How did you find him?"

"I tripped over him and he was just lying here." She wiped her eyes with her sleeve, which she then used to daub the side of his head. Steve groaned and his eyelids fluttered.

"Did you call for a doctor?"

"He hates doctors," she said, cradling him in her arms. "Go get Jeremy and Isaac to help carry him back for now."

"Back in five." No point arguing with her. His legs burned as he stood upright. He gave her shoulder a quick squeeze and ran back to the trail. He patted his pockets; he must have left his phone in either the kitchen or the front hall.

Ahead of him, his back lawn glowed. The moon seemed as bright as the sun in contrast to the dark woods. He headed for the walkout beneath his balcony, which led into the basement. From there, he'd call an ambulance, check the circuit breaker again, and then fetch Jeremy. What a stupid, stupid night.

~ CHAPTER TWENTY-NINE ~

Marcia slowed the car as she approached Lucy's store. After checking the street signs, she parked. Bulldozers and steamrollers crouched on the gravel as if readying to pounce on her and she hesitated before getting out. Construction machinery always creeped her out, especially when they sat empty. She imagined their lights flicking on, smoke billowing out of their engines, and roaring to life to come after her.

During the rest of the drive in, a crazy theory had taken root in her brain. She wanted to bounce it off Lucy: instead of summoning a ghost or poltergeist, she'd released a form of energy that was making everyone butt heads with each other. She'd never raged on Thomas like that before. Nor was he usually such a dick; all night he'd been obnoxious. Yet that didn't sound right either. Whatever, it was worth a shot.

She stood on the narrow concrete step and scrutinized the various parking signs again, all of which contradicted each other. Permit only, no standing, loading zone, two hours only. Her heart thrummed in her chest, her nerves still frayed from earlier.

"Fuck it." She turned and pounded on the door next to the shop. Her knocks echoed inside. She glanced at both sides of the doorway, hoping she hadn't just knocked at the wrong place. Lucy's store was to her right and the window for another business was on her left. A grimy, yellowed buzzer set into the doorframe caught her eye and she pushed down.

"Just a minute," Lucy's voice slurred through the intercom.

While Marcia waited, she applied some lip balm, keeping her eyes on the monster machinery that she swore had just inched closer. Footsteps tromped down. Lucy opened the door, rubbing her eyes.

"Sorry to wake you," Marcia said.

Lucy stood, wavering on her feet, her face puffy and swollen. She wore a leopard print robe over zebra-striped pajamas and her feet had been stuffed into fun fur slippers. She was a walking petting zoo of fuzzy polyester.

"You okay, hon?" Marcia asked as Lucy curled her fists against her eyes and rubbed them again.

She nodded and edged aside enough for Marcia to enter.

"Since last night, things have been really weird."

Lucy squinted up at her. Definitely not a morning person.

"Something has taken over Thomas's house and all of us as well. I'm not saying it was you who caused anything, but maybe you can come and help fix it?"

Lucy stood, looking bewildered. "I don't know what I can do. He's right, I'm a fraud."

"No you're not." Marcia stooped so that she was eye level with her. "I know Tom was a jerk. There's no excusing what they were planning and yes, I was in on it too. He's my oldest friend, and what can I say. I suck."

"I should have never gone." Lucy stared at her feet and fiddled with the sash on her robe. "I was just going to go through the motions and planned to tell him I couldn't sense anything. That he was just letting himself get spooked by the weird noises that all old houses make."

"Really?" Marcia howled. "That is hilarious! I wish you had."

Lucy sighed. "It kind of backfired."

The headlights from that pickup truck earlier flashed in her mind. A sick feeling formed in the pit of her stomach once more. "Can you come back there with me? Please?"

Lucy stood, catatonic. Marcia had half a mind of just picking her up and throwing her into the car; she looked light enough. From the second she'd met Lucy she'd liked her, but also sensed she was exactly like Thomas in so many ways. Bad ways. Defeated too easily, too proud, and stubborn as all hell. If she didn't get Lucy back there tonight, Thomas would be with Jenn for good. "I'll drop you home afterward; I can do some free marketing for you through the company I work for where I could—"

"I don't know what you want me to do. I don't understand what happened, even."

"See my hand," Marcia said, in a much gentler tone than she'd used with Thomas. She held her bandaged hand up to her. "I grew up working in my parents' restaurant and got the worst slice of my life earlier. That knife moved by itself."

Lucy furrowed her brow at her.

"Earlier tonight we were all crammed in Steve's SUV to go downtown. It took on a life of its own and crashed straight into the gate. When I went by it again about twenty minutes later, it looked fine! But at the time, I was sure we were all going to—"

"So it's all in your heads?"

"No! It was all like—" Marcia groaned, trying to figure how to describe it. She decided to change her tack. "Even if you planned to fake the whole séance, you didn't do the protection ritual, and you know better than to *ever* neglect doing that. *Something* was definitely summoned."

"It was fake!" Lucy stared at her, wide-eyed, and then her gaze fell to the linoleum floor again.

"Just come. Please?"

"I need to get dressed." Lucy started back up the stairs. "May as well come up."

*   *   *

Lucy put on a pair of black leggings, a loose, black and white cotton dress, then struggled into the same red cardigan she'd been wearing earlier that afternoon. After running a brush through her hair, she led Marcia down into the store via the back staircase.

"Excuse the carpet," Lucy said, leading her past the tiny table where Thomas had first told his cockamamie story to her. Without the incense smoke clouding everything, it looked so grimy and worn. Vacuuming only did so much and she'd never steam-cleaned it. "It hasn't been replaced since I was a kid."

"You grew up here?" Marcia asked, holding up the strands of beads for her to pass under.

"Since I was eleven. In the apartment between this one and my place now. My dad used to run a convenience store out of here when I was in my teens."

"Does he own the building?"

Lucy nodded. "He did. I inherited it from him and can't bring myself to move even though I probably should."

"I'm sorry," Marcia said. "How old were you?"

"Seventeen. So not that young, but it was very sudden."

"Thomas lost his mom a couple of years ago, but she'd been sick for nearly a decade. A few months before that, his uncle—her brother—was killed in a car wreck. I don't think he's ever allowed himself to grieve."

"Hm," Lucy said, her chest tightening. She didn't want to feel sorry for him. As she stared at the wall of shelves behind her cash register, she tried to blink away the welling tears so she could find where she kept her book of clearing rituals. If what Marcia had told her upstairs were true, this would take a lot more than a little sage and some candles.

Marcia lifted out a notebook with red binding, where Lucy had written, "banishing" in black marker. "Is this something you might need?"

"Yes, thanks!" She took it and crammed it into her leather satchel. Pointing to a row of glass jars on the top shelf, she asked, "Can you get that down for me? And the one with the grey stuff in it as well?"

Marcia set them on the counter. "What's in there?"

"Sea salt." Lucy squatted behind her display cabinet and fished out white and black candles, incense and matches. She turned to the medicine chest and fumbled through her collection of crystals, the ones customers she never allowed customers to touch. Tourmaline for sure. Then she lifted out her favorite chunk of amethyst. It was rough, but the deepest shade of purple she'd ever seen. Further back, she kept a collection of Vogel crystals and Lemurian seed crystals.

"What sign is Thomas?" Lucy asked.

"Hm, Leo, I think? His birthday's at the end of the month."

"That would explain a few things," Lucy mumbled. Pete had been a Leo, too. She'd dated men born under other star signs, yet none of them stoked a fire in her the way those born under the sun ever did. Tad was a Pisces, a water sign, and he was definitely a wet blanket.

Marcia smiled and resumed browsing one of the palm reading flyers. Ruby, it was, then. Thankfully, she kept a raw chunk handy. Dark pink and opaque, nobody ever guessed what it was whenever she showed it to them.

A cardboard box jingled as Lucy lifted it out, startling Marcia. Her Tibetan bells. She stuffed them, the crystals, a box of chalk, matches, candles, and packets of various herbs into her satchel. She fiddled with the zipper tab. "What else."

Marcia chuckled. "You don't sound too sure."

"I've done minor cleansing rituals my whole life out of habit," Lucy said. "My grandmother taught me. I learned some other techniques from my friend Athena as well. Usually, someone has just moved into a new place and complained of feeling a bad vibe, or little things have started going awry. Not where people were getting into car wrecks or slicing their wrists."

She closed the satchel, slung the strap over her shoulder, and led Marcia out the front door of her shop.

"Do you mind driving?" Marcia asked, dangling her keys in front of her. "I think I'm still tripping on meds. The drive to get here felt like hours."

Lucy took the keys from her, but a glance at Marcia's face reminded her of the real reason. She got into the driver's seat anyway and hoped there'd be no trucks stalking her, deer jumping into the road or a stoned, drag racing trust fund brat of the kind who'd collided with her father's car.

"Are you okay?" Marcia asked.

"I'm fine." She was thankful her mother made her drive out to the suburbs twice a month to do grocery shopping. She could do this.

~ CHAPTER THIRTY ~

Jeremy felt as though he and Isaac had been wandering through the maze of corridors and tiny rooms for hours. Marcia's eerie calls had stopped, thank God, but they were trapped on the second floor of the house. No matter which way they went, they found no stairs. Just a long hallway that kept turning back on itself, with doors on each side. Each time he opened a new door, it led at random into yet another bedroom or study or out into the hall again. It was like being lost in a house whose floor plan had been designed by Escher.

"There's no end to this!" Jeremy stared out into the same wood flooring with the same doors along each side, all with thick wood frames and round, bronze doorknobs. The faded damask wallpaper above the wainscoting was the only thing that looked different. He swore it had been navy earlier. Now it was brown and beige.

He checked over his shoulder at the door they'd used to enter the room and said to Isaac, "Close that one and open it again."

Isaac shrugged and did as asked. No hallway now, instead it opened to a bare closet roughly a foot deep, with a single rod inside. A couple of wire hangers dangled from it. He stared blankly, closed the door, and then opened it again. Same closet.

"Let's try to find a room with some windows," Jeremy said, brandishing the flashlight. He was going to go insane if he didn't get his bearings soon.

Taking one side of the hall each, they opened every door and looked in.

"I see curtains, at least." Isaac said. Jeremy followed him into a large room with a plush, royal blue carpet. His flashlight swept across thick velvet drapes. Isaac yanked a cord to open them.

He gulped and joined Isaac staring out the window. Relief flooded into him; it looked out onto the driveway. But his Honda was still gone. The sight of empty gravel next to Tom's car should have eased his mind. It meant Marcia wasn't trapped anywhere in the house.

"Something's wrong," he said.

"I know. Since when does his house come this far out on the side? There's no wall near to his garage. It should be just grass and trees or shrubs or something."

Jeremy backed away from the window. He hoped they wouldn't have to resort to knotting bed sheets together and climbing down as if they were breaking out of prison.

"This will sound insane, but I have an idea."

He turned and said, "Yeah?"

Isaac shuffled from side to side, hands thrust in his jeans pockets, and said, "Try to picture finding a way back down. Stairs, an elevator, a dumbwaiter, anything."

"Why not." As flakey as Isaac could get, he had moments of genius. At this point, he was willing to try anything. Jeremy closed his eyes and tried to picture Thomas's elegant wooden staircase with the spherical newel at each end. Once it was firmly in his mind he said, "Fine. Let's go."

They left the room. At the end of the hallway, he spotted a door that was narrower and lower than the rest. He pulled it open and shone the flashlight in. Stairs! Not the set he was looking for, but they'd do. To fit through the doorframe, he had to squeeze in sideways. The plaster walls felt as if they were pressing against him as he went down. The unfinished wood steps were worn smooth and they ended in a cramped hall that must have once been used by servants.

At the end of the passage, Jeremy pressed against a heavy, rough-grained door. He dreaded what might be waiting for them on the other side. It opened into the dining room and he almost wanted to pass out with relief at the sight of that awful wallpaper.

Isaac shone his flashlight around the various hutches and china cabinets. "This place is pretty sweet. Makes me wonder why he always has us eat in the kitchen."

"Whatever," Jeremy said, checking the time on his phone. Marcia had been gone for close to an hour and it took every fiber of muscle in his body not to try calling her. She'd come back on her own time, she always did. Best not to pester her.

They went out into the main hall, calling for Thomas and Jenn. On their way to the library, Jeremy listened out for their voices or footsteps. "They should be back by now, surely."

"Maybe they got lost outside?" Isaac edged toward the front door.

"His property is maybe two acres, surrounded by a twelve-foot fence. There's nowhere for them to go!" He flung his arms against his sides. If Marcia came back, he didn't want her to have to search for him. She would, too, she could never stay in one place. Where was she, anyway? With each passing minute, the house felt more like a prison. He took his phone out of his pocket, hesitated, and put it back. She hated him checking up on her.

"None of them are answering," Isaac said, texting on his phone.

"Did you try Marcia?"

Isaac nodded.

"Dammit," Jeremy whispered, growing even more agitated. His body felt wired. Fresh air and a brisk walk would rid him of some of his excess energy, he hoped, and he'd hear her car if it was coming up the driveway. "Let's do a quick check outside."

*   *   *

Thomas crept along the second-floor hallway. Still no sign of Isaac or Jeremy and now he wondered if he'd hallucinated everything in the forest as well. While searching through his house, he kept hearing Jenn's voice or seeing her flounce past him, vanishing the second he tried to look directly at her. His candle flickered higher, sending long shadows swirling around him. He rubbed his eyes, really feeling the bottle of wine he'd drunk earlier.

"It's all in my mind," he said to himself as the shadows took on a more threatening posture. His landline had no dial tone, he couldn't find his cell phone, and Jenn was somewhere in the woods, nursing Steve, who he hated, but didn't want dying on either of them. Listening for footsteps, he hissed, "Jeremy! Isaac!"

211

He opened the door to his bedroom. He recoiled as if he'd spied a cobra rearing and about to launch itself at him. When he peeked back in, nothing appeared to be out of the ordinary. No suspicious bulge under his bedcovers or behind his curtains, and his closet door was firmly closed.

Metronomic footsteps tapped in the attic above and a chill spread through his veins.

"Jeremy!" Thomas lumbered to the end of the hallway. He stopped at the door that opened to the stairs leading up to the attic. "Jeremy! Isaac! Are you up there? Steve's been hurt!"

To his right, the corridor disappeared into a void. Since when was there a corridor *there*?

"This way," hissed a voice that sounded like neither of them.

He froze, staring into the abyss. There was something hypnotic about seeing into absolutely nothing. He squinted, trying to make out any shape in the shadows or the faintest glimmer of light. He shone his flashlight into it and stepped forward. The floor disappeared from beneath his feet.

~ CHAPTER THIRTY-ONE ~

Lucy drove up the road toward Thomas's house, glad no one was behind her. The headlights flashed across a cluster of white, flower-strewn crosses, then the mangled remains of some unfortunate, furry critter. To settle her nerves, she had Marcia fill her in more about Thomas's life, about how his uncle's savings had dwindled as they sought experimental treatments for his mother, how he'd had to fight his absentee sister over the remains of the estate, as well as his and Jenn's dysfunction.

"So she never once visited." Lucy slowed outside the gate. She felt the same dread as that day in the store with Athena when she'd spotted Thomas lurking outside the front window. The idea of seeing or talking to him again terrified her more than any entity she might have to face.

"Look." Marcia pointed to a black SUV sitting on the lawn to their left. The rear bumper of the vehicle was inches away from the trunk of a giant oak tree. "Ask anyone at the house. It *crashed* into the gate and a spike went right through the windshield, almost impaling Jenn. Now? Nothing!"

"Weird." Lucy couldn't stop staring at the SUV as she drove around it. She swallowed, her mouth parched, her stomach doing somersaults. The house loomed up ahead of them like a witch's castle. She parked behind the Karmann Ghia and got out, a chill spreading down her arms in spite of the warm breeze.

Marcia took the lead up the front steps. "I hope they're okay in there."

Lucy trotted up after her and the front door sprung open on its own. "My God," she mumbled as they stepped inside.

The house was eerily quiet like a cemetery at the stroke of midnight. A LED lantern sat on the bottom step next to the chaise lounge, casting the entrance in a harsh white glow. She clutched her satchel to her chest and stared around. Gone was the beauty she'd taken in that first visit. All the furniture looked ancient and worn, in various stages of disrepair.

Marcia stooped, about to pick up the lantern.

"Marsh, is that you?" Jeremy called from the library.

"Oh thank God." Marcia ran inside. Lucy followed, scanning the room for Thomas. She dreaded seeing him again, but best to get it over with. Jeremy and Isaac huddled at the round table, shivering as if they were on an ice floe.

Marcia sat on her husband's lap, kissed his forehead and asked, "Are you guys okay?"

"Better now," Jeremy said, squeezing her tight. Lucy stared at the white candles burning, sending long, sharp shadows skulking along the walls above. The ceiling seemed lower than she recalled and a subterranean gloom hung in the air.

"Where's Thomas?" Marcia asked.

Jeremy cast his eyes at Lucy and hunched his shoulders.

"Guess I should start the cleansing ritual," Lucy said, fighting the urge to race out, a dark energy oppressing her. While she'd always conducted her rituals with religious sincerity, she'd never sensed such a malevolence before, similar to being under the gaze of a murderer. Her mind's eye was clouded with black soot and grime. Goose pimples spread on her arms.

She took out her book on banishing rituals and flipped through. For the first time in her life, she worried her spells would do nothing. They'd always been just a ritual she performed, not really thinking about whether there really was some entity or energy in her house that needed clearing to begin with. It had always been one of those persistent superstitions, like avoiding stepping on cracks in the sidewalk or trying not to spill salt. Still, everyone was waiting for her to do *something*.

She set her satchel on one of the empty seats across from Jeremy, took out a small white bowl, and tore open some packets of herbs. As she'd done the night before, she set them alight and ground up the ashes.

"Are you all right?" Isaac asked.

Realizing how hard she was clutching the pestle, Lucy mumbled, "I hope so."

"Did Steve and Jenn go home?" Marcia asked.

"They're all missing," Isaac said. "We looked everywhere."

Fear flared in Lucy. What were they hiding?

"Fuck." Marcia stood again and took out her phone. "How long have they been gone for?"

Jeremy said, "Half an hour or so?"

Lucy caught him and Isaac glancing at each other; it was the second time she'd glimpsed them exchanging strange looks. "How about you guys stay here while I go look for them?" Lucy asked. She expected one of them to protest, but they all nodded.

Marcia asked, "Anything you want us to do?"

"Don't move from here. Or if you do, stay where I can find you easily." Hoping they'd heed her, Lucy hurried out and picked up the lantern by the foot of the staircase. All of them were far too subdued to be pulling any kind of prank on her. That didn't mean they wouldn't get bored or antsy and start wandering off.

She checked every room on the main floor first. A massive dining room, a study, the kitchen, a formal living room and a sunroom room filled with orchids. She tried a light switch, nothing. At the kitchen window she peered out across the moonlit back yard; no one. She came back down the hall, peeked into the library to make sure they were still sitting in there, and crept up the stairs to the second floor.

She knew it was a large house going by the outside, but this was crazy. The hallway went on and on, so many bedrooms and bathrooms and more empty rooms with doors on the far side that opened back out to where she swore she'd just left.

As she explored each room, she regretted not asking for a tour when she'd had the chance. Then she remembered the railing that ran along between the main staircase and the upper landing. The instant she called it into her mind, she spotted it at the end of the hall.

On her right, she came across a bedroom that looked lived in. The blinds were partially opened and moonlight streamed in from outside. Beneath, clothes had been slung over the back of a leather chair. The bed's comforter and sheets were rumpled. This had to be Thomas's room. It *felt* like his room. In a hushed voice, she called, "Thomas!" and nudged the door further open. "Tom!"

His bedroom was a less cluttered version of her own, with old-fashioned lamps, wood carvings, and wall hangings that appeared to be high-end Sari fabric. A piece of burgundy silk shimmered in the light of her lantern, drawing her in.

"What are *you* doing in here?"

She bristled and whipped around. Thomas stood behind her, dressed in a fuzzy grey housecoat and holding a glass of water. His eyes were puffy from sleep, his mouth turned to a frown. Surely, Jeremy and Isaac had checked his bedroom. "Marcia brought me."

"What for?"

"You called me too. You said some kind of entity was plaguing your house."

"Hm. Must have been a ruse," he said pushing past her. "I went to bed ages ago and only got up because I had to pee. And I was thirsty. Hate how that works. Is everyone gone yet?"

She furrowed her brow as he crossed the room. He stripped off his robe and stood, wearing nothing but a pair of black boxer briefs. He'd have a nice body if he exercised more; he was quite doughy in the middle. Not that she was athletic either, she reminded herself with a twinge of guilt.

"Do you mind?" he said. "Jenn should be back any minute."

"Then why did Marcia bring me here, why'd you call earlier?"

"She's got it into her stupid head that I fancy you. You of all people." His eyes glowed darkly with contempt as he stepped closer. He leaned closer, his breath reeking of red wine. "Jenn is The One for me, even if my all friends hate her. I mean those breasts of hers. They're even more fabulous now that she's—"

Lucy staggered backward, her throat clenching, and she prayed her eyes weren't turning red. "What about all those things you said were going on? You called *me*!"

"You ran off, so how could I get any good footage? I have to get this episode out in four days!"

She stared down at her feet, humiliated and heartbroken.

"Yes, it was all a ruse," he said, circling around her. "And you fell for it because you're so gullible. You'll believe anything so long as it's complete and utter bullshit. It's the truth you can't stand, the truth about anything." He lifted her chin and stared into her face, reveling in her anguish. "Why did you come back here anyway? Do you have a crush on me? Loads of women do."

"I don't!" she protested, wishing she meant it.

He laughed. "You realize I'm involved with someone else, right? I mean, she might be a two-timing bitch, but she's absolutely gorgeous. You're not even in the same league."

She glared up at him, wishing she could set him on fire with her gaze. He had the same haughty look as those mean girls back in seventh grade.

"She has a real career, as well. She got promoted to VP of Marketing at this tech company a few months ago. She now pulls in more than a hundred grand, plus bonuses. Sure beats being a carnie."

"A carnie! You asshole!" Lucy lunged at him and stumbled into darkness.

Thomas had evaporated.

She stared around the empty bedroom and went back out into the hallway, panting, and heart racing. No trace of him anywhere. What the …

Halfway back downstairs, she stopped and sat on one of the steps, trying to steady herself. What an absolute mind-fuck. No wonder none of them had been able to explain what was going on. In the bedroom with Thomas, everything had seemed so real. She thought back to that crack she'd seen in her basement, and Marcia's description of that SUV crashing into the gate. This went well beyond some collective hallucination or hysteria.

It also seemed to be growing worse for each of them.

~ CHAPTER THIRTY-TWO ~

Jenn stood on the lawn, shaking her head as Steve yanked at the iron gate. He gripped the bars and shook it like a monkey wanting to get out of a cage. "Come help, my head's fucking pounding here," he said. "You're pregnant, not an invalid."

"And I keep saying, let's go back up to the house where Tom has a first aid kit and a crap-ton of painkillers." Shame he wasn't still unconscious. He was way less annoying then.

He kept tugging at the gate. Fed up, she climbed into driver's side of the SUV. Yet as she sat on the black leather seat, panic welled in her. The vehicle was intact but the memories of them crashing, and that metal spear almost skewering her, were as vivid as if it had happened seconds ago.

All she wanted to do was go home, eat and sleep, wishing it was possible to do all three at once. She got out again and took his arm. "Come on; let's head back up to the house. Quit being such a pill."

He said nothing, letting her drag him back up the gravel driveway as if she was about to take him over her knee. She hated to admit it, but Tom was right. Steve was her karma. Even without the baby, she was stuck on him for reasons that totally escaped her. The guy could be the biggest douche, a brain-dead gym bunny into working out, sports, TV, and nothing else beyond his own reflection in the mirror, yet she was *in love* with him. Even the times she'd gone back to Tom and he'd been on his best behavior, she couldn't get her mind off Steve.

"Can we slow down?" he asked breathlessly. "My head is killing me."

"I'm sorry." She slowed to an amble, which made her even more anxious to get back to everyone. "You still can't remember what happened to you?"

He squeezed his eyes shut and pressed his fingers to his temple. "I was under the back porch hiding from Marcia."

"She took off an hour ago!" She gripped his waist and he started shuffling forward more quickly. "You need to get yourself checked out."

"I'll be *fine*."

They passed Marcia and Jeremy's silver Honda. The bitch was back. Every other time she'd seen the woman have a freak-out, she'd gone home, leaving Jeremy to find his own way. Not that he was better. He treated her like a frigging five-year-old.

She helped Steve up the front steps. He slumped down on the tiny wooden stool and rested his elbows on his knees. "You go in. I'll wait here."

"I'm not letting you out of my sight," she said, trying the door. It was locked. She held down the doorbell, and then remembered it didn't work anymore. If it wasn't something people could see, Tom let everything slide. She lifted the ring of the iron doorknocker and began hammering on it.

"Quit it!" Steve winced and stuck his fingers into his ears.

She pounded the door with her fist and yelled, "Tom! Open up!" Footsteps lumbered toward her from inside.

The door opened and Steve stood before her, teeth bared. She glanced at where he'd been sitting. Just bare wood and streaks of grey-blue paint on the seat now.

"What do you want?"

"What just happened?" She stumbled backward, pinching the flesh of her arm between her fingers. How had he gotten inside the house like that?

He screwed up his face, shaking his head at her. Blood streamed out of his wound, matting his blond hair and staining his light grey hoodie. "Are you on drugs or something? I'm bleeding, call a fucking doctor already."

She edged past him and found the handset Thomas kept on a side table at the far end of the chaise lounge. Her hands shook and she kept dropping it. "You said you didn't want a doctor."

"Always do what you tell me? I thought you had a mind of your own. You always said that–" He groaned, doubling over, and his eyes squeezed shut. "Holy fuck, my head, it's killing."

"Here, lie down." It was all she could do to avoid freaking out. She grabbed a phonebook for him to use as a pillow and lifted his legs up onto the chaise lounge. He curled up, writhing. She raced into the kitchen to fetch water and a dishtowel, then rummaged in the cupboards and found a bottle of cheap vodka.

By the time she came back out, he was rolling on the floor, clutching his head in his hands.

"Stay still!" She crouched next to him, her eyes burning. His body spasmed as if he were having a seizure. She grabbed the phone again to call 9-11 and instead of a dial tone, slow piano music played. Then one of those annoying electronic voices came on. "Your call is very important to us. Stay on the line and a customer service agent will be right with you."

"Get off! I need to use this!" she screamed. She pressed the button to hang up, then to call again.

The music kept playing. She threw the phone against the wall and shards of plastic dribbled along the hallway. She took her own phone out of her hoodie pocket and the same music played through the tiny speaker. Screaming, she was about to hurl it, too, when she found herself face to face with the legs of Steve's jeans. He was standing over her now. She looked up.

"Calm the fuck down," he said, taking her phone out of her hands. He perched on the end of the chaise lounge and glared at her. "You're not kidding about all those hormones making you crazy. Holy Jeez. You're going to be one psycho mama. No wonder Thomas is steering clear of you."

"He isn't the father. You know damn well who is!"

"Whatever." He slumped forward, elbows on his knees, and stared off. "You've been banging both of us for years! Until it's out and DNA tests are done, who knows."

"I left him *before* I started getting with you!" She swatted his shoulder, but he just leaned to the side and bobbed upright again. That fucking asshole. "I *wish* Tom was the dad. I know you don't want to be tied down, don't want to grow up, take on any responsibilities, or have to spend money on anyone but yourself. I should have never ... You're a fucking child-man!"

"You're unbelievable," he said, getting up. "I'm outta here." He turned and barged straight into Lucy, who'd just come down the stairs from the second floor.

*   *   *

"Hi," Lucy said, eying Steve as he sat upright on the chaise lounge. He squinted at her as if he'd just woken up from a night of weird dreams, and rubbed the side of his head. A teary-eyed Jenn gaped at each of them alternately and Lucy suspected she wasn't the only one having wild, phantasmagoric experiences. Now was definitely not the time to ask if they'd seen Thomas recently.

"Um, Isaac was looking for you." That seemed safe enough.

"He's in there," Jenn said, pointing her thumb to behind her.

"Guess we should join him, then." To Lucy's relief, both of them followed her into the library without a single snide remark. Whatever had gone on between them, they were spooked, too. They kept close to her like frightened animals around their mother. Which only added to the surrealness.

Marcia rose to her feet. "Everything okay?"

"That was so weird," Lucy said, still in a trance and feeling stung by Thomas's insults, even though she'd imagined them. She turned to make sure Steve and Jenn were still behind her. If she didn't keep double-checking everything around her, she feared reality itself would slip away.

"Did you find him?" Isaac asked.

She shook her head, desperate to get out of here. The stale air and negative energy had intensified, suffocating her. The whole house felt contaminated as if she'd stumbled onto the grounds around Chernobyl. She held her arms close to her body, not wanting to bump against anything.

Marcia returned to her seat at the round table and said, "Think we should start without him?"

Lucy checked over her shoulder; both Jenn and Steve were nodding like a pair of bobbleheads. No goofing around this time. She set her case on one of the leather chairs and dragged the round table away from under the chandelier, until it was closer to

221

the window overlooking the back yard. The cross-breeze coming through helped settle her nerves somewhat.

*   *   *

Light from outside illuminated Thomas's bedroom. He stared up, surprised to find himself sprawled on his back on the floor between his bed and one of his dressers. Last thing he remembered, he was falling through the floor. Only without the sensation of falling. It had been as if everything solid around him had dissolved in an instant. Sweaty and panting, he strained to move his head. From the neck down, he was paralyzed, some force pinning him to the floorboards. A weight crushed his chest. His skin tingled, electrified. He could hear his own heart, pulsing in his ears.

"Thomas," he heard Lucy calling, her voice faraway and alluring, one of Circe's sirens. He tried to say her name but no sound would come out of his throat. With all his might, he tried to lift one of his arms or legs to make noise. Her footsteps passed by in the corridor outside. He closed his eyes, willing her to come into his room and find him, help him back onto his feet.

His door creaked open. He squinted at the shadowy expanding lozenge, yet saw no one.

"Thomas," her voice echoed, muffled as if she were underwater.

The muscles in his throat constricted and he tried to speak. He managed an incoherent gurgle. The footsteps continued padding along the hall, fading to nothing. The more he struggled, the more terrified he grew. His arms were still his arms, yet whenever he tried moving either of them, he could feel them flailing only to realize they were still at his sides. His head buzzed and colorless lights flashed in front of his eyes.

~ CHAPTER THIRTY-THREE ~

Lucy felt everyone's gaze on her as she took a long piece of chalk out of a side pocket in her satchel. She began drawing on the bare surface of the table. The unfinished wood was perfect for marking on. No one said a word, faces solemn as they watched patiently. If only they'd been this accommodating the previous night.

She drew a rough pentagram inside a circle, then symbols for each of the elements inside the corresponding points. Steve looked at her quizzically.

"A banishing ritual," she said, thinking, hope it works.

She placed the black candle into the middle of her drawing and set it alight. Isaac eyed her questioningly and she said, "Black isn't evil or anything. It absorbs negative energy."

He nodded. She laid out the crystals on top of the lines of chalk. For the straight lines, she used wand-like Vogel crystals, laying them end to end. In between, she arranged the seed crystals, ruby, and black tourmaline. The shimmering spider web pattern grew harmonious, producing a sensation similar to gazing up at the constellations in a clear night sky. So far, so good.

She sat between Isaac and Jenn and everyone joined hands without her having to tell them to. She was glad for it; the easier they made this for her, the better the chance of her spell succeeding. According to her book, all participants had to be of the same mindset. Trying to quell her nervousness, she took a deep breath and said, "Everyone, close your eyes."

She took a second long, deep breath. Now that she'd created the necessary atmosphere and felt a circuit of energy pulsating between each of them, she didn't want to ruin it by consulting her notebook again. She'd have to wing it. Unlike the channeling, though, she'd done this before.

"Try to visualize light shining, filling the room."

Something upstairs thudded. Sensing a spike in tension, she opened her eyes. The library darkened. Everyone's brows were furrowed, likely sensing the same thing as her. The air felt thick and electrified. Her skin tingled unpleasantly.

Now that they had so much faith in her, she tried to calm down and remember what she was supposed to say next. Even the protection symbol she'd drawn was probably wrong. It wasn't just the order of each element she had to get right, but the direction she drew them in as well. She'd laid out the stones and crystals at random, letting intuition guide her without having studied her notes from the previous session first. She watched Jenn roll her lips into her mouth and wriggle in her seat. Across from her, Marcia's shoulders were hunched almost to her ears.

Mimicking Athena's soothing tone, she said, "See the light getting brighter. Picture an ember, starting to glow, sparking to life, a flame beginning to rise."

The pressure of other people's fingers on hers soothed her. She tried to picture a silvery-white flame leaping to life in front of her, spreading between them. "See that flame burning brighter, flickering higher."

Trying to keep her eyes focused on the orange glow above the candle flame, Lucy counted the seconds and exhaled through her mouth. The wind blew steadily through the open windows, curtains fluttering on two sides of their table. Outside, trees rustled and branches creaked. Upstairs, something thumped rhythmically, like an unlatched gate caught in a breeze. Rooted in the present, she said, "Picture the light."

"I can't see anything," Marcia said and Lucy glanced at her. Everything behind her faded and darkened. A shadow spread up and out like a bird of prey about to take flight, and swooped low over the table. She flinched and ducked her head. "I don't think it's working!"

"It will," Lucy said, "I promise. Just keep calm and stay focused." If she sounded declarative enough, she could convince herself, too. "Try to see white light."

A writing desk in the corner of the library slid across the room, crashing into the opposite wall. Jenn huddled into Steve and shrieked, "What light? I can't see anything!"

Isaac leapt up to examine the desk and Lucy said, "Stay at the table—don't break the circle! *Please*."

Jeremy hauled him back to his chair. Time for her to try another technique, which she'd always thought of as cheating. But if it worked, it worked. "Okay. Stare at the candle for a few seconds and then close your eyes, concentrating on the afterimage that remains."

Everyone seemed to calm; the tension lowered as if someone had turned a dial down several notches. Once their eyes were closed again, she said, "See that spot getting bigger and brighter, as bright as you can stand. Try to picture the brightness, imagine it. Like you've just stepped outside on a bright, summer afternoon from a dark movie theater and the sun is blinding you."

The windows rattled and the wind juddered. Distractions, she reminded herself. She shut her eyes tight, trying to block out extraneous noises.

"Blinding bright light," she said, glancing up at the sounds of creaking above. The chandelier swung overhead, jangling and spinning wildly on its chain. Jenn let go of her hand, hugged Steve tightly and buried her face into his sweatshirt.

The house shuddered, producing a fear similar to being out at sea in a hurricane. A pungent stench filled the room. Lucy gripped the fabric of Jenn's velour tracksuit. "Keep the circle!"

A crack, louder than a thunderbolt, struck somewhere outside. Lucy tried to steady herself; the entire room felt as if it was swaying from side to side on heaving ocean waves. Bile stung the back of her throat.

*   *   *

Sweat dripped down Thomas's temples and his breathing grew more rapid and shallow. He tried to concentrate on taking deeper breaths. He managed to hold in a lungful of air, which he then exhaled slowly. Breathing was the only part of his body he had any control over. He had no idea what time it was, or for how long he'd been on the floor. All he could do was hope he'd soon fall asleep and wake up feeling normal again.

The manner in which he was lying, with the skirt of his bed inches from the tip of his toe, there was no way he'd fallen out. Yet for the life of him, he couldn't remember what he'd been doing beforehand. He tried to stretch and still couldn't move a muscle. While his eyes felt as though they were open, he wasn't certain they really were. His bedroom seemed much larger and faint light scattered in odd directions, beyond the usual cracks between his wooden blinds or beneath the door.

Shadows spread closer to him from each corner of the room, unintelligible voices whispering and hissing all around, growing louder and more menacing. He shut his eyes tight. It's all in my mind. There is nothing in here with me. I'm already asleep and I just need to wake up.

*   *   *

Lucy grabbed Jenn's hand, shouting over the howling winds and groaning walls. The storm was illusory; the curtains remained still against the window frames. As further torment, the temperature dropped to where her breath puffed out in clouds. "We have to keep holding hands, we need a circle!"

Everyone at the table gripped the hand of whoever was next to them. "Keep your eyes closed and concentrate! Don't break the circle!" Lucy yelled, the words pouring out of her mouth on their own, as if some outside force were guiding her. "Picture bright light filling this room—from ceiling to floor! Brilliant blinding light! The light of an angel, Jesus, creation, whatever God you follow."

She peered out the corner of her eye. Beyond the window facing her, nothing. No trees, no lights or stars, nothing in the distance. She squinted toward the entrance to the library. Beyond the doorway, a void. Darker than any darkness she'd ever seen in her life. Terror spread through her and she forced her attention back to the candle flame trembling in the well of melted wax. This was all in their minds, she tried to remind herself, a collective hallucination. None of it was real. They were fine.

"Keep your eyes on the candle," she said and the flame burned more steadily. Warmth spread into her fingers from her neighbors' palms. In her mind's eye, crystalline light flared.

*   *   *

Thomas stared up at the vanishing ceiling, blackness enveloping the room. The air had grown stuffy, as if all the oxygen was leaching away, leaving him faint and dizzy. How stupid he'd been. For years, he'd wallowed in self-pity, hating his job, clinging to a miserable relationship so he didn't have to face life alone and only now could he see the vistas of possibilities open to him, only now when he was lying on his floor unable to move or speak, slowly suffocating. So many wasted years, wasted chances.

He gaped along his body, his bare feet lost in the shadows. Like a python beginning to devour him, the darkness consumed his calves, crept up past his knees, his thighs. Helpless, he watched his hands and forearms vanish. The lower half of his torso faded into the nothingness, sending him out of his mind with fear. This wasn't how he wanted to go. He wasn't ready yet. If he woke up still alive in the morning, he promised himself, he'd work on building his life back up. No more living in the past, ignoring the present, avoiding even thoughts of the future. Gathering any remaining strength he yelled, "Fine! You exist!"

The darkness slowed its advance. He hadn't been expecting that. He'd no idea what made him shout it, but he was too relieved it had had an effect, that he *could* shout for that matter, to think about the whys and hows. Filled with a renewed burst of energy he yelled, "Whatever you are, you exist! Okay? You exist in your own right, completely independent of my own mind!"

He wriggled his shoulders, dizzy with gratitude he was able to move again. He freed his arm and watched it materialize. "I believe," he called out. "Whatever you are, you're real!" The darkness retreated and he propped himself up on his elbows.

"You're real because I created you!" His mind flooded with how he'd externalized every negative thought and emotion until it had taken on a life of its own. Lucy had unwittingly channeled all the conflict and tension, enabling this monster of his to manifest. Now another being seemed to be counteracting it.

He stared in awe at the manganese light flooding into his room. This was amazing, being in a presence completely different from anything he'd ever before experienced or imagined possible. He couldn't see or hear it, but he could feel energy radiating all around, similar to being near a powerful magnetic or electrical field or under the warmth of the sun but even that couldn't fully express it. When he looked more closely at the coruscating whorls and eddies, he sensed his mother, his uncle, and everyone else he'd ever lost. They never really had left him; they would always exist so long as he kept them in his memory.

*   *   *

Lucy feared her attempt at spell-casting had only intensified whatever curse she'd unleashed. The walls of the library had vanished and in the brief glimpse she allowed herself to take, she saw nothing but endless wasteland, devoid of any life. The moon hung at a strange angle. The few stars she could see through the haze looked misaligned. She fixed her gaze on the candle, forcing the alien landscape into the margins of her vision.

Her chair slid away from the table and she clasped Jenn and Isaac's hands. Everyone's chairs were shifting backward, a force tearing their circle apart. Tightening her grip on their fingers, Lucy stretched her arms, her shoulders aching from the strain.

"Keep your eyes closed and keep trying to see the light, growing brighter and brighter!"

Jenn's chair jerked and she slipped out of Lucy's grasp. Hooking her fingers into Isaac's, Lucy reached for Jenn's flailing arm. A ghostly figure flew past her head and she ducked, then she felt stronger, larger fingers clasping her wrist.

Thomas knelt next to her and squeezed her hand. Lucy grinned at him and said to everyone, "Close your eyes and try to feel light flowing inside your body!"

The library darkened, their faces and outstretched arms and hands barely visible in the failing candlelight. Only one on the table between them remained lit.

"Feel the light! Pouring out of your body!" She shut her eyes and tried to visualize light exploding all around them. Thomas's fingers locked into hers and her inner light began to intensify.

She tried to steady her voice and speak more slowly, in a more soothing tone. She imagined herself as Athena, sitting cross-legged on her living room sofa, speaking in that smooth, buttermilk tone of hers.

"Feel yourself ... filling the entire house ... with brilliant, shining light. Bright as the sun ... growing steadily brighter."

Finally, she felt it again, a current circulating between them, pulsating from one hand to the next. The walls and bookshelves solidified and all of them were able to edge their seats closer to the table. The air felt lighter and fresher. She braved opening her eyes. Ethereal light emanated from each person.

Everyone else's eyes opened and each face grew radiant as they marveled at the light shimmering, coruscating, around and between them in all directions.

Their energy flooded the library, phantom shadows retreating into the corners. Blinding light spread beyond the room, the walls and ceiling dissolving in the brightness. A brilliant white flashed like a nuclear explosion.

~ CHAPTER THIRTY-FOUR ~

Lucy lifted her head from the table and squinted into the sunlight streaming in through the window. It was morning, well after dawn. A cool, damp breeze fluttered the curtains. While at first, she hadn't the slightest clue where she was or how long she'd been here, peace radiated all around her. She felt as if she'd just woken up from a wonderful, magical dream and traces of that realm still lingered.

She opened her eyes wider to see Thomas passed out next to her, facing the other way, his head nested in his folded arms. Steve was awake, stretching out a crick in his neck. He looked uncharacteristically contemplative, combing his fingers tenderly through Jenn's mop of blonde hair. Her head was nestled in her arms, chalk smeared on the sleeve of her black velour hoodie. Isaac groaned and lurched forward. His chair had been leaning precariously against the side of a bookshelf. Next to him, a sleeping Marcia snuggled into Jeremy, who stared out, his eyes bleary and glazed.

Lucy turned her head around. The library wasn't the mess she expected it to be, the way it had been the other night. Books were still in orderly stacks. Glittering shards in the carpet were the only sign of disarray and on closer look, she realized they were her seed crystals, scattered like wedding rice. Some caught in the morning sunlight, scattering kaleidoscopic rainbows along the walls and ceiling.

"What time is it?" Jenn roused and sat upright. Steve slung his arm around her shoulder and cooed something in her ear that made her smile and blush. "How long were we asleep for?"

"At least a couple of hours," Lucy said. "Last I can remember, it was pitch dark in here."

"Me too." Marcia stretched and blinked a few times, sleepy-eyed. "What happened?"

Lucy hunched her shoulders. Despite the mess, the room had a feel similar to that of a placid lake at sunrise. Outside, a chorus of birds twittered.

"That was so trippy," Jenn gaped around. She straightened her back and placed her palms on her belly. "I swear I had this crazy out of body experience after that light flashed, where I was flying between galaxies."

"Tom, wake up." Isaac jabbed his side.

Thomas lifted his head and winced, his eyes swollen. Not a morning person, Lucy thought, giggling to herself. He reached over and gave her hand a squeeze. "Sleep all right?"

"I think I'm going to hurt later," Lucy said, thrilled at the touch of his warm, soft hand clasping hers. Even hung over, he was still so cute, especially how the corners of his mouth curled up.

"I'm in pain," he said, laying his head back down on the table. "They let me drink far too much last night."

"You did that all on your own, buddy," Jeremy said.

He sat up and pretended to frown. "You know I don't like leaving half-opened bottles of wine around. It goes off too fast."

"Then quit buying the same cheap shit all the time, or put it in the fridge," Jeremy said and Lucy giggled. Athena always lectured her about the exact same thing.

"You're not supposed to refrigerate red wine." Thomas yawned and got out of his chair. "Anyone else for a coffee? I have tea, too. Normal tea, I'm afraid," he said, craning closer to Jenn.

"Just some water or juice," she said. "Thanks."

Catching Lucy's eye, he jerked his head and she followed him into the kitchen. Jeremy and Marcia trailed behind them. Sunlight poured in through the picture window, making all the cupboards and countertops gleam. A machine hissed and the smell of freshly brewed coffee filled the air. Lucy leaned her knee on one of the benches in the breakfast nook and gazed out at an idyllic back yard.

Just beyond the door was a large wooden balcony. On the far side, steps led down to a stone patio surrounded by a beautiful rock garden. Unless Thomas hired a landscaper, which she doubted, he must be busy out there when he wasn't at work.

Once the coffee was ready, she'd ask if he would join her at the lacy cast iron table out there.

A hand clasped her shoulder and Thomas held a steaming mug of black coffee to her. "Sugar or cream?"

She took the cup from him and helped herself to the carton he set out. "Thanks."

Marcia slid into the bench across from her, blinking in the brightness. Caught in the sun, her eyes were the most incredible shade of emerald. Jeremy sat next to her and stared at Thomas setting more mugs and teaspoons onto the table. "Where the hell were you all night?" Jeremy asked.

Lucy sat down and Thomas squeezed in next to her. "In my bedroom. I passed out there for a bit."

"I checked in there like three times!" Jeremy said.

"Don't know how you could have missed me, I was sprawled out right in the middle of the floor." He stretched out a kink in his neck and blew over the top of his mug. "As for how I got that way? No idea."

Like Lucy, he put a lot of cream in his coffee. Once she'd stirred in some sugar, she took a sip. Dark roast and strong. Real coffee, in other words. "I checked too. Went right in. You weren't there."

"I must have been. I can't have just disappeared." He got up again and filled a fresh pot of water for the coffee maker. He then filled a glass of water, which he gulped down as he returned to the table. "God, I need this. So what happened?"

"Do you remember *anything*?" Marcia asked.

He winced and pressed his fingers to his temple, as if it hurt for him to shake his head. "I know Steve wandered off, so I went upstairs to search for him. Next thing I knew, I was on the floor in my bedroom. I must have passed out. Weird dreams, too. Next, I was in the library with you lot and no idea how I got there."

Lucy said, "You'd don't remember coming to the table. At all."

"Sorry," he said, shrinking from her. She hoped she hadn't upset him.

"Shame you missed it. I don't know how to describe it, other than that it was incredible." Marcia gazed off as if she was trying to return to some heavenly place in her mind. "Part of me feels as if I'm still there."

"You still never answered my question. What happened?"

Lucy eyed Marcia and Jeremy, giggling. "We're not sure."

"It was weird," Jeremy said, his voice gruff from sleepiness. "Whole house was shaking, it kept feeling like someone was stalking me, when Marcia took off I flipped out and when I went upstairs looking for you, I thought I heard her trapped in some room. It was nuts."

Marcia wrapped her fingers around her mug and nodded. "The drive when I went to fetch Lucy, ho-lee shit. That road seemed to go on forever and for half of it this crazy-ass pickup truck was tailgating me. At one point I thought a deer had jumped right in front of the car and I almost went off the road." She eyed Jeremy and shrugged. "Yeah, I didn't want to tell you."

Thomas snorted. "Speaking of worst nightmares, I was wandering in the forest out back, somewhere with Jenn and about to ask her to marry me. Then she had to pee or something."

Lucy laughed and covered her mouth with her hands.

"I plead temporary insanity. And too much wine." Slumping closer to Lucy, he said, "So what personal demons did you have to face down?"

She sucked her lips into her mouth, feeling her cheeks flush. She hoped they weren't turning red. She sensed he wanted to tell her more about what he'd experienced, but privately. "You didn't seem surprised to see me here."

"Yeah, about that," he said, a pained look on his face. "I owe you a huge apology. No excuses. I hate my career, but I've been too lazy to look for another job. I wasn't happy, but I was comfortable. As much as I wanted to insist on using someone else instead, what would that have accomplished? It was still an awful thing to do. To anyone."

His rueful smile made her melt. A dimple had pressed into one of his cheeks and there was a sad warmth in his eyes she'd seen before, that afternoon in the library before any of his friends had come over and she was talking about her travels to Russia.

"I forgive you. So long as you promise it never, ever ends up online."

"Why not? You should've seen Dave in the studio. He must have gone through the same segment a hundred times yesterday, trying to figure out what had happened. It was hilarious! I've always been of two minds about all that stuff whereas he … he was totally buggered by it, until he could convince himself it was nothing."

Now she was dying to see it. Her mood deflated at the thought of her store and how slow business had been lately. If she left now, and someone gave her a ride back, she should still be able to open on time. Ah, screw it. "It's okay. Business couldn't be worse, anyway."

He bumped against her and said, "You, my dear, have a lot to learn about online marketing. I couldn't even find a Facebook page or Twitter account and your website—no offense—looked as if you'd hand-coded it in HTML three."

"I have an Etsy account where I planned to sell stuff once I've learned how to knit better," she said, giggling while she cringed. Yet another thing Athena had been on her ass about for ages, getting with the times and technology.

Thomas slung his arm around her and pulled her against him, his t-shirt soft against her cheek. "I've been thinking about freelancing on the side. You can be my first client. I won't charge you, but I might expect some sort of favor in return. Free … books, perhaps?"

She felt like she was floating. It had been ages since a guy this hot had flirted with her and he was being so brazen, too. Just in time to send her hurtling back down to Earth, Jenn appeared at the threshold of the kitchen and cleared her throat.

Keeping her eyes fixed on Thomas, Jenn said, "I have to go."

To her relief, he made no move to get up. "Where's Steve gone to?"

"He went with Isaac to check on the SUV hoping it is still intact. Isaac said it was; I can't remember now either way."

The atmosphere in the kitchen tensed. They all eyed each

other, and Lucy remembered Marcia telling her about an accident last night. Jenn bowed her head and poked the arch of one of her feet with the toes of the other. "Steve kind of apologized, which is his way of saying he's going to try to give us another shot."

"I hope it works out," Thomas said.

"Thanks," she whispered, sucking in her breath. Lucy felt sorry for her and guilty for her own childish jealousy. Would she have behaved differently in Jenn's shoes? In all honesty, she probably wouldn't have.

"He'll come around," Jeremy said. "I had three other friends freak out the exact same way. He just has to get used to the idea."

"I hope you're right," she said.

"I'm always right." He winked, nudging Marcia. "Right?"

The front door creaked open and footsteps tromped up the hall toward them. Steve came up to Jenn, kissed her cheek, and said, "Hey babe, ride's waiting. We'll drop Isaac off and go out for breakfast somewhere, okay?"

That seemed to be Jeremy and Marcia's cue to leave too. Both of them got up and set their empty coffee mugs in the sink. Thomas nudged Lucy and said in a low, reluctant voice, "I suppose I should go see them out."

Not sure what to do, she trailed after them. Was he inviting her to stay for now? She stood near the foot of the stairs, watching everyone exchange hugs. Marcia pecked each of her cheeks and said, "Need a ride anywhere?"

Lucy eyed Thomas, who flashed a grin at her. Her heart leapt into her throat as he said to her, "I'm sure there're things in that satchel of yours you can't leave without. Those crystals must be quite pricy and it'll take a while to find them in all that mess."

"I'll visit your store again one of these days. This time during opening hours," Marcia said.

Lucy giggled. Her nerves were frazzled. In the space of a few hours, she'd gone from being convinced she was nothing but a deluded fraud, to someone who actually had the power to bring about peace and harmony. How it worked, exactly, she had no idea; all that mattered, was that it had.

Jeremy slapped Thomas's shoulder. "See ya, buddy."

Marcia kissed his cheek. "Bye, hon." She turned to Lucy and asked, "Sure you don't want a ride?"

"I'll get her home." Thomas hugged Lucy from behind, resting his chin on her top of her head. Normally she hated when tall guys did that with her, but with him, she hoped he'd never move.

Marcia followed Jeremy out, closing the door behind her.

"About time. I've been waiting for them all to leave for nearly twelve hours," Thomas said, leading her back into the kitchen. "Want to go sit on the deck? Looks quite nice out."

"Sure." Her insides fluttered as he opened the back door for her, and they stepped out onto the veranda. The sun blazed down overhead, tempered by a cool, morning breeze.

He took her to a wooden swing in the far right corner that she hadn't been able to see from the kitchen window. Camouflaged beneath the rambling branches of a cherry tree, the seat was shaded by a dark green canopy and matching cushions.

He stretched out on it and pulled her down next to him, holding her in his arms. "Today's Monday, isn't it."

"Yeah," she said, tensing. She should be opening her store by now. Screw it, she needed a break. Especially after last night. Since waking, she felt she'd entered some magical dream world and hated the thought of leaving it so soon. She wondered what the others would think later on, especially Steve and Jenn, who'd made such a joke of everything but had become so cooperative.

"Excuse me a sec." He shifted, pulling his phone out of his jeans pocket. There was just enough room for the two of them to lie comfortably while he texted.

"Good weather to pull a sickie, I think. I can't stand being indoors on days like this. Summers are short enough already."

"Me neither." She snuggled against him, his heart thumping into her back. "Before the construction started up, I used to set a card table out on the sidewalk to do my readings."

He set his phone on a nearby bench and kissed her temple. "You're very forgiving, I have to say. I like that in a person. Hell, I *need* that in a person."

She felt so comfortable as she rolled onto her back and said, "Even when you were being a total jackass, I knew there was a great guy in there somewhere. I just had to find him."

"Well, you are the psychic." Grinning, he tucked a stray lock of her hair behind her ear. "Wish I'd seen whatever magic it was you did last night. The library really did have a different feel to it this morning than it had in ages. The entire house, for that matter. As if unpleasant company had cleared out and someone had given everything a good scrub."

"You really don't remember anything? At all?" Self-doubt began creeping in again.

"I had a lot of wine last night. I mean, I remember things, but it was all sort of a chaotic haze and now I can't tell what was real and what wasn't. I had the most bizarre dreams you could imagine. Red wine always gives me the weirdest–"

"A dream," she said, stiffening. Maybe hanging out with him was a bad idea, their worldviews too far apart to ever be bridged. She also had a business to run.

"You're bound to be more familiar than I am with the varying states of consciousness. At the time, I genuinely could not tell which I was, asleep or awake. I couldn't move and these lights kept flashing in front of my eyes. I'd never experienced it before, but wondered whether it could be sleep paralysis or–"

"Sleep paralysis?"

He *was* trying, she reminded herself. She thought back to the reading she'd done for that blonde woman at the fair, who'd said she needed to cut people more slack. It was wise advice for her to follow as well.

He shrugged and said, "You know, when you rouse from deep sleep, but you're still in the R.E.M. stage. Generally, your body is paralyzed from the neck down so you can't act out your dreams. At the time it was terrifying, but looking back, it was a fascinating experience!"

"Did you get a buzzing in your ears or sense a presence in the room with you?" she asked.

"Yeah! It was quite something. I'd first heard of them after reading up on UFO abductions and such. My experience was remarkably similar. Well, apart from any nasty probes and such."

"Really?" She was surprised he showed interest in the subject.

Pulling her closer again, he said, "I'm a lot more open-minded about these things than I let on, you know. When my mum died, I sensed something. This light, but not one you could see, exactly. It's hard to describe. The room was filled with her. Most of the time I chalk it up to wishful thinking because I miss her so much, but then sometimes, I don't know."

She nuzzled her head into his chest and closed her eyes. The sun radiated into her skin, birds chirped and a breeze rustled through the trees. She could easily laze around like this the rest of the day.

He resumed twirling a lock of her hair, saying, "I wouldn't spend so much time debunking if I wasn't fascinated by all of it. I actually keep hoping to one day come across a real haunting or firm proof of an existence beyond what we can see and touch. That show gave me an excuse to look for it and get paid at the same time."

Feeling hot, she wriggled out of her cardigan. Something fell out of her pocket onto the wooden slats of the deck. The Tower card. Exactly as Athena had said, disruption wasn't always so bad. She shifted around so that they lay face to face. She gazed into his beautiful, twinkling eyes and they kissed.

ABOUT THE AUTHOR

Charlotte de Souza currently resides in Canada with her husband, two cats and several thousand books. We also own several beautiful thoroughbred horses, which are currently stabled at Woodbine Racetrack in Toronto. I have had a lifelong interest in all things occult and esoteric, although from a skeptical perspective.

www.charlottedesouza.wordpress.com
https://www.youtube.com/channel/UCw8KYPkBJDf7gkm2igq1ozg